DEAD OF NIGHT

Also by Peter Haining
   The Ghouls
   Mystery!
   The Ancient Mysteries
   Ghosts
   The Leprechaun's Kingdom
   Terror!
   Everyman's Book of Classic
      Horror Stories
   and many more

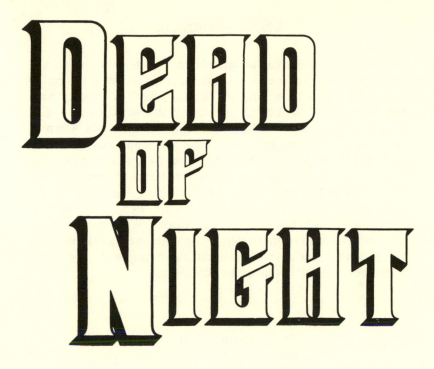

DEAD OF NIGHT

Horror Stories
from Radio, Television and Films

Edited by Peter Haining

Stein and Day/*Publishers*/New York

Acknowledgments

The editor and publishers are grateful to the following authors and their agents for permission to include copyright stories in this collection: A.D. Peters & Co. Ltd. for "The Ferryman" by Kingsley Amis and "De Mortuis" by John Collier; A.P. Watt and the Estate of E.F. Benson for "The Bus Conductor" and also the Estate of Algernon Blackwood for "King's Evidence"; Scott Meredith Literary Agency, Inc. for "The Weird Tailor" by Robert Bloch (reprinted by permission of the author and the author's agents, Scott Meredith Literary Agency, Inc., 845 Third Avenue, New York, New York 10022); BP Singer Features Inc. for "A Thing About Machines" by Rod Serling; and Douglas Rae for "The Pond" by Nigel Kneale. While every care has been taken to establish the owners of copyright in the stories included in this book, in the case of any accidental infringement, the Editor should be contacted in care of the publishers.

First published in the United States of America in 1983
All rights reserved, Stein and Day, Incorporated
Printed in the United States of America
Stein and Day/*Publishers*
Scarborough House
Briarcliff Manor, N.Y. 10510

Library of Congress Cataloging in Publication Data

Main entry under title:

Dead of night.

Contents: The bus conductor / E.F. Benson   Sweeney Todd, the demon barber / Thomas Prest   The middle toe of the right foot / Ambrose Bierce   [etc.]
    1. Horror tales, English. 2. Horror tales, American.
I. Haining, Peter.
PR1309.H6D4   1983   823'.0872'08   81-48444
ISBN 0-8128-2848-8   AACR2

For
BASIL COPPER
– a dead of night man, too

Contents

Preview

Horror has been very good to me over the years. Ghostly hauntings, ghastly monsters and the Undead rising have not only provided me with a livelihood, but at the same time enabled me to do one of the things I enjoy doing most: trying to frighten myself to death!

If you were to visit my sixteenth-century home in the Suffolk countryside you would find there were plenty of skeletons in the cupboards – but not the usual boney kind. They are literary skeletons: row upon row of books and magazines (many a hundred years old and more) in whose pages are shrouded dark and sinister tales from the pens of men and women who know all about the dead of night and what lurks there ...

For a good while now I have been something of a literary ghoul, a plunderer of deathless prose, a seeker after strange and horrid tales to satisfy you, the public's, seemingly unquenchable thirst for what is perhaps too simply defined as the 'horror story'. For the term can embrace fantasy, the weird and the bizarre, the outré and the unspeakable, as well as the fringes of science fiction. Much of this resurrection work has, naturally enough, resulted in the compiling of new anthologies, but my hard-won expertise (at the cost of dust-filled lungs and failing eyesight!) has also enabled me to contribute to those other important mediums of entertainment: films, television and the radio. Yet because all three are so ephemeral by nature, their material presented today and shelved tomorrow (though not necessarily forgotten), I have decided to give permanence to the best of this material in this collection.

The book has, in fact, a dual purpose. Firstly, it enables me to reprint some of the rare and now difficult to obtain stories which were most influential on me in the early years of my developing interest in the horror story genre. Secondly, it contains a selection of tales which represent my work as a consultant and which along the way introduced me to three of the nicest horror-makers you could wish to share a tomb with: Vincent Price, Christopher Lee and Peter Cushing. In a nut-shell, I could almost say this book is an autobiography of my life and horrid times!

It is my hope that in these pages both my own older generation of lovers of the macabre, as well as the present one, will discover much that is nostalgic, fascinating and, naturally enough, spine-chilling. Above all else, though, I trust the reader will be *entertained*, for the horror story which fails to do that fails in its most basic and important function.

The horror story has, as I said, been kind to me. In all the years since I first came across the genre as a small boy, I've never lost my enthusiasm for macabre fiction (blood, yes, enjoyment, no!), never felt I'd exhausted what is clearly a rich vein of literature (there is still many a tomb to be opened) and managed to keep my sanity through every frightening encounter (relatively speaking, I suppose!).

Before you go on to the tales themselves, I think I should just explain that I have called this collection *Dead of Night* as a mark of respect for the war-time British film of the same title which did much to spark my interest in ghost and horror stories and which, for my money, still remains unsurpassed of its kind. This is a view I know is shared by many other people who have seen it. The picture was actually the amalgamation of four stories, and one of these produced a moment of cinema as clearly etched on my memory today as it was when I first saw it over twenty years ago. The episode was based on the story which opens this collection, and that being the case it conveniently enables me to end this brief introduction and urge you to enter the world of the *Dead of Night*. Remember, though, that you go on at your own risk ...

Peter Haining

I

The Bus Conductor
E.F. Benson

The film Dead of Night *was released in 1945 when Britain was emerging from the nightmare of war, and I was just taking my first tentative steps into the darker regions of the imagination. Although I was hardly aware of the fact at the time, the film caused something of a stir due to its content and at least one national newspaper felt it should be banned from cinemas because the public had already suffered more than enough horrors during the war! This was not a view shared by the Censor, who passed it as suitable for adult audiences, and it then began to repay the faith of Ealing Studios, who made it, by earning the kind of critical and public acclaim that has since made it legendary. Basically,* Dead of Night *consists of four ghost stories told during the course of an evening by a group of guests staying in a lonely old house. Effective though each of the stories is, it is the linking theme and the weird ending which leaves the viewer's flesh crawling. Much of the credit for this must go to the story 'The Bus Conductor' on which it is based. This story also provided me with a moment of spine-tingling screen horror which I have never forgotten – the image of an old hearse-driver calling grimly after a young man, 'Room for one more!' If, by any chance, you have not seen the film, I think you will experience something of the same sensation by reading the pages which follow ...*

My friend, Hugh Grainger, and I had just returned from a two days' visit in the country, where we had been staying in a house of sinister repute which was supposed to be haunted by ghosts of a peculiarly fearsome and truculent sort. The house itself was all that such a house should be, Jacobean and oak-panelled, with long dark passages and high vaulted rooms. It stood, also, very remote, and was encompassed by a wood of sombre pines that muttered and whispered in the dark, and all the time that we were there a south-westerly gale with torrents of scolding rain had prevailed, so that by day and night weird voices moaned and fluted in the chimneys, a company of uneasy spirits held colloquy among the trees, and sudden tattoos and tappings beckoned from the window-panes. But in spite of these surroundings, which were sufficient in themselves, one would almost say, spontaneously to generate occult phenomena, nothing of any description had occurred. I am bound to add, also, that my own state of mind was peculiarly well adapted to receive or even to invent the sights and sounds we had gone to seek, for I was, I confess, during the whole time that we were there, in a state of abject apprehension, and lay awake both nights through hours of terrified unrest, afraid of the dark, yet more afraid of what a lighted candle might show me.

Hugh Grainger, on the evening after our return to town, had dined with me, and after dinner our conversation, as was natural, soon came back to these entrancing topics.

'But why you go ghost-seeking I cannot imagine,' he said, 'because your teeth were chattering and your eyes starting out of your head all the time you were there, from sheer fright. Or do you like being frightened?'

Hugh, though·generally intelligent, is dense in certain ways; this is one of them.

'Why, of course, I like being frightened,' I said. 'I want to be made to creep and creep and creep. Fear is the most absorbing and luxurious of emotions. One forgets all else if one is afraid.'

'Well, the fact that neither of us saw anything,' he said, 'confirms what I have always believed.'

'And what have you always believed?'

'That these phenomena are purely objective, not subjective, and that one's state of mind has nothing to do with the perception that perceives them, nor have circumstances or surroundings anything to do with them either. Look at Osburton. It has had the reputation of being a haunted house for years, and it certainly has all the accessories of one. Look at yourself, too, with all your nerves on edge, afraid to look round or light a candle for fear of seeing something! Surely there was the right man in the right place then, if ghosts are subjective.'

He got up and lit a cigarette, and looking at him – Hugh is about six feet high, and as broad as he is long – I felt a retort on my lips, for I could not help my mind going back to a certain period in his life, when, from some cause which, as far as I knew, he had never told anybody, he had become a mere quivering mass of disordered nerves. Oddly enough, at the same moment and for the first time, he began, to speak of it himself.

'You may reply that it was not worth my while to go either,' he said, 'because I was so clearly the wrong man in the wrong place. But I wasn't. You for all your apprehensions and expectancy have never seen a ghost. But I have, though I am the last person in the world you would have thought likely to do so, and, though my nerves are steady enough again now, it knocked me all to bits.'

He sat down again in his chair.

'No doubt you remember my going to bits,' he said, 'and since I believe that I am sound again now, I should rather like to tell you about it. But before I couldn't; I couldn't speak of it at all to anybody. Yet there ought to have been nothing frightening about it; what I saw was certainly a most useful and friendly ghost. But it came from the shaded side of things; it looked suddenly out of the night and the mystery with which life is surrounded.

'I want first to tell you quite shortly my theory about ghost-seeing,' he continued, 'and I can explain it best by a simile, an image. Imagine then that you and I and everybody in the world are like people whose eye is directly opposite a little tiny hole in a sheet of cardboard which is continually shifting and revolving and moving about. Back to back with that sheet of cardboard is another, which also, by laws of its own, is in perpetual but independent motion. In it too there is another hole, and when, fortuitously it would seem, these two holes, the one through which we are always looking, and the other in the spiritual plane, come opposite one another, we see through, and then only do the sights and sounds of the spiritual world become visible or audible to us. With most people these holes never come opposite each other during their life. But at the hour of death they do, and then they remain stationary. That, I fancy, is how we "pass over".

'Now, in some natures, these holes are comparatively large, and are constantly coming into opposition. Clairvoyants, mediums are like that. But, as far as I knew, I had no clairvoyant or mediumistic powers at all. I therefore am the sort of person who long ago made up his mind that he never would see a ghost. It was, so to speak, an incalculable chance that my minute spy-hole should come into opposition with the other. But it did: and it knocked me out of time.'

I had heard some such theory before, and though Hugh put it rather picturesquely, there was nothing in the least convincing or practical about it. It might be so, or again it might not.

'I hope your ghost was more original than your theory,' said I, in order to bring him to the point.

'Yes, I think it was. You shall judge.'

I put on more coal and poked up the fire. Hugh has got, so I have always considered, a great talent for telling stories, and that sense of drama which is so necessary for the narrator. Indeed before now, I have suggested to him that he should take this up as a profession, sit by the fountain in Piccadilly Circus, when times are, as usual, bad, and tell stories to the passers-by in the street. Arabian fashion, for reward. The most part of mankind, I am aware, do not like long stories, but to the few, among whom I number myself, who really like to listen to lengthy accounts of experiences, Hugh is an ideal narrator. I do not care for his theories, or for his similes, but when it comes to facts, to things that happened, I like him to be lengthy.

'Go on, please, and slowly,' I said. 'Brevity may be the soul of wit, but it is the ruin of story-telling. I want to hear when and where and how it all was, and what you had for lunch and where you had dined and what – '

Hugh began:

'It was the 24th of June, just eighteen months ago,' he said. 'I had left my flat, you may remember, and come up from the country to stay with you for a week. We had dined alone here – '

I could not help interrupting.

'Did you see the ghost here?' I asked. 'In this square little box of a house in a modern street?'

'I was in the house when I saw it.'

I hugged myself in silence.

'We had dined alone here in Graeme Street,' he said, 'and after dinner I went out to some party, and you stopped at home. At dinner your man did not wait, and when I asked where he was, you told me he was ill, and, I thought, changed the subject rather abruptly. You gave me your latch-key when I went out, and on coming back, I found you had gone to bed. There were, however, several letters for me, which required answers. I wrote them there and then, and posted them at the pillar-box opposite. So I suppose it was rather late when I went upstairs.

'You had put me in the front room, on the third floor, over-looking the street, a room which I thought you generally occupied yourself. It was a very hot night, and though there had been a moon when I started to my party, on my return the whole sky was cloud-covered, and it both looked and felt as if we might have a thunderstorm before morning. I was feeling very sleepy and heavy, and it was not till after I had got into bed that I noticed by the shadows of the window-frames on the blind that only one of the windows was open. But it did not seem worth while to get out of bed in order to open the other, though I felt rather airless and uncomfortable, and I went to sleep.

'What time it was when I awoke I do not know, but it was certainly not yet dawn, and I never remember being conscious of such an extraordinary stillness as prevailed. There was no sound either of foot-passengers or wheeled traffic; the music of life appeared to be absolutely mute. But now instead of being sleepy and heavy, I felt, though I must have slept an hour or two at most, since it was still quite dark, perfectly fresh and wide-awake, and the effort which had seemed not worth making before, that of getting out of bed and opening the other window, was quite easy now, and I pulled up the blind, threw it wide open, and leaned out, for somehow I parched and pined for air. Even outside the oppression was very noticeable, and though, as you know, I am not easily given to feel the mental effects of climate, I was aware of an awful creepiness coming over me. I tried to analyse it away, but without success; the past day had been pleasant, I looked forward to another pleasant day tomorrow, and yet I was full of some nameless apprehension. I felt, too, dreadfully lonely in this stillness before the dawn.

'Then I heard suddenly and not very far away the sound of some approaching vehicle; I could distinguish the tread of two horses walking at a slow foot's pace. They were, though yet invisible, coming up the street, and yet this indication of life did not abate that dreadful sense of loneliness which I have spoken of. Also in some dim unformulated way that which was coming seemed to me to have something to do with the cause of my oppression.

'Then the vehicle came into sight. At first I could not distinguish what it was. Then I saw that the horses were black and had long tails, and that what they dragged was made of glass, but had a black frame. It was a hearse. Empty.

'It was moving up this side of the street. It stopped at your door.

'Then the obvious solution struck me. You had said at dinner that your man was ill, and you were, I thought, unwilling to speak more about his illness. No doubt, so I imagined now, he was dead, and for some reason, perhaps because you did not want me to know anything about it, you were having the body removed at night. This, I must tell you, passed through my mind quite instantaneously, and it did not occur to me how unlikely it really was, before the next thing happened.

'I was still leaning out of the window, and I remember also wondering, yet only momentarily, how odd it was that I saw things – or rather the one thing I was looking at – so very distinctly. Of course, there was a moon behind the clouds, but it was curious how every detail of the hearse and the horses was visible. There was only one man, the driver, with it, and the street was otherwise absolutely empty. It was at him I was looking now. I could see every detail of his clothes, but from where I was, so high above him, I could not see his face. He had on grey trousers, brown boots, a black coat buttoned all the way up, and a straw hat. Over his shoulder there was a strap, which seemed to support some sort of little bag. He looked exactly like – well, from my description what did he look exactly like?'

'Why – a bus-conductor,' I said instantly.

'So I thought, and even while I was thinking this, he looked up at me. He had a rather long thin face, and on his left cheek there was a mole with a growth of dark hair on it. All this was as distinct as if it had been noonday, and as if I was within a yard of him. But – so instantaneous was all that takes so long in telling – I had not time to think it strange that the driver of a hearse should be so unfunereally dressed.

'Then he touched his hat to me, and jerked his thumb over his shoulder.'

' "Just room for one inside, sir," he said.

'There was something so odious, so coarse, so unfeeling about this that I instantly drew my head in, pulled the blind down again, and then, for what reason I do not know, turned on the electric light in order to see what time it was. The hands of my watch pointed to half-past eleven.

'It was then for the first time, I think, that a doubt crossed my mind as to the nature of what I had just seen. But I put out the light again, got into bed, and began to think. We had dined; I had gone to a party, had come back and written letters, had gone to bed and had slept. So how could it be half-past eleven? ... Or – *what* half-past eleven was it?

'Then another easy solution struck me; my watch must have stopped. But it had not; I could hear it ticking.

'There was stillness and silence again. I expected every moment to hear muffled footsteps on the stairs, footsteps moving slowly and smally under the weight of a heavy burden, but from inside the house there was no sound whatever. Outside, too, there was the same dead silence, while the hearse waited at the door. And the minutes ticked on and ticked on, and at length I began to see a difference in the light in the room, and knew that the dawn was beginning to break outside. But how had it happened then that if the corpse was to be removed at night it had not gone, and that the hearse still waited, when morning was already coming?

'Presently I got out of bed again, and with the sense of strong physical shrinking I went to the window and pulled back the blind. The dawn was coming fast; the whole street was lit by that silver hueless light of morning. But there was no hearse there.

'Once again I looked at my watch. It was just a quarter-past four. But I would swear that not half an hour had passed since it had told me that it was half-past eleven.

'Then a curious double sense, as if I was living in the present and at the same moment had been living in some other time, came over me. It was dawn on June 25th, and the street, as natural, was empty. But a little while ago the driver of a hearse had spoken to me, and it was half-past eleven. What was that driver, to what plane did he belong? And again *what* half-past eleven was it that I had seen recorded on the dial of my watch?

'And then I told myself that the whole thing had been a dream. But if you ask me whether I believed what I told myself, I must confess that I did not.

'Your man did not appear at breakfast next morning, nor did I see him again before I left that afternoon. I think if I had, I should have told you about all this, but it was still possible, you see, that what I had seen was a real hearse, driven by a real driver, for all the ghastly gaiety of the face that had looked up to mine, and the levity of his pointing hand. I might possibly have fallen asleep soon after seeing him, and slumbered through the removal of the body and the departure of the hearse. So I did not speak of it to you.'

There was something wonderfully straightforward and prosaic in all this; here were not Jacobean houses oak-panelled and surrounded by weeping pine-trees, and somehow the very absence of suitable surroundings made the story more impressive. But for a moment a doubt assailed me.

'Don't tell me it was all a dream,' I said.

'I don't know whether it was or not. I can only say that I believe myself to have been wide awake. In any case the rest of the story is – odd.'

'I went out of town again that afternoon,' he continued, 'and I may say that I don't think that even for a moment did I get the haunting sense of what I had seen or dreamed that night out of my mind. It was present to me always as some vision unfulfilled. It was as if some clock had struck the four quarters, and I was still waiting to hear what the hour would be.

'Exactly a month afterwards I was in London again, but only for the day. I arrived at Victoria about eleven, and took the Underground to Sloane Square in order to see if you were in town and would give me lunch. It was a baking hot morning, and I intended to take a bus from the King's Road as far as Graeme Street. There was one standing at the corner just as I came out of the station, but I saw that the top was full, and the inside appeared to be full also. Just as I came up to it the conductor who, I suppose, had been inside, collecting fares or what not, came out on to the step within a few feet of me. He wore grey trousers, brown boots, a black coat buttoned, a straw hat, and over his shoulder was a strap on which hung his little machine for punching tickets. I saw his face, too; it was the face of the driver of the hearse, with a mole on the left cheek. Then he spoke to me, jerking his thumb over his shoulder.

' "Just room for one inside, sir," he said.

'At that a sort of panic-terror took possession of me, and I knew I gesticulated wildly with my arms, and cried, "No, no!" But at that moment I was living not in the hour that was then passing, but in that hour which had passed a month ago, when I leaned from the window of your bedroom here just before the dawn broke. At this moment, too, I knew that my spy-hole had been opposite the spy-hole into the spiritual world. What I had seen there had some significance, now being fulfilled, beyond the significance of the trivial happenings of today and tomorrow. The Powers of which we know so little were visibly working before me. And I stood there on the pavement shaking and trembling.

'I was opposite the post-office at the corner, and just as the bus started my eye fell on the clock in the window there. I need not tell you what the time was.

'Perhaps I need not tell you the rest, for you probably conjecture it, since you will not have forgotten what happened at the corner of Sloane Square at the end of July, the summer before last. The bus pulled out from the pavement into the street in order to get round a van that was standing in front of it. At the moment there came down the King's Road a big motor going at a hideously dangerous pace. It crashed full into the bus, burrowing into it as a gimlet burrows into a board.'

He paused.

'And that's my story,' he said.

II

Sweeney Todd, The Demon Barber
Thomas Prest

If Dead of Night *was the film that played an important part in introducing me to the world of the macabre, then the now almost forgotten 'Master of Melodrama', Tod Slaughter, was the film star who sealed my love affair with horror. What imaginative-minded child could have resisted a name like Tod Slaughter, or the gloriously ghoulish titles of the roles he played on both screen and stage in the nineteen thirties, forties and fifties: Sweeney Todd, the Demon Barber; Spring Heeled Jack, the Terror of London; Burke of Burke and Hare, the Bodysnatchers; William Corder, the wicked squire of the murder in the Red Barn, and so on? Slaughter was a large, barrel-chested man of engaging personality, and though his style was pure ham he could transfix any audience as he slashed and murdered his victims with a bloody gusto that no actor before or since has matched. He captivated and terrified me, and I can vividly remember how I cowered in my seat peering through almost closed fingers whenever he hove into sight! Undoubtedly his best, and most famous, role was as the Demon Barber of Fleet Street, and indeed he became well-known by the nick-name of 'Sweeney'. Slaughter played the part of the infamous barber on the stage for almost fifty years until his death in 1956, and made one film version of the story for Ambassador Films in 1936. Wherever he appeared in the part it was customary for a souvenir booklet of the story to be sold, this being an abridged version of the original novel by Thomas Prest published in 1846. This novelisation is now extremely rare, and it is with pleasure as well as a feeling of pure nostalgia that I am returning it to print here. I think the reader may find his interest heightened all the more in the light of the latest revival of the Sweeney Todd story in the musical by Stephen Sondheim which owes a good deal to Prest's tale. But for me, though, there will only ever be one Demon Barber, and I still find it hard to write his name without a shudder!*

I

Near Temple Bar, at the end of Fleet Street, there stood, in the days of George II, a barber's establishment which was conducted by a man named Sweeney Todd. Its outward appearance would compare very unfavourably with any similar institution of the present day, which may also be said of most other businesses of that period, for shopkeepers merely hung out their signs and made little or no pretence of displaying their wares.

But Sweeney Todd's shop presented a mean, dirty, repulsive appearance, for in keeping with the custom of his profession he practised the minor arts of surgery, such as bleeding, and pulling out teeth; so, in addition to the parti-coloured pole projecting from the door, there was at the lower part of the window a row of porringers of pewter and blue and white delf, filled with coagulated blood; while some of the upper panes were adorned with a fanciful arrangement of rotten teeth; and as he united to his vocation the art of dressing and renovating wigs, he added the sign of a grizzly old peruke stuck on a wooden featureless block.

The unpleasant aspect of the exterior was well borne out by the dinginess that prevailed inside, where all the paraphernalia hinted at in the window was to be found in the frowsiest profusion.

At a bench within the shop stood Sweeney Todd dressing a wig, with his apprentice close at hand, timidly watching his movements. He was not a pleasant-looking man, this barber; his brows were low and sullen, his cheekbones high, his nose short and pugnacious, and his hard mouth and square jaw suggested brutal selfishness, which was encouraged by his powerful physique.

'Tobias Wragg,' growled Sweeney, without shifting his eyes from his work, 'you're a lucky dog! Don't you think you're a lucky dog to be here learning an honourable and lucrative profession under such a kind and respected master as myself? Eh?' A pause. 'Haven't you got a tongue?' Sweeney turned and scowled.

'Y'yes, sir,' trembled the boy, painfully uncertain as to what his master expected of him.

'Listen to me seriously, Tobias,' said Sweeney with emphasis, 'you are now my apprentice, bound to me body and soul until you are twenty-one. If you attend to business and merit my approval you may have a comfortable and profitable time with me – I shall not tell you what I expect from you, but I shall watch you, and if you turn out the sort of lad I hope, you will have nothing to complain of, and you may be a rich man some day; but, understand this, if you don't do what I require, if you go against me in any way, if you notice things that are not intended for you to notice, or if you talk outside of anything that takes place here, I'll slit your throat as sure as you are alive. Do you hear, you lout?'

The poor boy, greatly alarmed, was about to give an assurance that he would always do his best to please, when the door was opened and a young man attired in nautical style, and bearing on his good-looking face the bronze of tropical skies, entered the shop. This was Mark Ingestre, whose fate closely concerns this story. Sweeney turned from his work and scrutinised his visitor whilst awaiting his commands.

'Good day to you, Mr Barber, may I trouble you to shave me?' said he.

'Why, of course, you may,' answered Sweeney, 'and I venture to remark that I have rarely shaved a face so gloriously tanned as yours. I presume you have been sailing under sunny skies?'

'Yes, I have known what a hot sun is; but I went to the East for a purpose, determined not to return until it was accomplished. And now I am back again in dear old London with my first great object achieved, and the rest soon will be. But I am in haste to visit my dearest friend, and perhaps you can assist me. I find that Mr Oakley, the spectacle maker, has left Fleet Street – do you know his present address?'

'I do, sir,' replied Sweeney. 'He now lives in Fore Street, and outside you will see the big pair of spectacles that adorned his shop in Fleet Street. Sit down, sir – this chair, please.'

Sweeney always tried to learn as much as possible concerning his patrons, so while he prepared to commence operations he remarked that he had heard much of the wealth of the Indies, but those he knew who had been there had but little to show for their toil. He hoped his visitor had fared better.

'I admit that for a long time I had no luck,' said Mark, 'but when a man can show a packet like this he has little to complain of.' As he spoke he produced a beautifully wrought gold casket. Sweeney was all attention.

'That's wonderfully fine,' he said.

'But not so fine as the contents. Look!' said Mark, opening the box and displaying some magnificent pearls. Sweeney's little eyes glittered.

'I don't know anything about pearls, but they look grand. I shouldn't think you'd take less than a hundred pounds for them.'

'A hundred pounds!' laughed Mark, 'why they are worth £12,000.'

'Really! Well, I'm proud of the honour of shaving you,' said the barber. 'Tobias, go to Mr Crick, in Butcher Row, and ask him if he can oblige me with change for a guinea.'

'I can accommodate you with that,' remarked Mark, putting his hand into his pocket.

'Many thanks,' smiled Todd, 'but it is not so much the change I require as a little outstanding matter which I hope the appearance of my apprentice may bring to his mind.'

He followed Tobias to the door as if to give him further instructions, but his object was to put on the catch. Then, having rapidly lathered Mark's chin, he took a few deliberate steps towards a large cupboard, which he opened, and keeping his eyes on his visitor, who lay with his head back waiting for the shaving to commence, Todd inserted his arm and grasped a lever: there followed a swift, soft, churning sound, the floor opened, and the chair with its burden disappeared. In a few seconds *the chair rose empty*.

Sweeney closed the cupboard, scattered sawdust where it had been disturbed, and picked up the casket. 'Just as well that didn't go with him,' he muttered, as he raised the catch on the door, 'although I shall have to see what else he has got shortly. It is well I waited for this, although I am rich enough without it, and prudence prompts me to get away before my greed of gold proves my undoing.'

Tobias returned at this moment, and so quietly that he startled Sweeney, who hastily thrusting the casket under his apron, turned furiously upon his unfortunate apprentice demanding to know what he meant by creeping back like a spy. He answered that he was afraid of disturbing him in the act of shaving somebody. Unfortunately he saw Mark's hat and stick, and thoughtlessly called Sweeney's attention to them, which infuriated him beyond measure, and he was about to rush at the boy when a negro's head appeared in the doorway.

'Well, Satan, what do you want?' roared Todd.

'Massa Ingestre, where he be?'

'How should I know where he is? Who is he?'

'He came here for shave. I wait for him outside.'

'Well, he's gone, and you go after him.'

'He not gone. I wait outside all time.'

It took Sweeney all his time to get rid of the black, and he was much rattled about it, for he felt there was danger in store for him. Many remarks had been made about mysterious disappearances during the past few months, and many enquiries had been made at his shop by friends of the missing ones, who were stated to have set out intending to call at the barber's, and in consequence he was greatly agitated, for he felt that Tobias had only to mention the hat, stick, and casket, to provide a rope for his neck.

'Yes,' he muttered, 'I'll get away as soon as I can, without a word to anyone.'

But avarice held him in a grip, and while he planned a disappearance he was considering how to dispose of the pearls. Sounds of a brawl in the street reached him, but he was too depressed to seek the reason. The door opened, and amid jeers and shouts, a gentleman entered the shop. Sweeney could hardly believe his eyes – here was the very man to help him out of his first perplexity, Mr Parmine, the eminent goldsmith and jeweller.

'Good evening, Mr Todd,' he said, 'I have been molested

unfortunately in the street just now, my hat was knocked off and my wig snatched, but although I recovered it there is too much mud on it for comfort, so please do your best to set it right.'

Sweeney was thinking hard. He realised that Tobias was in the way. 'Tobias, you can go home, and see that you are early in the morning.' He followed Tobias to the door, and quietly released the catch.

While he endeavoured to restore the outraged glory of the wig Todd spoke casually about precious stones in order that he might lead to the sale of the pearls. Mr Parmine remarked that precious stones were in no demand, the only things asked for being pearls.

'I have some pearls that I might dispose of,' said Sweeney; 'would you care to buy them?'

'Where are they?' asked Mr Parmine.

'Here,' and Sweeney handed him the casket looking keenly at his face to read his thoughts. Mr Parmine was a jeweller of experience, but with all his self-control he did not entirely conceal his surprise.

'H'm. They look well, don't they? Wonderful how cleverly they get up these imitations! The box is not bad either. What do you think of £50 for the lot?'

'I would rather not tell you what I think,' said Sweeney, striving to keep his temper. 'Hand them over!'

'Well, now I come to look at them a little closer, I think, perhaps, I might be able to manage a little more. Shall we say £100?'

'No,' said Todd savagely. 'I know what their value is and so do you.'

'What do you think they are worth then?'

'Twelve thousand pounds, and I am willing to sell them to you so that you can make a substantial profit, but I want no nonsense or haggling.'

'Well, if they are genuine – I didn't think they were – I daresay I can find a purchaser for £11,000; if so I will advance £8,000.'

'That will satisfy me. I will call tomorrow morning for the money.'

'I am afraid I shall not be able to let you have it – there are important matters to be considered first. A string of valuable pearls cannot be bought like common trinkets; the vendor must give every satisfaction as to how he came by them.'

'And who, may I enquire, will question a man of your standing in the trade?' asked Sweeney, trying to be calm.

'That is not the point; if I give you a large sum for an article I am entitled to know how it came into your possession as a safeguard against possible future complications.'

'That is to say that you don't care how I came to possess the property provided I sell it to you at a thief's price, but if I want its real value you mean to be particular.'

'For a man in your position to possess a £12,000 string of pearls requires explanation and I insist that it is given before a magistrate. Come!'

Mr Parmine, casket in hand, turned towards the door, but as he did so Sweeney sprang upon him with the howl of a fiend. The suddenness of the attack, and the blind fury with which it was delivered, gave him an advantage, and he forced the jeweller towards the fatal chair, intending to strangle him in it, for he could not hold him there and manipulate the lever; but scarcely had he thrown him in the chair than the trap-door opened without assistance, and Sweeney was only just able to save himself from disappearing with his victim.

Sweeney was terribly alarmed at his narrow escape, and his blood ran cold when he contemplated the failure of his trap. He kicked the casket on the floor and cursed it. What was he to do now! He dare not allow anyone in the shop with the trap exposed, for there was another chair on the underneath side, which rose as the other descended. If the shop were closed the authorities, with so many rumours afloat, were sure to investigate matters. For some time he sat on a *safe* chair utterly bewildered. He was not addicted to strong liquors, but eventually he rose, and going to his parlour, drank several glasses of brandy in succession.

II

The abode of Mr Oakley in Fore Street has no counterpart in the City today; it was one of those picturesque old houses with small windows and quaint architecture which are dear to all artists; in front the small garden, bright with flowers, did not destroy the commercial aspect denoted by the huge pair of spectacles over the door although the workshop was in the rear.

Soon after the events we have just narrated, a military-looking man in a cloak arrived at the gate, and taking hesitating steps up the pathway, he paused in uncertainty. From the parlour window Johanna Oakley watched the stranger, and thinking she might solve his difficulty, she went out and asked if she could assist him. Her beauty and deep melancholy made an instant impression on him, and he enquired if she was Miss Oakley.

'Yes,' she replied, turning a shade paler, 'tell me, have you come about Mark? You look serious – don't tell me any evil has befallen him. He was to have been here three days ago, but he never came. Have you come from him?'

'I have not come from him, Miss Oakley. I am Colonel Jefferey, his friend; and knowing that this was his destination, and that he carried articles of great value – for he returned from India an affluent man – I have come to tell you all I know of his movements, and consider with you what steps should be taken to trace him. After leaving the ship in the river he went with his black servant to a barber's in Fleet Street. His man waited outside, but he never saw his master again. The barber told him Mark had gone, but the man says that is impossible.'

'Hush! Here comes my mother,' said Johanna, 'she had better not see you yet. Conceal yourself behind this curtain.'

Mr Oakley entered with his wife, who, noticing her daughter's distressed appearance, exclaimed, 'Why, child, how pale and ill you look. I must positively speak to Dr Lupin about you.'

'Dr Lupin may be all very well as a parson,' remarked Mr Oakley, 'but I don't see what he can have to do with Johanna looking pale.'

'A pious man takes an interest in everything and everybody,' his wife replied.

'Then he must be the most intolerable bore in existence, and I don't wonder at his being kicked out of people's houses.'

'If the good man has been kicked he glories in it. You would like to see him murdered on account of his holiness, but you won't say as much when he comes to tea this afternoon.'

'What!' exclaimed her husband, 'haven't I told you a hundred times I won't have him in my house?'

'And haven't I told you twice that number that he shall come to tea? I've asked him and he is coming.'

'But, my dear – '

'It's no use your talking. Oh, dear!' she gasped, 'you have brought on a palpitation – you always do. I must have some brandy.'

'Poor girl,' thought Mr Oakley, as he followed her from the room, 'she has been a good wife, although she has changed of late. I ought to be more considerate.'

Colonel Jefferey reappeared at Johanna's behest, and with a sad heart she heard the story of Mark's adventures, and his disappearance whilst on his way to present her with the pearls.

She cared nothing for the pearls, she said; she would rather have Mark than all the pearls in the world, and in order to learn how the Colonel's efforts progressed she agreed to meet him in Temple Gardens that day week at six o'clock if nothing transpired previously.

As he was about to depart, Johanna exclaimed, 'Dr Lupin! How unfortunate!' and the Colonel again retired behind the curtain.

'Yes, maiden,' said Lupin, 'I am that chosen vessel whom the profane call "Mealy Mouth". I come hither at the bidding of thy respected mother to partake of a vain mixture which rejoiceth in the name of tea.'

'Allow me to pass, if you please, Dr Lupin.'

'Thou art disrespectful considering the honour intended for thee. Thy mother has intended thee to be my wedded wife,' and the slimy hypocrite approached her with extended arms.

'Hands off, or you'll repent it!' exclaimed Johanna.

He still persisted, and the sound of Miss Oakley's alarm proved too much for Colonel Jefferey's self-control; he rushed from his concealment and belaboured the reverend gentleman with the scabbard of his sword with great heartiness. Then, leaving Dr Lupin roaring, and holding a black eye, he escaped out of the door while Johanna locked it after him.

III

A few doors up Bell Yard, at the end of Fleet Street, there was about this time a noted pie-shop kept by a Mrs Lovett, whose wares were in such request by lawyer's clerks and sundry others that at certain hours the place was positively besieged by crowds of epicures who swore there were no pies like them. Tobias often had a pie there when a customer gave him a tip, but it puzzled him how his master knew of it.

One afternoon a shabbily-dressed young man presented himself in the shop, and before he could say anything, Mrs Lovett told him to go away as she never gave anything to beggars.

'I'm not a beggar, marm,' he said, 'I've been unfortunate and I'm looking out for a situation. I hoped you might be able to give me one.'

'What, a dilapidated creature like you!'

'That's where you're wrong, marm; it's manners not togs that make the gentleman. It ain't long ago that I kept my own vehicle.'

'Indeed!'

'Yes, I had the best barrow of greens that ever came out of Clare Market, but some villain sneaked it, and I haven't recovered – but I shall.'

'According to what I see of you if ever you are prosperous your insolence will be unbearable. But what employment could I give you except pie-making? What do you know of that?'

'Oh, I was with a baker for four months – I could soon learn your ways.'

Mrs Lovett looked thoughtful. 'I have a man already, but if I give you a trial can you furnish me with a character?'

'A character? No one knows me. The baker died, and I lost the rest when I lost my barrow.'

'No one knows you? Well, come tomorrow morning and I'll show you what to do.'

In the morning he arrived, and in answer to Mrs Lovett, said his name was Jarvis Williams. Raising a trap-door behind the shop she pointed to some stone stairs: 'By this passage, Jarvis, we descend to the furnace and the ovens, where I will show you how to make the pies, feed the fires, and make yourself generally useful.'

They descended into the bakehouse, a gloomy cellar of vast dimensions and sepulchral appearance; a fitful glare issued from various low-arched entrances in which an oven was placed, and there was a counter with pies on a tray.

'I suppose I'm to have someone to help me in this situation,' said Jarvis. 'One pair of hands could never do the work of such a place.'

'Aren't you satisfied?'

'Oh, yes, only you spoke about having a man.'

'He has gone to his friends – to some of his oldest friends, who will be glad to see him. So now say the word, and let me know if you have any scruples.'

'No scruples, but one objection. I should like to leave when I please.'

'Make your mind easy on that score,' replied Mrs Lovett, 'I never keep anybody many hours after they are dissatisfied. As long as you are industrious you will get on well, but as soon as you begin to get idle and neglect my orders you will receive a piece of information that may – '

'May what?'

'There is no occasion for it yet, but after a time, when you get well fed you may need it, and then you will go to your old friends. Now I must leave you.'

'What a queer way of talking that woman has,' thought Jarvis, 'she seems to have a double meaning all the time. And what a singular-looking place too – nothing visible but darkness. It would be unbearable if it wasn't for the pies.'

Jarvis was at liberty to help himself to as many as he liked, but circumstances blunted his appetite, and before long he discovered he was a prisoner in the gloomy vault. The iron-cased doors above defied all his efforts to escape, and day by day his hopes grew less, until one day he heard strange sounds on the other side of the wall, which he apprehended to be evil. He waited in trepidation as the sounds grew more distinct, and after much suspense a part of the wall gave way, and through the aperture appeared a face – the face of Mr Parmine.

'Who are you?' demanded Jarvis boldly.

'I am the victim of a murderer,' said Mr Parmine, 'and if you are not in league with him you will help me to escape.'

'I should be only too glad to escape myself, for I've been a prisoner for days.'

'Then it's no use my coming in to you, so you had better join me and we will get out somehow. These vaults are no doubt connected with St Dunstan's if we can find its direction.'

'I can tell you that. This is Bell Yard; so turn your back on it and you look towards St Dunstan's.'

'Then come quickly, for I hear footsteps.'

IV

When Sweeney recovered somewhat from his agitation he decided that his only hope of temporary safety depended upon his ability to restore the trap-door to its former condition. He had a certain amount of mechanical skill, but he was handicapped by lack of suitable implements; still he worked at it until far into the night, and although he could not restore its original action, he contrived to fix it so that it would remain rigid under a man's weight.

Then thoroughly exhausted by mental and bodily fatigue, he threw himself upon a couch and slept for some hours. As soon as he was thoroughly awake he arose, and sliding back a panel in the wall he descended many stairs until he reached a vault beneath the trap-door where he expected to find his victims with their brains dashed out. *They were gone!* and not a trace of them to be seen except some blood upon the stones.

Sweeney was aghast – he could only think the worst. Had Mrs Lovett been there?

Mrs Lovett was his mistress and partner in crime, but no one ever saw them together, for his house backed on to hers, and they met by means of mysterious underground passages entirely unknown to the outer world. By a passage known only to himself and his paramour, he made his way towards the pie-shop, and manipulating a secret spring he caused the wall to open like a door, and he entered the bakehouse.

Sweeney had developed a habit of talking to himself: 'I have too many enemies to be safe. I will dispose of them one by one, till no evidence remains against me. My first step must be to stop the tongue of Tobias Wragg. I need not take his life, for that may be of use to me later; but confinement in a lunatic asylum will silence him. Mrs Lovett, too, grows scrupulous and dissatisfied. I've watched her for some time and fear she intends mischief. A little poison when next she visits me may remove any unpleasantness in that direction. Ha! Who – '

Sweeney turned and saw Mrs Lovett at his elbow, and she was in a very bad temper.

'Sweeney Todd!' said Mrs Lovett in a hard voice.

'Well!' replied Sweeney calmly.

'Since I discover that you intend treachery, I demand my share of the plunder this instant – an equal share of the results of our bloodshed.'

'You shall have it,' said Sweeney, with indifference.

'I mean to,' she almost shrieked, 'every penny!'

'Well, all right, be patient. But don't forget that you are greatly in my debt. Remember that I set you up in business – that I taught you the trade secret' – here he drew his fingers significantly across his throat – 'I have kept you in clothes – '

'Clothes!'

'Yes, and you have kept all the profits of the pie-shop, and they belong to me – '

'You want to rob me,' she screamed, 'but I will show you that I will have my due'; and suddenly drawing a knife, she said, 'Now, villain, the whole of the wealth that blood has purchased for me, or I'll slaughter you where you stand!'

'Fool! you should know that Sweeney Todd always calculates his chances,' and springing backwards he drew a pistol from his breast and fired, and Mrs Lovett fell.

'Now the furnace can consume the body and destroy the evidence of any guilt,' he muttered as he opened the furnace door and thrust the body into it.

Immediately the deed was done Todd saw that he had precipitated the end, for the swarm of disappointed pie-eaters would certainly cause an enquiry to be made. How long could he remain with safety?

V

During the next few days Todd was away a great deal, and Tobias was left in charge of the shop, with instructions to do the best he could, and keep his tongue under control. One day, whilst alone, he was startled to hear strange sounds in the barber's parlour (which, of course, was locked in his absence), and still more amazed when the face of Jarvis Williams emerged.

'Phew! out at last,' he exclaimed. 'Why, Toby, old chum, just fancy dropping on you. My word, I have had a time. Where's Todd?'

They were old acquaintances, both hailing from Clare Market; so Jarvis imparted to Tobias the story of his adventures, including what he had heard from Mr Parmine, who had endeavoured to escape by way of St Dunstan's, and also that he had witnessed the murder of Mrs Lovett, whose pies were made of human flesh – poor Tobias felt very sick when he heard that. In return, Tobias gave him the story of Mark Ingestre, the hat, stick, casket, and black servant, and was giving other incidents when Sweeney returned.

Master Williams moved towards the door. 'Well?' said Sweeney questionably. 'It's all right,' said Jarvis. 'I came to see if my father was here, but he's gone,' and away he went. Sweeney looked after him doubtingly; then turning to Tobias he demanded what '*that* fellow' wanted, only to receive the same answer.

'Who else has been?'

'Colonel Jefferey and the black servant kept coming.'

'What did you tell them?'

'Nothing, except that you were out, and I didn't know when you would return.'

'Are you sure that was all?'

'Yes; I never said a word about the things left behind, or the gold casket you had.'

'I *had*, villain!' yelled Todd, and in a burst of ungovernable fury he seized a knife and sprang after his apprentice, who dodged round tables and chairs in terror. But Sweeney heard the rattling of a coach on the cobbles cease at his door: he was evidently expecting it, for he put up the knife and opened the door. 'I'll let you off this time – come, we'll go for a ride. Get in,' he said, pointing to the coach; but Tobias, afraid, refused to move, so Todd called the driver, and the boy's chance of dodging was ended.

They rode to a private mad-house at Peckham, kept by a man named Jonas Fogg, with whom Todd had had previous transactions, and who appeared to know what was expected of him. Todd had some conversation with Fogg, explaining that Tobias suffered from delusions, and was liable to make dangerous statements concerning himself, but he hoped that twelve months' treatment in Fogg's humane institution would restore him to reason, and for that period Todd would pay in advance. Having arranged everything, Sweeney departed, while poor Tobias was taken before the master who caused him to be put in a dark cell, and into a strait jacket if he offered any resistance.

While Fogg was rubbing his hands with satisfaction at receiving twelve months' keep for a patient *who might die in two months*, he little thought how this event would terminate.

When Jarvis Williams left Todd's shop he felt uneasy about Tobias, and he hovered near the shop considering. Soon he saw a coach of ominous appearance arrive, and, later, Tobias was bundled into it and it rumbled away.

Londoners of that day were capable pedestrians, having to depend on their legs for the accomplishment of their travels, and Jarvis thought nothing of following the coach to its destination. For some time it crawled, but afterwards the pace mended, and a journey of about four miles saw the end.

When Sweeney came out alone, Jarvis set off at a good speed towards Clare Market, where some of the toughest rascals in London were to be found, and gathering nearly a score of them they started to the rescue of Tobias.

A leisurely journey to Peckham enabled them to arrange plans *en route*.

It was an awkward place to enter without permission – high walls had to be scaled if they could not gain access from the front door, and that had a grating in it through which a porter scrutinised all visitors. Fortunately the names of the establishment and its proprietor were prominently displayed outside, so Jarvis, having arranged his gang in crouching attitudes where they could not been seen from inside, rang the bell.

'What do you want?' said a voice through the grating.

'Mr Sweeney Todd sent me with an urgent message for Mr Fogg, and I would like to see him,' said Jarvis.

After a brief delay and sounds of bolts and chains being withdrawn, the door opened; Jarvis stepped inside and immediately a desperate rush swept the porter off his feet, and, notwithstanding his strength, he was tied up, legs and arms, before he could resist. Fogg, hearing the noise, put his head out of his room, and they swooped down on him, demanding that Tobias should be produced at once. Fogg, although terrified, tried to equivocate, but they handled him so roughly that he shouted for his attendants, and as they appeared, one by one, they were overpowered, and Tobias was released.

The money Todd had paid was lying on the table, and Fogg would have conveyed it to his pocket if a blow on his hand with a cudgel had not interfered with his plans and allowed his visitors to pocket it instead. They successfully hunted for refreshments, and then, after ransacking the place and releasing all the unfortunate inmates, they left Fogg and his satellites bound hand and foot and departed. Their offence was a hanging one in those days, but they felt certain they need not fear Jonas Fogg.

VI

The figures of Adam and Eve on St Dunstan's Church were striking the hour of six when Colonel Jefferey arrived in Temple Gardens to keep his appointment with Johanna Oakley. She was already there, pale and beautiful, and trembling with anxiety. Unfortunately the Colonel could add but little to what she already knew; he could only tell her of several uneventful visits to the barber's, although he was convinced that Todd could unravel the mystery, and he added that he was in communication with an expert crime investigator.

Johanna thanked him in spite of his ill-success, and she

looked so lovely in her distress that the Colonel decided in the event of Mark never returning to strain all his energies to make her his own; but he was a man of honour and a true friend, and while there was the slightest hope remaining he would not relax his efforts on her behalf. They walked together to Fleet Street, and as she would not accept his offer to escort her home, they parted opposite Todd's shop. The Colonel was going towards Bow Street when a mysterious voice muttered in his ear, 'You seek news of a missing friend; if you will come with me I may be able to help you,' and turning he saw an individual whose features were concealed by a mask.

'I must first know who and what you are before I consent to be guided by a man who hides his features behind a mask,' said the Colonel.

'I wear this mask for other purposes than concealment,' said the man, 'but since you distrust me I will leave you and you will remain without the information you desire.'

'Stay, friend, have you no token to prove your sincerity?'

'Yes, and one that will appeal to you,' he replied, at the same time putting the casket of pearls into his hand.

'Good heavens!' he exclaimed, 'This convinces me – where do you wish me to go?'

'To the shop of Sweeney Todd, the barber, where you will learn something that will surprise you.'

The shop, being only a few yards away, was soon reached, and Colonel Jefferey received the surprise he was promised, for the shop was occupied by constables, and the stranger, removing his mask, revealed the malignant features of Sweeney Todd. The barber, pointing to the Colonel said, 'This is the man who murdered Mark Ingestre, and if you search him you will find the casket of pearls in his possession.'

Colonel Jefferey was astounded; but as the constables gathered round he held out the casket.

'There is no necessity for searching. That villain handed them to me in the street just now as a guarantee of good faith, telling me that if I would visit this shop with him the mystery of Mark Ingestre's disappearance would be cleared up. If Mark has been murdered he is the murderer.'

'You may have a satisfactory explanation,' said the leader of the constables, 'but this is a murder charge, and it is my duty to take you before a magistrate.'

'I am quite ready,' said the Colonel.

Sweeney was chuckling to himself over his cleverness, when the officer said, 'You must come as well.'

'Of course,' replied Sweeney, 'but I'll follow on as I have something to do first.'

'You will come now; there is a counter-charge of murder against you.'

'Nonsense!' said Sweeney, 'why, I've handed the murderer over to you. I'll come on as a witness afterwards.'

'Bring him along!'

And Sweeney joined the party with a constable holding each of his arms.

Let us now refer to certain matters that may seem to require explanation. The Church of St Dunstan's (it was pulled down and rebuilt 1831-3) was an ancient affair that stood 30 feet south of the present church, and beneath it there were extensive underground passages and vaults stretching away in various directions, which few people had ever heard of or suspected to exist. Sweeney Todd, by accident, made the discovery, and after many nocturnal explorations, he concluded that they were entirely forgotten, and that it was safe for him to use them for his own purposes.

A conversation with a skilful mechanic gave him the idea of the trap-door, which they made between them, and when it was completed Sweeney tested its efficiency upon the unsuspecting mechanic, and became the sole possessor of the secret. He worked cautiously, murdering many, and grew rich, but the disposal of the bodies troubled him, as he had to bury them beneath the stones underground.

He had been intimate with Mrs Lovett for some time when he discovered that a passage could be made to communicate with a shop in Bell's Yard, and he installed her in it as an expert pie manufacturer. Then the horrible idea occurred to him that it would be both profitable and expedient if she used the flesh of the dead for her pies, and if any of their assistants suspected anything – *they went to their friends*.

At last the mechanism of the death-trap failed, and Mr

Parmine escaped, because of its irregular action, instead of throwing him on his head, caused him to turn a somersault and fall on his feet, sustaining only minor injuries.

Sweeney Todd prided himself upon his cunning, but little he dreamt what it would do for him. He expected to be at liberty to depart after giving evidence against Colonel Jefferey, but both were detained until the morning. This was a bitter disappointment to Sweeney, who had everything ready for a flight which, during his frequent absences, he had arranged with the captain of a ship in the Thames, who was to sail about midnight – and time and tide wait for no man.

When they appeared before the magistrate Sweeney had a shock which paralysed him with terror; for there, seated beside the magistrate, was the murdered Mr Parmine, and confronting him were Tobias Wragg, Jarvis Williams, Mark Ingestre's black servant, and the captain of the ship he was to have sailed in. It seemed that constables and watchmen had been keeping an eye on Todd, and he was aware of it; and in order to gain the few hours he required to join the ship he endeavoured to betray Colonel Jefferey, but with a fatal result to himself. Every word that went to clear the Colonel struck a blow at Sweeney, with the result that he was committed for trial at the Old Bailey, while Colonel Jefferey went free.

When the trial opened, Sweeney was staggered to see the murdered Mark Ingestre sitting with Colonel Jefferey, and the effect on his nerves was disastrous. It was stated that Mark would have appeared before, but he was too badly injured to be moved, and that but for the defect in the trap he would have been killed. He owed his escape to Mr Parmine.

The evidence of Mark Ingestre and his black servant, of Tobias Wragg, Jarvis Williams, Mr Parmine, and others was overwhelming, and when the judge pronounced sentence of death Sweeney was in a state of abject collapse, from which he never recovered.

His hanging was a great event, for the public were more bitter against him than any other malefactor on record, and especially violent were those who found themselves unwitting cannibals through his instrumentality, and he was pelted all the way to the gallows, his escort having great difficulty in preventing the mob from tearing him limb from limb.

It is satisfactory to record that Mark and Johanna had a happy time in store, and that Fortune was kind to the others who deserved it. Being parted from his treasure embittered Todd's last hours, but it probably did good elsewhere, for Jarvis Williams appeared abundantly supplied with money, possibly due to his subterranean investigations, and by his instrumentality Tobias and his mother were installed in the pie-shop, which they thereafter conducted in exemplary style.

III

The Middle Toe of the Right Foot
Ambrose Bierce

As I have indicated, films had a strong influence on my early interest in the macabre, but the radio, and later television, also played an important part. Although television had begun in Britain on a small scale before the Second World War, it was closed down during the hostilities, and only made a gradual return after 1945. In a great many households – and that of my parents was typical – the 'goggle box' did not find its place in the corner of the living-room until that eventful decade was almost over. The radio set, in fact, was King: and its wide-ranging programmes delighted huge audiences. The developing ghoul in me latched on to two programmes in particular, Appointment With Fear and, later, the spooky stories read by 'The Ghost Man' Algernon Blackwood. Appointment With Fear was a weekly series of programmes in which the storyteller, tantalisingly referred to as 'The Man in Black', related stories that ranged from the fantastic to the horrifying. Although the series had been devised by that talented mystery writer John Dickson Carr (who wrote many of the scripts), it was the voice of 'The Man in Black' that made the programme what it was. Deep and resonant, it suggested horrors that the listener could easily conjure up in his own imagination. This, indeed, was the great strength of radio over television where the horror story was concerned: the audience 'saw' in their minds far more vivid terrors than any screen could show. I soon joined the millions who listened with bated breath and quickening pulse each week, often huddled beside the radio set in a room illuminated only by the flickering flames of a winter fire. 'The Man in Black' was Valentine Dyall and it is good to be able to report that he is still busily engaged in acting today. Of all the stories he narrated, none has stayed more firmly fixed in my memory than 'The Middle Toe of the Right Foot', and I can hear his voice all over again as soon as I start reading the following lines ...

I

It is well known that the old Manton house is haunted. In all the rural district near about, and even in the town of Marshall, a mile away, not one person of unbiased mind entertains a doubt of it; incredulity is confined to those opinionated people who will be called 'cranks' as soon as the useful word shall have penetrated the intellectual demesne of the Marshall *Advance*. The evidence that the house is haunted is of two kinds: the testimony of disinterested witnesses who have had ocular proof, and that of the house itself. The former may be disregarded and ruled out on any of the various grounds of objections which may be urged against it by the ingenious; but facts within the observation of all are fundamental and controlling.

In the first place, the Manton house has been unoccupied by mortals for more than ten years, and with its outbuildings is slowly falling into decay – a circumstance which in itself the judicious will hardly venture to ignore. It stands a little way off the loneliest reach of the Marshall and Harriston road, in an opening which was once a farm and is still disfigured with strips of rotting fence and half covered with brambles over-running a stony and sterile soil long unacquainted with the plough. The house itself is in tolerably good condition, though badly weather-stained and in dire need of attention from the glazier, the smaller male population of the region having attested in the manner of its kind its disapproval of dwellings without dwellers. The house is two stories in height, nearly square, its front pierced by a single doorway flanked on each side by a window boarded up to the very top. Corresponding windows above, not protected, serve to admit light and rain to the rooms of the upper floor. Grass and weeds grow pretty rankly all about, and a few shade trees, somewhat the worse for wind and leaning all in one direction, seem to be making a concerted effort to run away. In short, as the Marshall town humorist explained in the columns of the *Advance*, 'the proposition that the Manton house is badly haunted is the only logical conclusion from the premises.' The fact that in this dwelling Mr Manton thought it expedient one night some ten years ago to rise and cut the throats of his wife and two small children, removing at once to another part of the country, has no doubt done its share in directing public attention to the fitness of the place for supernatural phenomena.

To this house, one summer evening, came four men in a waggon. Three of them promptly alighted, and the one who had been driving hitched the team to the only remaining post of what had been a fence. The fourth remained seated in the waggon. 'Come,' said one of his companions, approaching him, while the others moved away, in the direction of the dwelling – 'this is the place.'

The man addressed was deathly pale and trembled visibly. 'By God!' he said harshly, 'this is a trick, and it looks to me as if you were in it.'

'Perhaps I am,' the other said, looking him straight in the face and speaking in a tone which had something of contempt in it. 'You will remember, however, that the choice of place was, with your own assent, left to the other side. Of course if you are afraid of spooks – '

'I am afraid of nothing,' the man interrupted with another oath, and sprang to the ground. The two then joined the others at the door, which one of them had already opened with some difficulty, caused by rust of lock and hinge. All entered. Inside it was dark, but the man who had unlocked the door produced a candle and matches and made a light. He then unlocked a door on their right as they stood in the passage. This gave them entrance to a large, square room, which the candle but dimly lighted. The floor had a thick carpeting of dust, which partly muffled their footfalls. Cobwebs were in the angles of the walls and depended from the ceiling like strips of rotting lace, making undulatory movements in the disturbed air. The room had two windows in adjoining sides, but from neither could anything be seen except the rough inner surfaces of boards a few inches from the glass. There was no fireplace, no furniture; there was nothing. Besides the cobwebs and the dust, the four men were the only objects there which were not a part of the architecture. Strange enough they looked in the yellow light of the candle. The one who had so reluctantly alighted was especially 'spectacular' – he might have been called sensational. He was of middle age, heavily built, deep chested and broad-shouldered. Looking at his figure, one would have said that he had a giant's strength; at his face, that he would use it like a giant. He was clean shaven, his hair rather closely cropped and grey. His low forehead was seamed with wrinkles above the eyes, and over the nose these became vertical. The heavy black brows followed the same law, saved from meeting only by an upward turn at what would otherwise have been the point of contact. Deeply sunken beneath these, glowed in the obscure light a pair of eyes of uncertain colour, but, obviously enough, too small. There was something forbidding in their expression, which was not bettered by the cruel mouth and wide jaw. The nose was well enough, as noses go; one does not expect much of noses. All that was sinister in the man's face seemed accentuated by an unnatural pallor – he appeared altogether bloodless.

The appearance of the other men was sufficiently commonplace: they were such persons as one meets and forgets that he met. All were younger than the man described, between whom and the eldest of the others, who stood apart, there was apparently no kindly feeling. They avoided looking at one another.

'Gentlemen,' said the man holding the candle and keys, 'I believe everything is right. Are you ready, Mr Rosser?'

The man standing apart from the group bowed and smiled.

'And you, Mr Grossmith?'

The heavy man bowed and scowled.

'You will please remove your outer clothing.'

Their hats, coats, waistcoats, and neckwear were soon removed and thrown outside the door, in the passage. The man with the candle now nodded, and the fourth man – he who had urged Mr Grossmith to leave the waggon – produced from the pocket of his overcoat two long, murderous-looking bowie knives, which he drew from the scabbards.

'They are exactly alike,' he said, presenting one to each of the two principals – for by this time the dullest observer would have understood the nature of this meeting. It was to be a duel to the death.

Each combatant took a knife, examined it critically near the candle and tested the strength of blade and handle across his lifted knee. Their persons were then searched in turn, each by the second of the other.

'If it is agreeable to you, Mr Grossmith,' said the man holding the light, 'you will place yourself in that corner.'

He indicated the angle of the room farthest from the door, to which Grossmith retired, his second parting from him with a grasp of the hand which had nothing of cordiality in it. In the angle nearest the door Mr Rosser stationed himself, and, after a whispered consultation, his second left him, joining the other near the door.

At that moment the candle was suddenly extinguished, leaving all in profound darkness. This may have been done by a draught from the open door; whatever the cause, the effect was appalling!

'Gentlemen,' said a voice which sounded strangely unfamiliar in the altered condition affecting the relations of the senses, 'gentlemen, you will not move until you hear the closing of the outer door.'

A sound of trampling ensued, the closing of the inner door; and finally the outer one closed with a concussion which shook the entire building.

A few minutes later a belated farmer's boy met a waggon which was being driven furiously toward the town of Marshall. He declared that behind the two figures on the front seat stood a third with its hands upon the bowed shoulders of the others, who appeared to struggle vainly to free themselves from its grasp. This figure, unlike the others, was clad in white, and had undoubtedly boarded the waggon as it passed the haunted house. As the lad could boast a considerable former experience with the supernatural thereabout, his word had the weight justly due to the testimony of an expert. The story eventually appeared in the *Advance*, with some slight literary embellishments and a concluding intimation that the gentlemen referred to would be allowed the use of the paper's columns for their version of the night's adventure. But the privilege remained without a claimant.

II

The events which led up to this 'duel in the dark' were simple enough. One evening three young men of the town of Marshall were sitting in a quiet corner of the porch of the village hotel, smoking and discussing such matters as three educated young men of a Southern village would naturally find interesting. Their names were King, Sancher, and Rosser. At a little distance, within easy hearing but taking no part in the conversation, sat a fourth. He was a stranger to the others. They merely knew that on his arrival by the stage coach that afternoon he had written in the hotel register the name Robert Grossmith. He had not been observed to speak to anyone except the hotel clerk. He seemed, indeed, singularly fond of his own company – or, as the *personnel* of the *Advance* expressed it, 'grossly addicted to evil associations.' But then it should be said in justice to the stranger that the *personnel* was himself of a too convivial disposition fairly to judge one differently gifted, and had, moreover, experienced a slight rebuff in an effort at an 'interview'.

'I hate any kind of deformity in a woman,' said King, 'whether natural or – or acquired. I have a theory that any physical defect has its correlative mental and moral defect.'

'I infer, then,' said Rosser, gravely, 'that a lady lacking the advantage of a nose would find the struggle to become Mrs King an arduous enterprise.'

'Of course you may put it that way,' was the reply; 'but, seriously, I once threw over a most charming girl on learning, quite accidentally, that she had suffered amputation of a toe. My conduct was brutal, if you like, but if I had married that girl I should have been miserable and should have made her so.'

'Whereas,' said Sancher, with a light laugh, 'by marrying a gentleman of more liberal views she escaped with a cut throat.'

'Ah, you know to whom I refer! Yes, she married Manton, but I don't know about his liberality; I'm not sure but he cut her throat because he discovered that she lacked that excellent thing in woman, the middle toe of the right foot.'

'Look at that chap!' said Rosser in a low voice, his eyes

fixed upon the stranger.

That person was obviously listening intently to the conversation.

'That's an easy one,' Rosser replied, rising. 'Sir,' he continued, addressing the stranger, 'I think it would be better if you would remove your chair to the other end of the verandah. The presence of gentlemen is evidently an unfamiliar situation to you.'

The man sprang to his feet and strode forward with clenched hands, his face white with rage. All were now standing. Sancher stepped between the belligerents.

'You are hasty and unjust,' he said to Rosser; 'this gentleman has done nothing to deserve such language.'

But Rosser would not withdraw a word. By the custom of the country and the time, there could be but one outcome to the quarrel.

'I demand the satisfaction due to a gentleman,' said the stranger, who had become more calm. 'I have not an acquaintance in this region. Perhaps you, sir,' bowing to Sancher, 'will be kind enough to represent me in this matter.'

Sancher accepted the trust – somewhat reluctantly, it must be confessed, for the man's appearance and manner were not at all to his liking. King, who during the colloquy had hardly removed his eyes from the stranger's face, and had not spoken a word, consented with a nod to act for Rosser, and the upshot of it was that, the principals having retired, a meeting was arranged for the next evening. The nature of the arrangements has been already disclosed. The duel with knives in a dark room was once a commoner feature of South-western life than it is likely to be again. How thin a veneering of 'chivalry' covered the essential brutality of the code under which such encounters were possible, we shall see.

III

In the blaze of a midsummer noonday, the old Manton house was hardly true to its traditions. It was of the earth, earthy. The sunshine caressed it warmly and affectionately, with evident unconsciousness of its bad reputation. The grass greening all the expanse in its front seemed to grow, not rankly, but with a natural and joyous exuberance, and the weeds blossomed quite like plants. Full of charming lights and shadows, and populous with pleasant-voiced birds, the neglected shade trees no longer struggled to run away, but bent reverently beneath their burdens of sun and song. Even in the glassless upper windows was an expression of peace and contentment, due to the light within. Over the stony fields the visible heat danced with a lively tremor incompatible with the gravity which is an attribute of the supernatural.

Such was the aspect under which the place presented itself to Sheriff Adams and two other men who had come out from Marshall to look at it. One of these men was Mr King, the sheriff's deputy; the other, whose name was Brewer, was a brother of the late Mrs Manton. Under a beneficent law of the State relating to property which has been for a certain period abandoned by its owner, whose residence cannot be ascertained, the sheriff was the legal custodian of the Manton farm and the appurtenances thereunto belonging. His present visit was in mere perfunctory compliance with some order of a court in which Mr Brewer had an action to get possession of the property as heir to his deceased sister. By a mere coincidence the visit was made on the day after the night that Deputy King had unlocked the house for another and very different purpose. His presence now was not of his own choosing: he had been ordered to accompany his superior, and at the moment could think of nothing more prudent than simulated alacrity in obedience. He had intended going anyhow, but in other company.

Carelessly opening the front door, which to his surprise was not locked, the sheriff was amazed to see, lying on the floor of the passage into which it opened, a confused heap of men's apparel. Examination showed it to consist of two hats, and the same number of coats, waistcoats, and scarves, all in a remarkably good state of preservation, albeit somewhat defiled by the dust in which they lay. Mr Brewer was equally astonished, but Mr King's emotion is not on record. With a new and lively interest in his own actions, the sheriff now unlatched and pushed open a door on the right, and the three entered. The room was apparently vacant – no; as their eyes became accustomed to the dimmer light, something was visible in the farthest angle of the wall. It was a human figure – that of a man crouching close in the corner. Something in the attitude made the intruders halt when they had barely passed the threshold. The figure more and more clearly defined itself. The man was upon one knee, his back in the angle of the wall, his shoulders elevated to the level of his ears, his hands before his face, palms outward, the fingers spread and crooked like claws; the white face turned upward on the retracted neck had an expression of unutterable fright, the mouth half open, the eyes incredibly expanded. He was stone dead – dead of terror! Yet, with the exception of a knife, which had evidently fallen from his own hand, not another object was in the room.

In the thick dust which covered the floor were some confused footprints near the door and along the wall through which it opened. Along one of the adjoining walls, too, past the boarded-up windows, was the trail made by the man himself in reaching his corner. Instinctively in approaching the body the three men now followed that trail. The sheriff grasped one of the out-thrown arms; it was as rigid as iron, and the application of a gentle force rocked the entire body without altering the relation of its parts. Brewer, pale with terror, gazed intently into the distorted face. 'God of mercy!' he suddenly cried, 'it is Manton!'

'You are right,' said King, with an evident attempt at calmness: 'I knew Manton. He then wore a full beard and his hair long, but this is he.'

He might have added: 'I recognised him when he challenged Rosser. I told Rosser and Sancher who he was before we played him this horrible trick. When Rosser left this dark room at our heels, forgetting his clothes in the excitement, and driving away with us in his shirt – all through the discreditable proceedings we knew whom we were dealing with, murderer and coward that he was!'

But nothing of this did Mr King say. With his better light he was trying to penetrate the mystery of the man's death. That he had not once moved from the corner where he had been stationed, that his posture was that of neither attack nor defence, that he had dropped his weapon, that he had obviously perished of sheer terror of something that he *saw* –

these were circumstances which Mr King's disturbed intelligence could not rightly comprehend.

Groping in intellectual darkness for a clue to his maze of doubt, his gaze, directed mechanically downward, as is the way of one who ponders momentous matters, fell upon something which, there, in the light of day, and in the presence of living companions, struck him with an invincible terror. In the dust of years that lay thick upon the floor – leading from the door by which they had entered, straight across the room to within a yard of Manton's crouching corpse – were three parallel lines of footprints – light but definite impressions of bare feet, the outer ones those of small children, the inner a woman's. From the point at which they ended they did not return; they pointed all one way. Brewer, who had observed them at the same moment, was leaning forward in an attitude of rapt attention, horribly pale.

'Look at that!' he cried, pointing with both hands at the nearest print of the woman's right foot, where she had apparently stopped and stood. 'The middle toe is missing – it was Gertrude!'

Gertrude was the late Mrs Manton, sister to Mr Brewer.

IV

King's Evidence
Algernon Blackwood

The second radio influence on my youth was Algernon Blackwood who was a superb teller of weird stories which he presented under the nom-de-plume of 'The Ghost Man'. Blackwood is rightly regarded as one of the best horror story writers of the twentieth century, and it comes as no surprise to find that much of his work is still readily available in print. One of his great strengths as a writer was the fact that he had travelled widely and experienced a great many things of a supernatural and occult nature – devil worship in Germany, for instance, and a haunting in New York, to quote just two instances. Indeed when he wrote or told a story you had the feeling he had actually experienced what he was describing – and this gave all his work a special quality which has made it highly regarded by enthusiasts of the macabre. There are quite a number of his stories that could be included here as typical of his literary style and evocative of his broadcasts, but I have selected 'King's Evidence' because it does not appear in his collected works and I'm very fond of it. It also seems particularly appropriate for a collection such as this because it reaches its climax in the dead of night ...

When Flanagan left his nursing home that November afternoon the last rays of the red sunset lay over Regent's Park. It was very still. The air was raw, but the sky was clear, if with a hint of possible fog to come.

Flanagan was on his way to South Kensington by the Underground. He was in high spirits. His fear of open spaces – agoraphobia so-called – at last was really cured. He no longer dreaded to cross a square, a lawn, a field. This terrible affliction, inherited from shell-shock, was a thing of the past, thank heaven. For months he had been unable even to cross the open garden of the home. Gradually, the specialists had weaned him from that awful terror. Already he had made small journeys alone. Now he was fit for a longer effort.

'It'll do you good,' said the Matron, seeing him off. 'Go and have tea with your pal. An open space won't bother you a bit, and anyhow there are no open spaces on the Underground. Be back for dinner at 7.0.'

And Tim Flanagan, young Canadian soldier, who knew nothing of London beyond the precincts of his nursing home, started off full of confidence. Exact directions – first right, second left, etc., lay in his pocket. To a man of the backwoods it was child's play. He took the Underground at Regent's Park and reached South Kensington easily, of course. Then, leaving the train twenty minutes later and coming up to street level, he entered a world of blackness he had never known before, though he had read about it – a genuine London pea-soup fog.

'Gosh!' he said to himself. 'This is the real thing!'

The station hall itself was darkened with all its lights. He faced a wall of opaque, raw, stifling gloom that stung his eyes and bit into his throat. The change was so sudden, it amazed him. But the novelty at first stimulated him, accustomed as he was to the clear Canadian air. It seemed unbelievable, but it was true. He watched the people grope their way out into the street – and vanish. He hesitated. A slight shiver ran over him.

'Come on now, Tim Flanagan!' he said. 'You know the directions by heart,' – and he plunged down into the filthy blackness of the open street. First to the right, second to the left – and within five minutes he was completely lost.

He stood still, aware suddenly that he must keep himself in hand. He repeated calmly the directions he knew so well. But got them mixed. How many turns had he made so far? He wasn't sure. Memory was already out of gear a little. Too dark to read the paper in his pocket. Nothing to help him – no stars, wind, scent, sound of running water, moss on the north side of the trees.

Groping figures emerged, vanished, reappeared, dissolved. He heard shuffling feet, sticks tapping. Saw an occasional taxi crawling by the kerb, the passenger walking. They loomed, faded, were gone. A swirl in the fog showed a faint light, and he staggered towards it and recognized an island. Thank heaven for that refuge! A figure or two arrived and left as he stood there, clutching the lamp-post. They asked the way, choking, he asked the way, coughing. They lurched off and the murk covered them. Like blind fish, he thought, on the ocean bed. But his confusion and bewilderment became serious, with unpleasant symptoms he thought done with for ever. There were no carts, no taxis now, no figures either. He was alone, an empty space about him – the two things he dreaded most. He waved his stick. It struck nothing solid. In spite of the cold, he was sweating. And panic slowly raised its ugly head.

'I must get across to the pavement. I must cross that open space. I *must* ...!'

It took him fifteen minutes, most of the way on his hands and knees, but the moment of collapse was close as he crawled along pluckily by the pavement railings – then saw a slight thickening of the fog beneath the next lamp, grotesquely magnified. Was it real? It moved. It moved towards him. It was a human being. If it was a human being he could speak to – be with – he would be saved. It came close up against his face. It was a woman.

He gasped out at it, pulling himself up by the railing.

'Lost your way like me, Ma'am? D'you know where you are? Morley Place I'm looking for. For heaven's sake ...'

His voice stopped dead. The woman was peering down at him. He saw her face quite clearly – the brilliant, frightened eyes, the skin white like linen. She was young, wrapped in a dark fur coat. She had beauty – beauty of a sort. He didn't care who or what she was. To him she meant – safety only.

There was no answer to his questions. She whispered – as though speech was difficult: 'Where am I? I came out so suddenly. I can't find my way back ...' and was gone from his side into the swirling fog.

And Flanagan, without an instant's hesitation, went after her. He *must* be with a human being. She moved swiftly, seemed sure of her way, she never faltered. Terrified he might lose sight of her, he kept breathlessly at her heels. She uttered no sound, no cry, not once did she turn her head. But her unfaltering speed helped to restore his own confidence. She knew her way now beyond all question. But two things struck

him as odd – first that she made no sound – he heard no footsteps – second that she left a curious faint perfume in the air, a
perfume that made him uneasy – connecting it somehow with
misery and pain.

Abruptly then she swerved, so abruptly that he almost
touched her, and passed through an iron gate – across a tiny
garden to a house.

She did not turn her head, but he heard her queer
whispering voice again: 'I've found it. Now I can get back.'

'May I come in too?' he cried, exhausted. 'Don't leave me!
If I'm left alone I shall go mad!'

There was no answer. She passed like a feather up the stone
steps and vanished into the house. The front door, he noticed,
was ajar already. Nor did she close it behind her. He followed
her – into a pitchblack hall, then collapsed in a heap on the
stone floor. But he was safe. The open spaces of the street were
behind him. He heard a door open and close upstairs.
Complete silence followed.

A couple of minutes later he struggled to his feet, switched
on his electric torch, and realized at once that the house was
untenanted. Dust-sheets covered the hall furniture. Through a
door, half open, he saw pictures screened on the walls,
brackets draped. But companionship – human companionship was what he wanted – and *must* have – or his mind would
go. He was shaking like a leaf. So he crept upstairs on tiptoe
and reached the landing. Then stood still. His knees felt like
blotting-paper.

He saw a long corridor with closed doors. And he cautiously
tried three in succession – empty rooms, furniture under dust-
sheets, blinds down, mattresses rolled up. At the fourth door
he knew he was right, for the strange, unpleasant odour
caught his nostrils. And this time he knew instantly why it
brought pain and misery – anaesthetic, ether or chloroform.

His next glance showed him the young woman lying in her
fur coat on the bed. The body lay at full length. Motionless.
He had seen death too often to be mistaken, much less afraid.
He stole up, felt her cheek, still warm. An hour or so ago she
was alive. He gently raised a closed eyelid, but hurriedly let it
fall again, and in the presence of death instinctively he took off
his hat, laying it on the bed. His hand then, moving towards

the heart, encountered a hard knob – the head of a long steel
hat-pin driven up to its hilt. But his own private terror was
now lost in something greater. He drew the pin out slowly and
placed it on her breast. And in doing so he noticed a blood
stain on his finger. At which instant there was a loud clanging
noise downstairs – the front-door being closed. A frenzied
realization of his position blazed into his mind – a dead
woman, alone together in an empty house, blood on my hand,
fingerprints on the door-handle and pin, body still warm,
police!

The sinister combination cleared his brain. Heart racing
madly, he switched out his light, and darted across the
landing to the room opposite – seeing as he ran the flicker of
an electric torch on banisters and ceiling, as the man holding
it rapidly climbed the stairs. He managed it just in time.
Through the crack of his own door he saw the outline of the
man slip into the room where the dead – the murdered –
woman lay and close the door carefully behind him. Only his
outline had been visible, blurred in the deep shadows behind
the torch he carried.

The one thing Flanagan knew was that he must get away
instantly. He crept out, stole along the landing on tiptoe, and
began the perilous descent with the utmost caution. Each time
a board creaked, his heart missed a beat. He tested each step.
Half-way down, to his horror, his foot tripped in a rod – with
an uproar like a handgrenade in his forgotten trenches.
Concealment was now impossible. He took the last flight in a
leap, shot across the hall, tore open the front door, just as his
pursuer, with torch in hand, had reached the top of the stairs.
The light flashed down on to him for a second? He wasn't
sure. He banged the door, and plunged headlong into the
welcome all-obscuring fog outside.

He ran wildly, fast as he could, across the little garden out
into the street. The fog held no terrors for him now. His one
object was to put distance between him and that house of
death. Sense of direction he had none. There was no sound of
steps behind him. For ten, fifteen minutes, he raced along. He
must have gone a long way – a mile at least – when his legs
failed him, his mind went black, his strength was gone, and
the terror of open spaces rose over him like ice. He dropped in

his tracks clinging to the cold, wet area railing – one thought only hideously clear in his brain before it stopped functioning – he had left his hat beside the body on the bed.

Unconsciousness followed. He had no recollection exactly – till a voice sounded, a man's voice, kindly.

'Can I be of any assistance? Come, let me help you. Take my arm. I'm a physician. Luckily, too, you're just outside my house ...'

And Flanagan felt himself half dragged, half pushed into a warm, well-lit hall, the stranger having opened the door with a latchkey. A few minutes later, he was sipping whiskey before a blazing fire, trying to stammer his thanks and gratitude.

'Got lost,' he managed to say, 'agor – agoraphobia, sir, you know ... shell-shock ... you've saved me ...'

And some fifteen minutes later, whiskey, warmth and experienced human sympathy had worked wonders. The doctor's handling of the terrified youth was masterly. Flanagan found fuller control come back. He even smoked a cigarette with pleasure.

'You know,' the doctor was saying in his pleasant, gentle voice, 'I rather guessed it might be shell-shock. I've seen so many cases ...' as Flanagan now began to take him in more fully; elderly, with a very determined, implacable look sometimes behind what was a good, almost a benevolent face. A man not to be trifled with, he felt. 'And I'm encouraged', the doctor went on smilingly, 'to hazard a second guess – that you've had another violent shock too – quite recently.' He looked hard into Flanagan's eyes. 'Am I not right – eh? Yes, I felt sure of it.' There came a little pause. 'Now, why not tell me about it,' came the suggestion, soothingly, yet with more authority in the tone. 'It will help you – relieve your mind. Suppression is bad, remember. And we're complete strangers to one another. I don't know your name. You don't know mine. Tell me about it. Confession,' he laughed, 'is good for the soul, they say ...'

Flanagan hesitated. 'It's too incredible,' he mumbled, though burning to get it out of him. 'You just couldn't believe it, sir.'

In the end he told it, all of it, faithfully.

'Pretty tall story, isn't it, sir?'

'Tall, yes,' came the quiet reply, 'but not incredible – as I know from many a strange experience.' He paused and sipped his drink. 'In fact, as one confidence deserves another,' he went on, '*I* might now tell *you* of an oddly similar case that came my way. It may make you feel more comfortable,' he added with skilful tact, 'to hear *my* story. I won't give names, of course. It's about an officer at the front – great friend of mine – middle-aged, rich, just married to a young girl – a cheap, pleasure-loving sort, utterly worthless, I'm afraid. While he was fighting for his country, she took a lover. Planned to run away. Only somehow the husband got wind of it out in France. He got leave, too, just in the nick of time ...'

'Well rid of her,' Flanagan put in.

'Perhaps,' said the doctor. 'Only he determined to make that riddance final.'

Flanagan gasped, but not audibly. And that implacable look on the other's face had hardened him a little. He listened more closely, he watched more closely, too. He was thinking hard. Reflecting. A touch of uneasiness stirred in him.

'Go on, please,' he said.

The doctor went on; in a lowered tone. 'They met, he found out, this guilty pair, in an empty house, a house belonging to the husband. And the woman, using her latchkey, slipped in. She left the door ajar for the lover. She found death waiting for her. It was a *painless* death. Her lover, for some reason, was late. The fog possibly. It must have been a night rather like this, I gather ...'

'The lover,' Flanagan whispered, for his voice failed him somehow, 'the lover didn't come, you mean?'

'A man *did* come in,' was the doctor's quiet answer, 'but he hardly tallied with the description the husband had. A stranger, apparently. Saw the door ajar and came in for shelter perhaps – just as you might have done.'

Flanagan felt a shiver run down his spine. 'And the husband,' he asked under his breath, 'where was *he* all this time?'

'Oh,' came the answer at once, 'waiting outside – concealed in the fog. Watching. He saw the man go in, of course. Five minutes later he went in after him.'

Flanagan stood up with a sudden jerk. 'I'll be going,' he

said abruptly, and added some words of mumbled thanks. The doctor said nothing. He too rose to his feet. They passed into the hall.

'But you can't go out in the fog like that,' said the doctor, quietly enough. 'Why, you've got no hat. Here, I'll lend you one.' And he casually took a hat from a row on the rack and Flanagan mechanically put it on his head. He didn't shake the offered hand. Perhaps he hadn't seen it. He went out.

The fog had lifted a bit. He found his station easily. Open spaces did not bother him.

In the bright light of the train he took off the borrowed hat and looked it over. It was his own hat.

V

The Sire de Malétroit's Door
Robert Louis Stevenson

Television did not enter my family home until the late 1940s – but when it did it was to have a startling effect on my fascination with the macabre. Much of my early viewing was naturally confined to children's programmes which ran between five and six o'clock: then came the great night when I was allowed to stay up and see a play. My parents' choice of suitable adult viewing for my impressionable young mind has puzzled me to this day – although I'm obviously glad they took the view they did – for it was a season of dramas based on the works of Robert Louis Stevenson, ranging from Dr Jekyll and Mr Hyde *to 'The Body Snatcher' and 'The Sire de Malétroit's Door'. Although the names of the actors who appeared have long since escaped me, the production of those grim tales on the tiny, black and white screen was unforgettable. In those days television had to be watched in a darkened room, and the voices of the characters seemed to echo eerily from the set. These facts, plus Stevenson's terrifying stories, added a new dimension to my world of horror. Although I recall* Dr Jekyll and Mr Hyde *as the best of all the productions, there is obviously not room here for the entire novel: instead I have settled for another programme I particularly enjoyed – the strange tale of 'The Sire de Malétroit's Door' which is now almost forgotten amongst Stevenson's works. It also seems appropriate because in 1951 I saw an American film version of the same story entitled* The Strange Door *starring Boris Karloff and Charles Laughton and it immediately served to remind me of those first evenings when television brought nightmares into my own living room!*

Denis de Beaulieu was not yet two-and-twenty, but he counted himself a grown man, and a very accomplished cavalier into the bargain. Lads were early formed in that rough, warfaring epoch; and when one has been in a pitched battle and a dozen raids, has killed one's man in an honourable fashion, and knows a thing or two of strategy and mankind, a certain swagger in the gait is surely to be pardoned. He had put up his horse with due care, and supped with due deliberation; and then, in a very agreeable frame of mind, went out to pay a visit in the grey of the evening. It was not a very wise proceeding on the young man's part. He would have done better to remain beside the fire or go decently to bed. For the town was full of the troops of Burgundy and England under a mixed command; and though Denis was there on safe-conduct, his safe-conduct was like to serve him little on a chance encounter.

It was September 1429; the weather had fallen sharp; a flighty piping wind, laden with showers, beat about the township; and the dead leaves ran riot along the streets. Here and there a window was already lighted up; and the noise of men-at-arms making merry over supper within, came forth in fits and was swallowed up and carried away by the wind. The night fell swiftly; the flag of England, fluttering on the spire-top, grew ever fainter and fainter against the flying clouds – a black speck like a swallow in the tumultuous, leaden chaos of the sky. As the night fell the wind rose, and began to hoot under archways and roar amid the tree-tops in the valley below the town.

Denis de Beaulieu walked fast and was soon knocking at his friend's door; but though he promised himself to stay only a little while and make an early return, his welcome was so pleasant, and he found so much to delay him, that it was already long past midnight before he said good-bye upon the threshold. The wind had fallen again in the meanwhile; the night was as black as the grave; not a star, nor a glimmer of moonshine, slipped through the canopy of cloud. Denis was ill-acquainted with the intricate lanes of Château Landon; even by daylight he had found some trouble in picking his way; and in this absolute darkness he soon lost it altogether. He was certain of one thing only – to keep mounting the hill; for his friend's house lay at the lower end, or tail, of Château Landon, while the inn was up at the head, under the great church spire. With this clue to go upon he stumbled and groped forward, now breathing more freely in open places where there was a good slice of sky overhead, now feeling along the wall in stifling closes. It is an eerie and mysterious position to be thus submerged in opaque blackness in an almost unknown town. The silence is terrifying in its possibilities. The touch of cold window bars to the exploring hand startles the man like the touch of a toad; the inequalities of the pavement shake his heart into his mouth; a piece of denser darkness threatens an ambuscade or a chasm in the pathway; and where the air is brighter, the houses put on strange and bewildering appearances, as if to lead him farther from his way. For Denis, who had to regain his inn without attracting notice, there was real danger as well as mere discomfort in the walk; and he went warily and boldly at once, and at every corner paused to make an observation.

He had been for some time threading a lane so narrow that he could touch a wall with either hand, when it began to open out and go sharply downward. Plainly this lay no longer in the direction of his inn; but the hope of a little more light tempted him forward to reconnoitre. The land ended in a terrace with a bartizan wall, which gave an outlook between high houses, as out of an embrasure, into the valley lying dark and formless several hundred feet below. Denis looked down, and could discern a few tree-tops waving and a single speck of brightness where the river ran across a weir. The weather was clearing up, and the sky had lightened, so as to show the outline of the heavier clouds and the dark margin of the hills. By the uncertain glimmer, the house on his left hand should be a place of some pretensions; it was surmounted by several pinnacles and turret-tops; the round stern of a chapel, with a fringe of flying buttresses, projected boldly from the main block; and the door was sheltered under a deep porch carved with figures and overhung by two long gargoyles. The windows of the chapel gleamed through their intricate tracery with a light as of many tapers, and threw out the buttresses and the peaked roof in a more intense blackness against the sky. It was plainly the hotel of some great family of the neighbourhoood; and as it reminded Denis of a town house of his own at Bourges, he stood for some time gazing up at it and mentally gauging the skill of the architects and the consideration of the two families.

There seemed to be no issue to the terrace but the lane by which he had reached it; he could only retrace his steps, but he had gained some notion of his whereabouts, and hoped by this means to hit the main thoroughfare and speedily regain the inn. He was reckoning without that chapter of accidents which was to make this night memorable above all others in his career; for he had not gone back above a hundred yards before he saw a light coming to meet him, and heard loud voices speaking together in the echoing narrows of the lane. It was a party of men-at-arms going the night round with torches. Denis assured himself that they had all been making free with the wine-bowl, and were in no mood to be particular about safe-conducts or the niceties of chivalrous war. It was as like as not that they would kill him like a dog and leave him where he fell. The situation was inspiriting but nervous. Their own torches would conceal him from sight, he reflected; and he hoped that they would drown the noise of his footsteps with their own empty voices. If he were but silent and fleet he might evade their notice altogether.

Unfortunately, as he turned to beat a retreat, his foot rolled upon a pebble; he fell against the wall with an ejaculation, and his sword rang loudly on the stones. Two or three voices demanded who went there – some in French, some in English; but Denis made no reply, and ran the faster down the lane. Once upon the terrace, he paused to look back. They still kept calling after him, and just then began to double the pace in pursuit, with a considerable clank of armour, and great tossing of the torchlight to and fro in the narrow jaws of the passage.

Denis cast a look around and darted into the porch. There he might escape observation, or – if that were too much to expect – was in a capital posture whether for parley or defence. So thinking, he drew his sword and tried to set his back against the door. To his surprise, it yielded behind his weight; and though he turned in a moment, continued to swing back on oiled and noiseless hinges, until it stood wide open on a black interior. When things fall out opportunely for the person concerned, he is not apt to be critical about the how or why, his own immediate personal convenience seeming a sufficient reason for the strangest oddities and revolutions in our sublunary things; and so Denis, without a moment's hesitation, stepped within and partly closed the door behind him to conceal his place of refuge. Nothing was further from his thoughts than to close it altogether; but for some inexplicable reason – perhaps by a spring or a weight – the ponderous mass of oak whipped itself out of his fingers and clanked to, with a formidable rumble and a noise like the falling of an automatic bar.

The round, at that very moment, debouched upon the terrace and proceeded to summon him with shouts and curses. He heard them ferreting in the dark corners; the stock of a lance even rattled along the outer surface of the door behind which he stood; but these gentlemen were in too high a humour to be long delayed, and soon made off down a corkscrew pathway which had escaped Denis's observation, and passed out of sight and hearing along the battlements of the town.

Denis breathed again. He gave them a few minutes' grace for fear of accidents, and then groped about for some means of opening the door and slipping forth again. The inner surface was quite smooth, not a handle, not a moulding, not a projection of any sort. He got his finger-nails round the edges and pulled, but the mass was immovable. He shook it, it was as firm as a rock. Denis de Beaulieu frowned and gave vent to a little noiseless whistle. What ailed the door? he wondered. Why was it open? How came it to shut so easily and so effectually after him? There was something obscure and underhand about all this that was little to the young man's fancy. It looked like a snare; and yet who could suppose a snare in such a quiet by-street and in a house of so prosperous and even noble an exterior? And yet – snare or no snare, intentionally or unintentionally – here he was, prettily trapped; and for the life of him he could see no way out of it again. The darkness began to weigh upon him. He gave ear; all was silent without, but within and close by he seemed to catch a faint sighing, a faint sobbing rustle, a little stealthy creak – as though many persons were at his side, holding themselves quite still, and governing even their respiration with the extreme of slyness. The idea went to his vitals with a shock, and he faced about suddenly as if to defend his life. Then, for the first time, he became aware of a light about the level of his eyes and at some distance in the interior of the house – a vertical thread of light, widening towards the bottom, such as might escape between two wings of arras over a doorway. To see anything was a relief to Denis; it was like a piece of solid ground to a man labouring in a morass; his mind seized upon it with avidity; and he stood staring at it and trying to piece together some logical conception of his surroundings. Plainly there was a flight of steps ascending from his own level to that of this illuminated doorway; and indeed he thought he could make out another thread of light, as fine as a needle and as faint as phosphorescence, which might very well be reflected along the polished wood of a handrail. Since he had begun to suspect that he was not alone, his heart had continued to beat with smothering violence, and an intolerable desire for action of any sort had possessed itself of his spirit. He was in deadly peril, he believed. What could be more natural than to mount the staircase, lift the curtain, and confront his difficulty at once? At least he would be dealing with something tangible; at least he would be no longer in the dark. He stepped slowly forward with out-stretched hands, until his foot struck the bottom step; then he rapidly scaled the stairs, stood for a moment to compose his expression, lifted the arras and went in.

He found himself in a large apartment of polished stone. There were three doors; one in each of three sides; all similarly curtained with tapestry. The fourth side was occupied by two large windows and a great stone chimney-piece, carved with the arms of the Malétroits. Denis recognised the bearings, and was gratified to find himself in such good hands. The room was strongly illuminated; but it contained little furniture except a heavy table and chair or two, the hearth was innocent of fire, and the pavement was but sparsely strewn with rushes clearly many days old.

On a high chair beside the chimney, and directly facing Denis as he entered, sat a little old gentleman in a fur tippet. He sat with his legs crossed and his hands folded, and a cup of spiced wine stood by his elbow on a bracket on the wall. His countenance had a strongly masculine cast; not properly human, but such as we see in the bull, the goat, or the domestic boar; something equivocal and wheedling, something greedy, brutal, and dangerous. The upper lip was inordinately full, as though swollen by a blow or a toothache; and the smile, the peaked eyebrows, and the small, strong eyes were quaintly and almost comically evil in expression. Beautiful white hair hung straight all round his head, like a saint's, and fell in a single curl upon the tippet. His beard and moustache were the pink of venerable sweetness. Age, probably in consequence of inordinate precautions, had left no mark upon his hands, and the Malétroit hand was famous. It would be difficult to imagine anything at once so fleshy and so delicate in design; the taper, sensual fingers were like those of one of Leonardo's women; the fork of the thumb made a dimpled protuberance when closed; the nails were perfectly shaped and of a dead, surprising whiteness. It rendered his aspect tenfold more redoubtable, that a man with hands like these should keep them devoutly folded in his lap like a virgin martyr — that a man with so intense and startling an expression of face should sit patiently on his seat and contemplate people with an unwinking stare, like a god, or a god's statue. His quiescence seemed ironical and treacherous, it fitted so poorly with his looks.

Such was Alain, Sire de Malétroit.

Denis and he looked silently at each other for a second or two.

'Pray step in,' said the Sire de Malétroit. 'I have been expecting you all the evening.'

He had not risen, but he accompanied his words with a smile, and a slight but courteous inclination of the head. Partly from the smile, partly from the strange musical murmur with which the Sire prefaced his observation, Denis felt a strong shudder of disgust go through his marrow. And what with disgust and honest confusion of mind, he could scarcely get words together in reply.

'I fear,' he said, 'that this is a double accident. I am not the person you suppose me. It seems you were looking for a visit; but for my part, nothing was further from my thoughts — nothing could be more contrary to my wishes — than this intrusion.'

'Well, well,' replied the old gentleman indulgently, 'here you are, which is the main point. Seat yourself, my friend, and put yourself entirely at your ease. We shall arrange our little affairs presently.'

Denis perceived that the matter was still complicated with some misconception, and he hastened to continue his explanations.

'Your door ...' he began.

'About my door?' asked the other, raising his peaked eyebrows. 'A little piece of ingenuity.' And he shrugged his shoulders. 'A hospitable fancy! By your own account, you were not desirous of making my acquaintance. We old people look for such reluctance now and then; and when it touches our honour, we cast about until we find some way of overcoming it. You arrive uninvited, but believe me, very welcome.'

'You persist in error, sir,' said Denis. 'There can be no question between you and me. I am a stranger in this countryside. My name is Denis, damoiseau de Beaulieu. If you see me in your house, it is only – '

'My young friend,' interrupted the other, 'you will permit me to have my own ideas on that subject. They probably differ from yours at the present moment,' he added with a leer, 'but time will show which of us is in the right.'

Denis was convinced he had to do with a lunatic. He seated himself with a shrug, content to wait the upshot; and a pause ensued, during which he thought he could distinguish a hurried gabbling as of prayer from behind the arras immediately opposite him. Sometimes there seemed to be but one person engaged, sometimes two; and the vehemence of the voice, low as it was, seemed to indicate either great haste or an agony of spirit. It occurred to him that this piece of tapestry covered the entrance to the chapel he had noticed from without.

The old gentleman meanwhile surveyed Denis from head to foot with a smile, and from time to time emitted little noises like a bird or a mouse, which seemed to indicate a high degree of satisfaction. This state of matters became rapidly insupportable; and Denis, to put an end to it, remarked politely that the wind had gone down.

The old gentleman fell into a fit of silent laughter, so prolonged and violent that he became quite red in the face. Denis got upon his feet at once, and put on his hat with a flourish.

'Sir,' he said, 'if you are in your wits, you have affronted me grossly. If you are out of them, I flatter myself I can find better employment for my brains than to talk with lunatics. My conscience is clear; you have made a fool of me from the first moment; you have refused to hear my explanations; and now there is no power under God will make me stay here any longer; and if I cannot make my way out in a more decent fashion, I will hack your door in pieces with my sword.'

The Sire de Malétroit raised his right hand and wagged it at Denis with the fore and little fingers extended.

'My dear nephew,' he said, 'sit down.'

'Nephew!' retorted Denis, 'you lie in your throat'; and he snapped his fingers in his face.

'Sit down, you rogue!' cried the old gentleman, in a sudden, harsh voice, like the barking of a dog. 'Do you fancy,' he went on, 'that when I had made my little contrivance for the door I had stopped short with that? If you prefer to be bound hand and foot till your bones ache, rise and try to go away. If you choose to remain a free young buck, agreeably conversing with an old gentleman – why, sit where you are in peace, and God be with you.'

'Do you mean I am a prisoner?' demanded Denis.

'I state the facts,' replied the other. 'I would rather leave the conclusions to yourself.'

Denis sat down again. Externally he managed to keep pretty calm; but within, he was now boiling with anger, now chilled with apprehension. He no longer felt convinced that he was dealing with a madman. And if the old gentleman was sane, what, in God's name, had he to look for? What absurd or tragical adventure had befallen him? What countenance was he to assume?

While he was thus unpleasantly reflecting, the arras that overhung the chapel door was raised, and a tall priest in his robes came forth and, giving a long, keen stare at Denis, said something in an undertone to Sire de Malétroit.

'She is in a better frame of spirit?' asked the latter.

'She is more resigned, messire,' replied the priest.

'Now the Lord help her, she is hard to please!' sneered the old gentleman. 'A likely stripling – not ill-born – and of her own choosing, too? Why, what more would the jade have?'

'The situation is not usual for a young damsel,' said the other, 'and somewhat trying to her blushes.'

'She should have thought of that before she began the dance! It was none of my choosing, God knows that: but since she is in it, by our lady, she shall carry it to the end.' And then addressing Denis, 'Monsieur de Beaulieu,' he asked, 'may I present you to my niece? She has been waiting your arrival, I may say, with even greater impatience than myself.'

Denis had resigned himself with a good grace – all he desired was to know the worst of it as speedily as possible; so he rose at once, and bowed in acquiescence. The Sire de Malétroit followed his example and limped, with the assistance of the chaplain's arm, towards the chapel-door. The priest pulled aside the arras, and all three entered. The building had considerable architectural pretensions. A light groining sprang from six stout columns, and hung down in two rich pendants from the centre of the vault. The place terminated behind the altar in a round end, embossed and honeycombed with a superfluity of ornament in relief, and pierced by many little windows shaped like stars, trefoils, or wheels. These windows were imperfectly glazed, so that the night air circulated freely in the chapel. The tapers, of which there must have been half a hundred burning on the altar, were unmercifully blown about; and the light went through many different phases of brilliancy and semi-eclipse. On the steps in front of the altar knelt a young girl richly attired as a bride. A chill settled over Denis as he observed her costume; he fought with desperate energy against the conclusion that was being thrust upon his mind; it could not – it should not – be as he feared.

'Blanche,' said the Sire, in his most flute-like tones, 'I have brought a friend to see you, my little girl; turn round and give him your pretty hand. It is good to be devout; but it is necessary to be polite, my niece.'

The girl rose to her feet and turned towards the new-comers. She moved all of a piece; and shame and exhaustion were expressed in every line of her fresh young body; and she held her head down and kept her eyes upon the pavement, as she came slowly forward. In the course of her advance, her eyes fell upon Denis de Beaulieu's feet – feet of which he was justly vain, be it remarked, and wore in the most elegant accoutrement even while travelling. She paused – started, as if his yellow boots had conveyed some shocking meaning – and glanced suddenly up into the wearer's countenance. Their eyes met; shame gave place to horror and terror in her looks; the blood left her lips; with a piercing scream she covered her face with her hands and sank upon the chapel floor.

'That is not the man!' she cried. 'My uncle; that is not the man!'

The Sire de Malétroit chirped agreeably. 'Of course not,' he said, 'I expected as much. It was so unfortunate you could not remember his name.'

'Indeed,' she cried, 'indeed, I have never seen this person till this moment – I have never so much as set eyes upon him – I never wish to see him again. Sir,' she said, turning to Denis, 'if you are a gentleman, you will bear me out. Have I ever seen you – have you ever seen me – before this accursed hour?'

'To speak for myself, I have never had that pleasure,' answered the young man. 'This is the first time, messire, that I have met with your engaging niece.'

The old gentleman shrugged his shoulders.

'I am distressed to hear it,' he said. 'But it is never too late to begin. I had little more acquaintance with my own late lady ere I married her; which proves,' he added, with a grimace, 'that these impromptu marriages may often produce an excellent understanding in the long-run. As the bridegroom is to have a voice in the matter, I will give him two hours to make up for lost time before we proceed with the ceremony.' And he turned towards the door, followed by the clergyman.

The girl was on her feet in a moment. 'My uncle, you cannot be in earnest,' she said. 'I declare before God I will stab myself rather than be forced on that young man. The heart rises at it; God forbids such marriages; you dishonour your white hair. Oh, my uncle, pity me! There is not a woman in all the world but would prefer death to such a nuptial. Is it possible,' she added, faltering – 'is it possible that you do not believe me – that you still think this' – and she pointed at Denis with a tremor of anger and contempt – 'that you still think *this* to be the man?'

'Frankly,' said the old gentleman, pausing on the threshold, 'I do. But let me explain to you once and for all, Blanche de Malétroit, my way of thinking about this affair. When you took it into your head to dishonour my family and the name that I have borne, in peace and war, for more than threescore years, you forfeited, not only the right to question my designs, but that of looking me in the face. If your father had been alive, he would have spat on you and turned you out of doors. His was the hand of iron. You may bless your God you have only to deal with the hand of velvet, mademoiselle. It was my duty to get you married without delay. Out of pure goodwill, I have tried to find your own gallant for you. And I believe I have succeeded. But before God and all the holy angels, Blanche de Malétroit, if I have not, I care not one jackstraw. So let me recommend you to be polite to our young friend; for upon my word, your next groom may be less appetising.'

And with that he went out, with the chaplain at his heels; and the arras fell behind the pair.

The girl turned upon Denis with flashing eyes.

'And what, sir,' she demanded, 'may be the meaning of all this?'

'God knows,' returned Denis gloomily. 'I am a prisoner in this house, which seems full of mad people. More I know not; and nothing do I understand.'

'And pray how came you here?' she asked.

He told her as briefly as he could. 'For the rest,' he added, 'perhaps you will follow my example, and tell me the answer to all these riddles, and what, in God's name, is like to be the end of it.'

She stood silent for a little, and he could see her lips tremble and her tearless eyes burn with a feverish lustre. Then she pressed her forehead in both hands.

'Alas, how my head aches!' she said wearily – 'to say nothing of my poor heart! But it is due to you to know my story, unmaidenly as it must seem. I am called Blanche de Malétroit: I have been without father or mother for – oh! for as long as I can recollect, and indeed I have been most unhappy all my life. Three months ago a young captain began to stand near me every day in church. I could see that I pleased him; I am much to blame, but I was so glad that any one should love me; and when he passed me a letter, I took it home with me and read it with great pleasure. Since that time he has written many. He was so anxious to speak with me, poor fellow! and kept asking me to leave the door open some evening that we might have two words upon the stair. For he knew how much my uncle trusted me.' She gave something like a sob at that, and it was a moment before she could go on. 'My uncle is a hard man, but he is very shrewd,' she said at last. 'He has performed many feats in war, and was a great person at court, and much trusted by Queen Isabeau in old days. How he came to suspect me I cannot tell; but it is hard to keep anything from his knowledge; and this morning, as we came from mass, he took my hand in his, forced it open, and read my little billet, walking by my side all the while. When he had finished, he gave it back to me with great politeness. It contained another request to have the door left open; and this has been the ruin of us all. My uncle kept me strictly in my room until evening, and then ordered me to dress myself as you see me – a hard mockery for a young girl, do you not think so? I suppose, when he could not prevail with me to tell him the young captain's name, he must have laid a trap for him: into which, alas! you have fallen in the anger of God. I looked for much confusion; for how could I tell whether he was willing to take me for his wife on these sharp terms? He might have been trifling with me from the first; or I might have made myself too cheap in his eyes. But truly I had not looked for such a shameful punishment as this! I could not think that God would let a girl be so disgraced before a young man. And now I have told you all; and I can scarcely hope that you will not despise me.'

Denis made her a respectful inclination.

'Madam,' he said, 'you have honoured me by your confidence. It remains for me to prove that I am not unworthy of the honour. Is Messire de Malétroit at hand?'

'I believe he is writing in the salle without,' she answered.

'May I lead you thither, madam?' asked Denis, offering his hand with his most courtly bearing.

She accepted it; and the pair passed out of the chapel, Blanche in a very drooping and shamefast condition, but Denis strutting and ruffling in the consciousness of a mission, and the boyish certainty of accomplishing it with honour.

The Sire de Malétroit rose to meet them with an ironical obeisance.

'Sir,' said Denis, with the grandest possible air, 'I believe I am to have some say in the matter of this marriage; and let me tell you at once, I will be no party to forcing the inclination of this young lady. Had it been freely offered to me, I should have been proud to accept her hand, for I perceive she is as good as she is beautiful; but as things are, I have now the honour, messire, of refusing.'

Blanche looked at him with gratitude in her eyes; but the old gentleman only smiled and smiled until his smile grew positively sickening to Denis.

'I am afraid,' he said, 'Monsieur de Beaulieu, that you do not perfectly understand the choice I have to offer you. Follow me, I beseech you, to this window.' And he led the way to one of the large windows which stood open on the night. 'You observe,' he went on, 'there is an iron ring in the upper masonry, and reeved through that a very efficacious rope. Now, mark my words: if you should find your disinclination to my niece's person insurmountable, I shall have you hanged out of this window before sunrise. I shall only proceed to such an extremity with the greatest regret, you may believe me. For it is not at all your death that I desire, but my niece's establishment in life. At the same time, it must come to that if you prove obstinate. Your family, Monsieur de Beaulieu, is very well in its way; but if you sprang from Charlemagne, you should not refuse the hand of a Malétroit with impunity – not if she had been as common as the Paris road – not if she were as hideous as the gargoyle over my door. Neither my niece nor you, nor my own private feelings, move me at all in this matter. The honour of my house had been compromised; I believe you to be the guilty person; at least you are now in the secret; and you can hardly wonder if I request you to wipe out the stain. If you will not, your blood be on your own head! It will be no great satisfaction to me to have your interesting relics kicking their heels in the breeze below my windows; but half a loaf is better than no bread, and if I cannot cure the dishonour, I shall at least stop the scandal.'

There was a pause.

'I believe there are other ways of settling such imbroglios among gentlemen,' said Denis. 'You wear a sword, and I hear you have used it with distinction.'

The Sire de Malétroit made a signal to the chaplain, who crossed the room with long silent strides and raised the arras over the third of the three doors. It was only a moment before he let it fall again; but Denis had time to see a dusky passage full of armed men.

'When I was a little younger, I should have been delighted to honour you, Monsieur de Beaulieu,' said Sire Alain; 'but I am now too old. Faithful retainers are the sinews of age, and I must employ the strength I have. This is one of the hardest things to swallow as a man grows up in years; but with a little patience, even this becomes habitual. You and the lady seem to prefer the salle for what remains of your two hours; and as I have no desire to cross your preference, I shall resign it to your use with all the pleasure in the world. No haste!' he added, holding up his hand, as he saw a dangerous look come into Denis de Beaulieu's face. 'If your mind revolts against hanging, it will be time enough two hours hence to throw yourself out of the window or upon the pikes of my retainers. Two hours of life are always two hours. A great many things may turn up in even as little a while as that. And, besides, if I understand her appearance, my niece has still something to say to you. You will not disfigure your last hours by a want of politeness to a lady?'

Denis looked at Blanche, and she made him an imploring gesture.

It is likely that the old gentleman was hugely pleased at this symptom of an understanding; for he smiled on both, and added sweetly: 'If you will give me your word of honour, Monsieur de Beaulieu, to await my return at the end of the two hours before attempting anything desperate, I shall withdraw my retainers, and let you speak in greater privacy with mademoiselle.'

Denis again glanced at the girl, who seemed to beseech him to agree.

'I give you my word of honour,' he said.

Messire de Malétroit bowed, and proceeded to limp about the apartment, clearing his throat the while with that odd musical chirp which had already grown so irritating in the ears of Denis de Beaulieu. He first possessed himself of some papers which lay upon the table; then he went to the mouth of the passage and appeared to give an order to the men behind the arras; and lastly, he hobbled out through the door by which Denis had come in, turning upon the threshold to address a last smiling bow to the young couple, and followed by the chaplain with a hand-lamp.

No sooner were they alone than Blanche advanced towards Denis with her hands extended. Her face was flushed and excited, and her eyes shone with tears.

'You shall not die!' she cried, 'you shall marry me after all.'

'You seem to think, madam,' replied Denis, 'that I stand much in fear of death.'

'Oh no, no,' she said, 'I see you are no poltroon. It is for my own sake – I could not bear to have you slain for such a scruple.'

'I am afraid,' returned Denis, 'that you underrate the difficulty, madam. What you may be too generous to refuse, I may be too proud to accept. In a moment of noble feeling towards me, you forgot what you perhaps owe to others.'

He had the decency to keep his eyes upon the floor as he said this, and after he had finished, so as not to spy upon her confusion. She stood silent for a moment, then walked suddenly away, and falling on her uncle's chair, fairly burst out sobbing. Denis was in the acme of embarrassment. He looked round, as if to seek for inspiration, and seeing a stool, plumped down upon it for something to do. There he sat, playing with the guard of his rapier, and wishing himself dead a thousand times over, and buried in the nastiest kitchen-heap in France. His eyes wandered round the apartment, but found nothing to arrest them. There were such wide spaces between the furniture, the light fell so baldly and cheerlessly over all, the dark outside air looked in so coldly through the windows, that he thought he had never seen a church so vast, nor a tomb so melancholy. The regular sobs of Blanche de Malétroit measured out the time like the ticking of a clock. He read the device upon the shield over and over again, until his eyes became obscured; he stared into shadowy corners until he imagined they were swarming with horrible animals; and every now and again he awoke with a start, to remember that his last two hours were running, and death was on the march.

Oftener and oftener, as the time went on, did his glance settle on the girl herself. Her face was bowed forward and covered with her hands, and she was shaken at intervals by the convulsive hiccup of grief. Even thus she was not an unpleasant object to dwell upon, so plump and yet so fine, with a warm brown skin, and the most beautiful hair, Denis thought, in the whole world of womankind. Her hands were like her uncle's; but they were more in place at the end of her young arms, and looked infinitely soft and caressing. He remembered how her blue eyes had shone upon him, full of anger, pity, and innocence. And the more he dwelt on her perfections, the uglier death looked, and the more deeply was he smitten with penitence at her continued tears. Now he felt that no man could have the courage to leave a world which contained so beautiful a creature; and now he would have given forty minutes of his last hour to have unsaid his cruel speech.

Suddenly a hoarse and ragged peal of cockcrow rose to their ears from the dark valley below the windows. And this shattering noise in the silence of all around was like a light in a dark place, and shook them both out of their reflections.

'Alas, can I do nothing to help you?' she said, looking up.

'Madam,' replied Denis, with a fine irrelevancy, 'if I have said anything to wound you, believe me, it was for your own sake and not for mine.'

She thanked him with a tearful look.

'I feel your position cruelly,' he went on. 'The world has been bitter hard on you. Your uncle is a disgrace to mankind. Believe me, madam, there is no young gentleman in all France but would be glad of my opportunity, to die in doing you a momentary service.'

'I know already that you can be very brave and generous,' she answered. 'What I *want* to know is whether I can serve you – now or afterwards,' she added, with a quaver.

'Most certainly,' he answered, with a smile. 'Let me sit

beside you as if I were a friend, instead of a foolish intruder; try to forget how awkwardly we are placed to one another; make my last moments go pleasantly; and you will do me the chief service possible.'

'You are very gallant,' she added, with a yet deeper sadness ... 'very gallant ... and it somehow pains me. But draw nearer, if you please; and if you find anything to say to me, you will at least make certain of a very friendly listener. Ah! Monsieur de Beaulieu,' she broke forth – 'ah! Monsieur de Beaulieu, how can I look you in the face?' And she fell to weeping again with a renewed effusion.

'Madam,' said Denis, taking her hand in both of his, 'reflect on the little time I have before me, and the great bitterness into which I am cast by the sight of your distress. Spare me, in my last moments, the spectacle of what I cannot cure even with the sacrifice of my life.'

'I am very selfish,' answered Blanche. 'I will be braver, Monsieur de Beaulieu, for your sake. But think if I can do you no kindness in the future – if you have no friends to whom I could carry your adieux. Charge me as heavily as you can; every burden will lighten, by so little, the invaluable gratitude I owe you. Put it in my power to do something more for you than weep.'

'My mother is married again, and has a young family to care for. My brother Guichard will inherit my fiefs; and if I am not in error, that will content him amply for my death. Life is a little vapour that passeth away, as we are told by those in holy orders. When a man is in a fair way and sees all life open in front of him, he seems to himself to make a very important figure in the world. His horse whinnies to him; the trumpets blow and the girls look out of window as he rides into town before his company; he receives many assurances of trust and regard – sometimes by express in a letter – sometimes face to face, with persons of great consequence falling on his neck. It is not wonderful if his head is turned for a time. But once he is dead, were he as brave as Hercules or as wise as Solomon, he is soon forgotten. It is not ten years since my father fell, with many other knights around him, in a very fierce encounter, and I do not think that any one of them, nor so much as the name of the fight is now remembered. No, no, madam, the nearer you come to it, you see that death is a dark and dusty corner, where a man gets into his tomb and has the door shut after him till the judgment day. I have few friends just now, and once I am dead I shall have none.'

'Ah, Monsieur de Beaulieu!' she exclaimed, 'you forget Blanche de Malétroit.'

'You have a sweet nature, madam, and you are pleased to estimate a little service far beyond its worth.'

'It is not that,' she answered. 'You mistake me if you think I am so easily touched by my own concerns. I say so, because you are the noblest man I have ever met; because I recognise in you a spirit that would have made even a common person famous in the land.'

'And yet here I die in a mousetrap – with no more noise about it than my own squealing,' answered he.

A look of pain crossed her face, and she was silent for a little while. Then a light came into her eyes, and with a smile she spoke again.

'I cannot have my champion think meanly of himself. Any one who gives his life for another will be met in Paradise by all the heralds and angels of the Lord God. And you have no such cause to hang your head. For ... Pray, do you think me beautiful?' she asked, with a deep flush.

'Indeed, madam, I do,' he said.

'I am glad of that,' she answered heartily. 'Do you think there are many men in France who have been asked in marriage by a beautiful maiden – with her own lips – and who have refused her to her face? I know you men would half despise such a triumph; but believe me, we women know more of what is precious in love. There is nothing that should set a person higher in his own esteem; and we women would prize nothing more dearly.'

'You are very good,' he said; 'but you cannot make me forget that I was asked in pity and not for love.'

'I am not so sure of that,' she replied, holding down her head. 'Hear me to an end, Monsieur de Beaulieu. I know how you must despise me; I feel you are right to do so; I am too poor a creature to occupy one thought of your mind, although, alas! you must die for me this morning. But when I asked you to marry me, indeed, and indeed, it was because I respected and admired you, and loved you with my whole soul, from the very moment that you took my part against my uncle. If you had seen yourself, and how noble you looked, you would pity rather than despise me. And now,' she went on, hurriedly checking him with her hand, 'although I have laid aside all reserve and told you so much, remember that I know your sentiments towards me already. I would not, believe me, being nobly born, weary you with importunities into consent. I too have a pride of my own; and I declare before the holy mother of God, if you should now go back from your word already given, I would no more marry you than I would marry my uncle's groom.'

Denis smiled a little bitterly.

'It is a small love,' he said, 'that shies at a little pride.'

She made no answer, although she probably had her own thoughts.

'Come hither to the window,' he said, with a sigh. 'Here is the dawn.'

And indeed the dawn was already beginning. The hollow of the sky was full of essential daylight, colourless and clean; and the valley underneath was flooded with a grey reflection. A few thin vapours clung in the coves of the forest or lay along the winding course of the river. The scene disengaged a surprising effect of stillness, which was hardly interrupted when the cocks began once more to crow among the steadings. Perhaps the same fellow who had made so horrid a clangour in the darkness not half-an-hour before, now sent up the merriest cheer to greet the coming day. A little wind went bustling and eddying among the tree-tops underneath the windows. And still the daylight kept flooding insensibly out of the east, which was soon to grow incandescent and cast up that red-hot cannon-ball, the rising sun.

Denis looked out over all this with a bit of a shiver. He had taken her hand, and retained it in his almost unconsciously.

'Has the day begun already?' she said; and then, illogically enough: 'the night has been so long! Alas! what shall we say to my uncle when he returns?'

'What you will,' said Denis, and he pressed her fingers in his.

She was silent.

'Blanche,' he said, with a swift, uncertain, passionate utterance, 'you have seen whether I fear death. You must know well enough that I would as gladly leap out of that window into the empty air as lay a finger on you without your free and full consent. But if you care for me at all do not let me lose my life in a misapprehension; for I love you better than the whole world; and though I will die for you blithely it would be like all the joys of Paradise to live on and spend my life in your service.'

As he stopped speaking, a bell began to ring loudly in the interior of the house; and a clatter of armour in the corridor showed that the retainers were returning to their post, and the two hours were at an end.

'After all that you have heard?' she whispered, leaning towards him with her lips and eyes.

'I have heard nothing,' he replied.

'The captain's name was Florimond de Champdivers,' she said in his ear.

'I did not hear it,' he answered, taking her supple body in his arms, and covered her wet face with kisses.

A melodious chirping was audible behind, followed by a beautiful chuckle, and the voice of Messire de Malétroit wished his new nephew a good morning.

VI

The Hands of Mr Ottermole
Thomas Burke

If you were at all interested in horror in the nineteen fifties and sixties there was one name above all others that dominated the genre, Alfred Hitchcock, the British-born director whose now classic films earned him the accolade 'The Master of Suspense'. Indeed his name became synonymous with mystery and thrills on the screen and there is little dispute that its appearance above the title of any film was more important than that of virtually any actor he might cast to star in it. Like millions of other filmgoers I was enthralled by the superb movies he made during this period like Rear Window *(1954),* To Catch A Thief *(1955),* Vertigo *(1958),* Psycho *(1960),* The Birds *(1963), etc., etc.*

In the mid-fifties he also began appearing on television as the host of a series called Alfred Hitchcock Presents *in which he introduced a whole variety of nerve-tingling dramas based on stories by virtually all the best mystery and thriller writers. His appearance at the start of each presentation with a solomn look on his round, fat face as he made ghoulish observations and outrageous puns on the story to be unfolded — all in a sepulchral voice — was quite unforgettable. So successful did the series become that it ran until 1963, and then, after a title change to* The Alfred Hitchcock Hour, *continued until 1965 when it finally ceased.*

That year was an important one for me. For, after several years in journalism, I had entered the world of publishing and also begun drawing on my accumulated knowledge of the horror genre to assemble my first collections of macabre stories. And it was in 1965 that I was invited to 'ghost edit' a series of anthologies bearing Alfred Hitchcock's name. From the mid-fifties he had been the nominal editor of a successful monthly publication, Alfred Hitchcock's Mystery Magazine, *and my brief was to select from its pages the best material to fill six collections. This work took me to New York and a memorable meeting with the great man. He was kindness itself, and in reply to one of my questions told me that if there was a secret to the popularity of his work it was the fact that he utilised fears that anyone could identify with – fear of heights, of enclosed spaces, the fear of false accusation or arrest, and so on. As far as his own fears were concerned, he told me, 'I am terrified of sudden noises. This is a lamentable admission for a man of my supposed horrific aptitude, I know, but the slamming of a door sets my teeth on edge, and the bang of a firework also shatters my equanimity.' He also confessed that despite the enormous number of ghost and mystery stories he had read, 'If my wife tells me a ghost story then I'm certain I've heard someone in the house!'*

Naturally enough I have not picked one of the stories from my Hitchcock Anthologies for this collection, but instead what was perhaps the most outstanding short story ever to be featured on Alfred Hitchcock Presents *– 'The Hands of Mr Ottermole' by Thomas Burke. It was a dramatisation I know Hitchcock himself was particularly pleased with, and had undertones of his very first film,* The Lodger *made in 1926. It is the story of a maniac killer on the loose in London, and apart from also having been broadcast on the radio several times was called by Ellery Queen 'the best detective short story of all time'. How many other tales of horror can boast of being held in such high esteem by two great masters of mystery?*

At six o'clock of a January evening Mr Whybrow was walking home through the cobweb alleys of London's East End. He had left the golden clamour of the great High Street to which the tram had brought him from the river and his daily work, and was now in the chess-board of byways that is called Mallon End. None of the rush and gleam of the High Street trickled into these byways. A few paces south – a flood-tide of life, foaming and beating. Here – only slow shuffling figures and muffled pulses. He was in the sink of London, the last refuge of European vagrants.

As though in tune with the street's spirit, he too walked slowly, with head down. It seemed that he was pondering some pressing trouble, but he was not. He had no trouble. He was walking slowly because he had been on his feet all day, and he was bent in abstraction because he was wondering whether the Missis would have herrings for his tea, or haddock; and he was trying to decide which would be the more tasty on a night like this. A wretched night it was, of damp and mist, and the mist wandered into his throat and his eyes, and the damp had settled on pavement and roadway, and where the sparse lamplight fell it sent up a greasy sparkle that chilled one to look at. By contrast it made his speculations more agreeable, and made him ready for that tea – whether herring or haddock. His eye turned from the glum bricks that made his horizon, and went forward half a mile. He saw a gas-lit kitchen, a flamy fire and a spread tea-table. There was toast in the hearth and a singing kettle on the side and a piquant effusion of herrings, or maybe of haddock, or perhaps sausages. The vision gave his aching feet a throb of energy. He shook imperceptible damp from his shoulders, and hastened towards its reality.

But Mr Whybrow wasn't going to get any tea that evening – or any other evening. Mr Whybrow was going to die. Somewhere within a hundred yards of him another man was walking: a man much like Mr Whybrow and much like any other man, but without the only quality that enables mankind to live peaceably together and not as madmen in a jungle. A man with a dead heart eating into itself and bringing forth the foul organisms that arise from death and corruption. And that thing in man's shape, on a whim or a settled idea – one cannot know – had said within himself that Mr Whybrow should never taste another herring. Not that Mr Whybrow had injured him. Not that he had any dislike of Mr Whybrow. Indeed, he knew nothing of him save as a familiar figure about the streets. But, moved by a force that had taken possession of his empty cells, he had picked on Mr Whybrow with that blind choice that makes us pick one restaurant table that has nothing to mark it from four of five other tables, or one apple from a dish of half a dozen equal apples; or that drives Nature to send a cyclone upon one corner of this planet, and destroy five hundred lives in that corner, and leave another five hundred in the same corner unharmed. So this man had picked on Mr Whybrow, as he might have picked on you or me, had we been within his daily observation; and even now he was creeping through the blue-toned streets, nursing his large white hands, moving ever closer to Mr Whybrow's tea-table, and so closer to Mr Whybrow himself.

He wasn't, this man, a bad man. Indeed, he had many of the social and amiable qualities, and passed as a respectable man, as most successful criminals do. But the thought had come into his mouldering mind that he would like to murder somebody, and, as he held no fear of God or man, he was going to do it, and would then go home to *his* tea. I don't say that flippantly, but as a statement of fact. Strange as it may seem to the humane, murderers must and do sit down to meals after a murder. There is no reason why they shouldn't, and many reasons why they should. For one thing, they need to keep their physical and mental vitality at full beat for the business of covering their crime. For another, the strain of their effort makes them hungry, and satisfaction at the accomplishment of a desired thing brings a feeling of relaxation towards human pleasures. It is accepted among non-murderers that the murderer is always overcome by fear for his safety and horror at his act; but this type is rare. His own safety is, of course, his immediate concern, but vanity is a marked quality of most murderers, and that, together with the thrill of conquest, makes him confident that he can secure it, and when he has restored his strength with food he goes about securing it as a young hostess goes about the arranging of her first big dinner – a little anxious, but no more. Criminologists and detectives tell us that *every* murderer, however intelligent or cunning, always makes one slip in his tactics – one little slip that brings the affair home to him. But that is only half-true. It is true only of the murderers who are caught. Scores of murderers are not caught: therefore scores of murderers do not make any mistake at all. This man didn't.

As for horror or remorse, prison chaplains, doctors and lawyers have told us that of murderers they have interviewed under condemnation and the shadow of death, only one here and there has expressed any contrition for his act, or shown any sign of mental misery. Most of them display only exasperation at having been caught when so many have gone undiscovered, or indignation at being condemned for a perfectly reasonable act. However normal and humane they may have been before the murder, they are utterly without conscience after it. For what is conscience? Simply a polite nickname for superstition, which is a polite nickname for fear.

Those who associate remorse with murder are, no doubt, basing their ideas on the world-legend of the remorse of Cain, or are projecting their own frail minds into the mind of the murderer, and getting false reactions. Peaceable folk cannot hope to make contact with this mind, for they are not merely different in mental type from the murderer; they are different in their personal chemistry and construction. Some men can and do kill, not one man, but two or three, and go calmly about their daily affairs. Other men could not, under the most agonizing provocation, bring themselves even to wound. It is men of this sort who imagine the murderer in torments of remorse and fear of the law, whereas he is actually sitting down to his tea.

The man with the large white hands was as ready for his tea as Mr Whybrow was, but he had something to do before he went to it. When he had done that something, and made no mistake about it, he would be even more ready for it, and would go to it as comfortably as he went to it the day before, when his hands were stainless.

Walk on, then, Mr Whybrow, walk on; and as you walk, look your last upon the familiar features of your nightly journey. Follow your jack-o'-lantern tea-table. Look well upon its warmth and colour and kindness; feed your eyes with it, and tease your nose with its gentle domestic odours; for you will never sit down to it. Within ten minutes' pacing of you a pursuing phantom has spoken in his heart, and you are doomed. There you go – you and phantom – two nebulous dabs of mortality, moving through green air along pavements of powder-blue, the one to kill, the other to be killed. Walk on. Don't annoy your burning feet by hurrying, for the more slowly you walk, the longer you will breathe the green air of this January dusk, and see the dreamy lamplight and the little shops, and hear the agreeable commerce of the London crowd and the haunting pathos of the street-organ. These things are dear to you, Mr Whybrow. You don't know it now, but in fifteen minutes you will have two seconds in which to realize how inexpressibly dear they are.

Walk on, then, across this crazy chess-board. You are in Lagos Street now, among the tents of the wanderers of Eastern

Europe. A minute or so, and you are in Loyal Lane, among the lodging-houses that shelter the useless and the beaten of London's camp-followers. The lane holds the smell of them, and its soft darkness seems heavy with the wail of the futile. But you are not sensitive to impalpable things, and you plod through it, unseeing, as you do every evening, and come to Blean Street, and plod through that. From basement to sky rise the tenements of an alien colony. Their windows slot the ebony of their walls with lemon. Behind those windows strange life is moving, dressed with forms that are not of London or of England, yet, in essence, the same agreeable life that you have been living, and tonight will live no more. From high above you comes a voice crooning 'The Song of Katta'. Through a window you see a family keeping a religious rite. Through another you see a woman pouring out tea for her husband. You see a man mending a pair of boots; a mother bathing her baby. You have seen all these things before, and never noticed them. You do not notice them now, but if you knew that you were never going to see them again, you would notice them. You never *will* see them again, not because your life has run its natural course, but because a man whom you have often passed in the street has at his own solitary pleasure decided to usurp the awful authority of nature, and destroy you. So perhaps it's as well that you don't notice them, for your part in them is ended. No more for you these pretty moments of our earthly travail: only one moment of terror, and then a plunging darkness.

Closer to you this shadow of massacre moves, and now he is twenty yards behind you. You can hear his footfalls, but you do not turn your head. You are familiar with footfalls. You are in London, in the easy security of· your daily territory, and footfalls behind you, your instinct tells you, are no more than a message of human company.

But can't you hear something in those footfalls – something that goes with a widdershins beat? Something that says: *Look out, look out. Beware, beware.* Can't you hear the very syllables of *murd-er-er-, murd-er-er*? No; there is nothing in footfalls. They are neutral. The foot of villainy falls with the same quiet note as the foot of honesty. But those footfalls, Mr Whybrow, are bearing on to you a pair of hands, and there *is* something in hands. Behind you that pair of hands is even now stretching its muscles in preparation for your end. Every minute of your days you have been seeing human hands. Have you ever realized the sheer horror of hands – those appendages that are a symbol for our moments of trust and affection and salutation? Have you thought of the sickening potentialities that lie within the scope of that five-tentacled member? No, you never have; for all the human hands that you have seen have been stretched to you in kindness or fellowship. Yet, though the eyes can hate, and the lips can sting, it is only that dangling member that can gather the accumulated essence of evil, and electrify it into currents of destruction. Satan may enter into man by many doors, but in the hands alone can he find the servants of his will.

Another minute, Mr Whybrow, and you will know all about the horror of human hands.

You are nearly home now. You have turned into your street – Caspar Street – and you are in the centre of the chess-board. You can see the front window of your little four-roomed house. The street is dark, and its three lamps give only a smut of light that is more confusing than darkness. It is dark – empty, too. Nobody about; no lights in the front parlours of the houses, for the families are at tea in their kitchens; and only a random glow in a few upper rooms occupied by lodgers. Nobody about but you and your following companion, and you don't notice him. You see him so often that he is never seen. Even if you turned your head and saw him, you would only say 'Good evening' to him, and walk on. A suggestion that he was a possible murderer would not even make you laugh. It would be too silly.

And now you are at your gate. And now you have found your door key. And now you are in, and hanging up your hat and coat. The Missis has just called a greeting from the kitchen, whose smell is an echo of that greeting (herrings!) and you have answered it, when the door shakes under a sharp knock.

Go away, Mr Whybrow. Go away from that door. Don't touch it. Get right away from it. Get out of the house. Run with the Missis to the back garden, and over the fence. Or call the neighbours. But don't touch that door. Don't, Mr Whybrow, don't open ...

Mr Whybrow opened the door.

That was the beginning of what became known as London's Strangling Horrors. Horrors they were called because they were something more than murders: they were motiveless, and there was an air of black magic about them. Each murder was committed at a time when the street where the bodies were found was empty of any perceptible or possible murderer. There would be an empty alley. There would be a policeman at its end. He would turn his back on the empty alley for less than a minute. Then he would look round and run into the night with news of another strangling. And in any direction he looked nobody to be seen and no report to be had of anybody being seen. Or he would be on duty in a long quiet street, and suddenly be called to a house of dead people whom a few seconds earlier he had seen alive. And, again, whichever way he looked nobody to be seen; and although police whistles put an immediate cordon around the area, and all houses were searched, no possible murderer to be found.

The first news of the murder of Mr and Mrs Whybrow was brought by the station sergeant. He had been walking through Caspar Street on his way to the station for duty, when he noticed the open door of No 98. Glancing in, he saw by the gaslight of the passage a motionless body on the floor. After a second look he blew his whistle, and when the constables answered him he took one to join him in a search of the house, and sent others to watch all neighbouring streets, and make inquiries at adjoining houses. But neither in the house nor in the streets was anything found to indicate the murderer. Neighbours on either side, and opposite, were questioned, but they had seen nobody about, and had heard nothing. One had heard Mr Whybrow come home – the scrape of his latchkey in the door was so regular an evening sound, he said, that you could set your watch by it for half-past six – but he had heard nothing more than the sound of the opening door until the sergeant's whistle. Nobody had been seen to enter the house or leave it, by front or back, and the necks of the dead people carried no finger-prints or other traces. A nephew was called in to go over the house, but he could find nothing missing; and anyway his uncle possessed nothing worth stealing. The little money in the house was untouched, and there were no signs of any disturbance of the property, or even of struggle. No signs of anything but brutal and wanton murder.

Mr Whybrow was known to neighbours and work-mates as a quiet, likeable, home-loving man; such a man as could not have any enemies. But, then, murdered men seldom have. A relentless enemy who hates a man to the point of wanting to hurt him seldom wants to murder him, since to do that puts him beyond suffering. So the police were left with an impossible situation: no clue to the murderer and no motive for the murders; only the fact that they had been done.

The first news of the affair sent a tremor through London generally, and an electric thrill through all Mallon End. Here was a murder of two inoffensive people, not for gain and not for revenge; and the murderer, to whom, apparently, killing was a casual impulse, was at large. He had left no traces, and, provided he had no companions, there seemed no reason why he should not remain at large. Any clear-headed man who stands alone, and has no fear of God or man, can, if he chooses, hold a city, even a nation, in subjection; but your everyday criminal is seldom clear-headed, and dislikes being lonely. He needs, if not the support of confederates, at least somebody to talk to; his vanity needs the satisfaction of perceiving at first hand the effect of his work. For this he will frequent bars and coffee-shops and other public places. Then, sooner or later, in a glow of comradeship, he will utter the one ·word too much; and the nark, who is everywhere, has an easy job.

But though the doss-houses and saloons and other places were 'combed' and set with watches, and it was made known by whispers that good money and protection were assured to those with information, nothing attaching to the Whybrow case could be found. The murderer clearly had no friends and kept no company. Known men of this type were called up and questioned, but each was able to give a good account of himself; and in a few days the police were at a dead end. Against the constant public gibe that the thing had been done almost under their noses, they became restive, and for four days each man of the force was working his daily beat under a strain. On the fifth day they became still more restive.

It was the season of annual teas and entertainments for the children of the Sunday Schools, and on an evening of fog, when London was a world of groping phantoms, a small girl, in the bravery of best Sunday frock and shoes, shining face and new-washed hair, set out from Logan Passage for St Michael's Parish Hall. She never got there. She was not actually dead until half-past six, but she was as good as dead from the moment she left her mother's door. Somebody like a man, pacing the street from which the Passage led, saw her come out; and from that moment she was dead. Through the fog somebody's large white hands reached after her, and in fifteen minutes they were about her.

At half-past six a whistle screamed trouble, and those answering it found the body of little Nellie Vrinoff in a warehouse entry in Minnow Street. The sergeant was first among them, and he posted his men to useful points, ordering them here and there in the tart tones of repressed rage, and berating the officer whose beat the street was. 'I saw you, Magson, at the end of the lane. What were you up to there? You were there ten minutes before you turned.' Magson began an explanation about keeping an eye on a suspicious-looking character at that end, but the sergeant cut him short: 'Suspicious characters be damned. You don't want to look for suspicious characters. You want to look for *murderers*. Messing about ... and then this happens right where you ought to be. Now think what they'll say.'

With the speed of ill news came the crowd, pale and perturbed; and on the story that the unknown monster had appeared again, and this time to a child, their faces streaked the fog with spots of hate and horror. But then came the ambulance and more police, and swiftly they broke up the crowd; and as it broke the sergeant's thought was thickened into words, and from all sides came low murmurs of 'Right under their noses'. Later inquiries showed that four people of the district, above suspicion, had passed that entry at intervals of seconds before the murder, and seen nothing and heard nothing. None of them had passed the child alive or seen her dead. None of them had seen anybody in the street except themselves. Again the police were left with no motive and with no clue.

And now the district, as you will remember, was given over, not to panic, for the London public never yields to that, but to apprehension and dismay. If these things were happening in their familiar streets, then anything might happen. Wherever people met – in the streets, the markets and the shops – they debated the one topic. Women took to bolting their windows and doors at the first fall of dusk. They kept their children closely under their eye. They did their shopping before dark, and watched anxiously, while pretending they weren't watching, for the return of their husbands from work. Under the Cockney's semi-humorous resignation to disaster, they hid an hourly foreboding. By the whim of one man with a pair of hands the structure and tenor of their daily life were shaken, as they always can be shaken by any man contemptuous of humanity and fearless of its laws. They began to realize that the pillars that supported the peaceable society in which they lived were mere straws that anybody could snap; that laws were powerful only so long as they were obeyed; that the police were potent only so long as they were feared. By the power of his hands this one man had made a whole community do something new: he had made it think, and left it gasping at the obvious.

And then, while it was yet gasping under his first two strokes, he made his third. Conscious of the horror that his hands had created, and hungry as an actor who has once tasted the thrill of the multitude, he made fresh advertisement of his presence; and on Wednesday morning, three days after the murder of the child, the papers carried to the breakfast-tables of England the story of a still more shocking outrage.

At 9.32 on Tuesday night a constable was on duty in Jarnigan Road, and at that time spoke to a fellow-officer named Petersen at the top of Clemming Street. He had seen this officer walk down that street. He could swear that the street was empty at that time, except for a lame boot-black whom he knew by sight, and who passed him and entered a tenement on the side opposite that on which his fellow-officer was walking. He had the habit, as all constables had just then, of looking constantly behind him and around him, whichever way he was walking, and he was certain that the street was empty. He passed his sergeant at 9.33, saluted him, and answered his inquiry for anything seen. He reported that he had seen nothing, and passed on. His beat ended at a short distance from Clemming Street, and, having paced it, he turned and came again at 9.34 to the top of the street. He had scarcely reached it before he heard the hoarse voice of the sergeant: 'Gregory! You there? Quick. Here's another. My God, it's Petersen! Garotted. Quick, call 'em up!'

That was the third of the Strangling Horrors, of which there were to be a fourth and a fifth; and the five horrors were to pass into the unknown and unknowable. That is, unknown as far as authority and the public were concerned. The identity of the murderer *was* known, but to two men only. One was the murderer himself; the other was a young journalist.

This young man, who was covering the affairs for his paper, the *Daily Torch*, was no smarter than the other zealous newspaper men who were hanging about these byways in the hope of a sudden story. But he was patient, and he hung a little closer to the case than the other fellows and by continually staring at it he at last raised the figure of the murderer like a genie from the stones on which he had stood to do his murders.

After the first few days the men had given up any attempt at exclusive stories, for there was none to be had. They met regularly at the police station, and what little information there was they shared. The officials were agreeable to them, but no more. The sergeant discussed with them the details of each murder; suggested possible explanations of the man's methods; recalled from the past those cases that had some similarity; and on the matter of motive reminded them of the motiveless Neil Cream and the wanton John Williams, and hinted that work was being done which would soon bring the business to an end; but about that work he would not say a word. The Inspector, too, was gracefully garrulous on the theme of Murder, but whenever one of the party edged the talk towards what was being done in this immediate matter, he glided past it. Whatever the officials knew, they were not giving it to newspaper men. The business had fallen heavily upon them, and only by a capture made by their own efforts could they rehabilitate themselves in official and public esteem. Scotland Yard, of course, was at work, and had all the station's material; but the station's hope was that they themselves would have the honour of settling the affair; and however useful the co-operation of the Press might be in other cases, they did not want to risk a defeat by a premature disclosure of their theories and plans.

So the sergeant talked at large, and propounded one interesting theory after another, all of which the newspaper men had thought of themselves.

The young man soon gave up these morning lectures on the Philosophy of Crime, and took to wandering about the streets and making bright stories out of the effect of the murders on the normal life of the people. A melancholy job made more melancholy by the district. The littered roadways, the crestfallen houses, the bleared windows – all held the acid misery that evokes no sympathy: the misery of the frustrated poet. The misery was the creation of the aliens, who were living in this makeshift fashion because they had no settled homes, and would neither take the trouble to make a home where they *could* settle, nor get on with their wandering.

There was little to be picked up. All he saw and heard were indignant faces, and wild conjectures of the murderer's identity and of the secret of his trick of appearing and disappearing unseen. Since a policeman himself had fallen a victim, denunciations of the force had ceased, and the unknown was now invested with a cloak of legend. Men eyed other men, as though thinking: It might be *him*. It might be *him*. They were no longer looking for a man who had the air of a Madame Tussaud murderer; they were looking for a man, or perhaps some harridan woman, who had done these particular murders. Their thoughts ran mainly on the foreign set. Such ruffianism could scarcely belong to England, nor could the bewildering cleverness of the thing. So they turned to Rumanian gipsies and Turkish carpet-sellers. There, clearly, would be found the 'warm' spot. These Eastern fellows – they knew all sorts of tricks, and they had no real religion – nothing to hold them within bounds. Sailors returning from those parts had told tales of conjurers who made themselves invisible; and there were tales of Egyptian and Arab potions that were used for abysmally queer purposes. Perhaps it *was* possible to them; you never knew.

They were so slick and cunning, and they had such gliding movements; no Englishman could melt away as they could. Almost certainly the murderer would be found to be one of that sort – with some dark trick of his own – and just because they were sure that he *was* a magician, they felt that it was useless to look for him. He was a power, able to hold them in subjection and to hold himself untouchable. Superstition, which so easily cracks the frail shell of reason, had got into them. He could do anything he chose; he would never be discovered. These two points they settled, and they went about the streets in a mood of resentful fatalism.

They talked of their ideas to the journalist in half-tones, looking right and left, as though *HE* might overhear them and visit them. And though all the district was thinking of him and ready to pounce upon him, yet, so strongly had he worked upon them, that if any man in the street – say, a small man of commonplace features and form – had cried '*I* am the Monster!' would their stifled fury have broken into flood and have borne him down and engulfed him? Or would they not suddenly have seen something unearthly in that everyday face and figure, something unearthly in his everyday boots, something unearthly about his hat, something that marked him as one whom none of their weapons could alarm or pierce? And would they not momentarily have fallen back from this devil, as the devil fell back from the Cross made by the sword of Faust, and so have given him time to escape? I do not know; but so fixed was their belief in his invincibility that it is at least likely that they would have made this hesitation, had such an occasion arisen. But it never did. Today this commonplace fellow, his murder lust glutted, is still seen and observed among them as he was seen and observed all the time; but because nobody then dreamt, or now dreams, that he was what he was, they observed him then, and observe him now, as people observe a lamp-post.

Almost was their belief in his invincibility justified; for five days after the murder of the policeman Petersen, when the experience and inspiration of the whole detective force of London were turned towards his identification and capture, he made his fourth and fifth strokes.

At nine o'clock that evening, the young newspaper man,

who hung about every night until his paper was away, was strolling along Richards Lane. Richards Lane is a narrow street, partly a stall-market, and partly residential. The young man was in the residential section, which carries on one side small working-class cottages, and on the other the wall of a railway goods yard. The great wall hung a blanket of shadow over the lane, and the shadow and the cadaverous outline of the now deserted market stalls gave it the appearance of a living lane that had been turned to frost in the moment between breath and death. The very lamps, that elsewhere were nimbuses of gold, had here the rigidity of gems. The journalist, feeling this message of frozen eternity, was telling himself that he was tired of the whole thing, when in one stroke the frost was broken. In the moment between one pace and another silence and darkness were racked by a high scream and through the screams a voice: 'Help! help! *He's here!*'

Before he could think what movement to make, the lane came to life. As though its invisible populace had been waiting on that cry, the door of every cottage was flung open, and from them and from the alleys poured shadowy figures bent in question-mark form. For a second or so they stood as rigid as the lamps; then a police whistle gave them direction, and the flock of shadows sloped up the street. The journalist followed them, and others followed him. From the main street and from surrounding streets they came, some risen from unfinished suppers, some disturbed in their ease of slippers and shirt-sleeves, some stumbling on infirm limbs, and some upright, and armed with pokers or the tools of their trade. Here and there above the wavering cloud of heads moved the bold helmets of policemen. In one dim mass they surged upon a cottage whose doorway was marked by the sergeant and two constables; and voices of those behind urged them on with 'Get in! Find him! Run round the back! Over the wall!' and those in front cried: 'Keep back! Keep back!'

And now the fury of a mob held in thrall by unknown peril broke loose. He was here – on the spot. Surely this time he *could not* escape. All minds were bent upon the cottage; all energies thrust towards its doors and windows and roof; all thought was turned upon one unknown man and his extermination. So that no one man saw any other man. No man saw the narrow, packed lane and the mass of struggling shadows, and all forgot to look among themselves for the monster who never lingered upon his victims. All forgot, indeed, that they, by their mass crusade of vengeance, were affording him the perfect hiding place. They saw only the house, and they heard only the rending of woodwork and the smash of glass at back and front, and the police giving orders or crying with the chase; and they pressed on.

But they found no murderer. All they found was news of murder and a glimpse of the ambulance, and for their fury there was no other object than the police themselves, who fought against this hampering of their work.

The journalist managed to struggle though to the cottage door, and to get the story from the constable stationed there. The cottage was the home of a pensioned sailor and his wife and daughter. They had been at supper, and at first it appeared that some noxious gas had smitten all three in mid-action. The daughter lay dead on the hearthrug, with a piece of bread and butter in her hand. The father had fallen sideways from his chair, leaving on his plate a filled spoon of rice-pudding. The mother lay half under the table, her lap filled with the pieces of a broken cup and splashes of cocoa. But in three seconds the idea of gas was dismissed. One glance at their necks showed that this was the Strangler again; and the police stood and looked at the room and momentarily shared the fatalism of the public. They were helpless.

This was his fourth visit, making seven murders in all. He was to do, as you know, one more – and to do it that night; and then he was to pass into history as the unknown London horror, and return to the decent life that he had always led, remembering little of what he had done, and worried not at all by the memory. Why did he stop? Impossible to say. Why did he begin? Impossible again. It just happened like that; and if he thinks at all of those days and nights, I surmise that he thinks of them as we think of foolish or dirty little sins that we committed in childhood. We say that they were not really sins, because we were not then consciously ourselves: we had not come to realization; and we look back at that foolish little creature that we once were, and forgive him because he didn't know. So, I think, with this man.

There are plenty like him. Eugène Aram, after the murder of Daniel Clark, lived a quiet, contented life for fourteen years, unhaunted by his crime and unshaken in his self-esteem. Dr Crippen murdered his wife, and then lived pleasantly with his mistress in the house under whose floor he had buried his wife. Constance Kent, found Not Guilty of the murder of her young brother, led a peaceful life for five years before she confessed. George Joseph Smith and William Palmer lived amiably among their fellows untroubled by fear or by remorse for their poisonings and drownings. Charles Peace, at the time he made his one unfortunate essay, had settled down into a respectable citizen with an interest in antiques. It happened that, after a lapse of time, these men were discovered, but more murderers than we guess are living decent lives today, and will die in decency, undiscovered and unsuspected. As this man will.

But he had a narrow escape, and it was perhaps this narrow escape that brought him to a stop. The escape was due to an error of judgment on the part of the journalist.

As soon as he had the full story of the affair, which took some time, he spent fifteen minutes on the telephone, sending the story through, and at the end of the fifteen minutes, when the stimulus of the business had left him, he felt physically tired and mentally dishevelled. He was not yet free to go home; the paper would not go away for another hour; so he turned into a bar for a drink and some sandwiches.

It was then, when he had dismissed the whole business from his mind, and was looking about the bar and admiring the landlord's taste in watch-chains and his air of domination, and was thinking that the landlord of a well-conducted tavern had a more comfortable life than a newspaper man, that his mind received from nowhere a spark of light. He was not thinking about the Strangling Horrors; his mind was on his sandwich. As a public-house sandwich, it was a curiosity. The bread had been thinly cut, it was buttered, and the ham was not two months stale; it was ham as it should be. His mind turned to the inventor of this refreshment, the Earl of Sandwich, and then to George the Fourth, and then to the Georges, and to the legend of that George who was worried to know how the apple got into the apple-dumpling. He worried whether George would have been equally puzzled to know how the ham got into the ham sandwich, and how long it would have been before it occurred to him that the ham could not have got there unless somebody had put it there. He got up to order another sandwich, and in that moment a little active corner of his mind settled the affair. If there was ham in his sandwich, somebody must have put it there. If seven people had been murdered, somebody must have been there to murder them. There was no aeroplane or automobile that would go into a man's pocket; therefore that somebody must have escaped either by running away or standing still; and again therefore –

He was visualizing the front page story that his paper would carry if his theory were correct, and if – a matter of conjecture – his editor had the necessary nerve to make a bold stroke, when a cry of 'Time, gentleman, please! All out!' reminded him of the hour. He got up and went out into a world of mist, broken by the ragged discs of roadside puddles and the streaming lightning of motor buses. He was certain that he had *the* story, but, even if it were proved, he was doubtful whether the policy of his paper would permit him to print it. It had one great fault. It was truth, but it was impossible truth. It rocked the foundations of everything that newspaper readers believed and that newspaper editors helped them to believe. They might believe that Turkish carpet-sellers had the gift of making themselves invisible. They would not belive this.

As it happened, they were not asked to, for the story was never written. As his paper had by now gone away, and as he was nourished by his refreshment and stimulated by his theory, he thought he might put in an extra half-hour by testing that theory. So he began to look about for the man he had in mind – a man with white hair, and large white hands; otherwise an everyday figure whom nobody would look twice at. He wanted to spring his idea on this man without warning, and he was going to place himself within reach of a man armoured in legends of dreadfulness and grue. This might appear to be an act of supreme courage – that one man, with no hope of immediate outside support, should place himself at

the mercy of one who was holding a whole parish in terror.
But it wasn't. He didn't think about the risk. He didn't think
about his duty to his employers or loyalty to his paper. He was
moved simply by an instinct to follow a story to its end.

He walked slowly from the tavern and crossed into Fingal
Street, making for Deever Market, where he had hope of
finding his man. But his journey was shortened. At the corner
of Lotus Street he saw him – or a man who looked like him.
This street was poorly lit, and he could see little of the man:
but he *could* see white hands. For some twenty paces he stalked
him; then drew level with him; and at a point where the arch
of a railway crossed the street, he saw that this was his man.
He approached him with the current conversational phrase of
the district: 'Well, seen anything of the murderer?' The man
stopped to look sharply at him, then, satisfied that the
journalist was not the murderer, said:

'Eh? No, nor's anybody else, curse it. Doubt if they ever
will.'

'I don't know. I've been thinking about them, and I've got
an idea.'

'So?'

'Yes. Came to me all of a sudden. Quarter of an hour ago.
And I'd felt that we'd all been blind. It's been staring us in the
face.'

The man turned again to look at him, and the look and the
movement held suspicion of this man who seemed to know so
much. 'Oh? Has it? Well, if you're so sure, why not give us the
benefit of it?'

'I'm going to.' They walked level, and were nearly at the
end of the little street where it meets Deever Market, when the
journalist turned casually to the man. He put a finger on his
arm. 'Yes, it seems to me quite simple now. But there's still
one point I don't understand. One little thing I'd like to clear
up. I mean the motive. Now, as man to man, tell me, Sergeant
Ottermole, just *why* did you kill those inoffensive people?'

The sergeant stopped, and the journalist stopped. There
was just enough light from the sky, which held the reflected
light of the continent of London, to give him a sight of the
sergeant's face, and the sergeant's face was turned to him with
a wide smile of such urbanity and charm that the journalist's

eyes were frozen as they met it. The smile stayed for some seconds. Then said the sergeant: 'Well, to tell you the truth, Mister Newspaper Man, I don't know. I really don't know. In fact, I've been worried about it myself. But I've got an idea – just like you. Everybody knows that we can't control the workings of our minds. Don't they? Ideas come into our minds without asking. But everybody's supposed to be able to control his body. Why? Eh? We get our minds from lord-knows-where – from people who were dead hundreds of years before we were born. Mayn't we get our bodies in the same way? Our faces – our legs – our heads – they aren't completely ours. We don't make 'em. They come to us. And couldn't ideas come into our bodies like ideas come into our minds? Eh? Can't ideas live in nerve and muscle as well as in brain? Couldn't it be that parts of our bodies aren't really us, and couldn't ideas come into those parts all of a sudden, like ideas come into – into' – he shot his arms out, showing the great white-gloved hands and hairy wrists; shot them out so swiftly to the journalist's throat that his eyes never saw them – 'into *my hands!* '

VII

A Thing About Machines
Rod Serling

Although Alfred Hitchcock Presents *overshadowed all other mystery and horror programmes on television, I was also a fan of another American series which was first screened in the late 1950s and is still being re-run today,* The Twilight Zone. *The series was the brain-child of a talented screenwriter named Rod Serling who also employed the same technique as Hitchcock in personally introducing each episode. The stories were a mixture of the weird and the fantastic, the chilling and the bizarre, yet somehow never totally divorced from everyday life and therefore all the more impressive. In defining* The Twilight Zone, *Serling has written, 'It lies somewhere between the day and darkness, between sleeping and waking, reality and illusion. It's a place inhabited by outlandish people where strange things happen'. A factor that has also played a part in its popularity has been an uncanny ability to predict future events — like the story of 'The Doomsday Flight' about a bomb hoax on board an aircraft which was shown in July 1971 and then dramatically repeated in real life in the August of that same year on a BOAC 747 bound from Montreal to London. Several collections of stories from the series have already been published, but this following tale of Mr Bartlett Finchley's strange inability to cope with modern machinery and the terrifying repercussions, is here making its first book appearance. It has some of the flavour which Rod Serling has also been giving to his more recent series of television thrillers entitled* The Night Gallery ...

Mr Bartlett Finchley, tall, tart, and fortyish, looked across his ornate living room to where the television repairman was working behind his set and felt an inner twist of displeasure that the mood of the tastefully decorated room should be so damaged by the T-shirted, dungareed serviceman whose presence was such a foreign element in the room. He looked, gimlet-eyed, at the man's tool box lying on the soft pile of the expensive carpet like a blot on Mr Finchley's escutcheon which emphasized symmetry above all! Mr Finchley, among other things, was both a snob and fastidious. And snobbery and fastidiousness were not simply character traits with him; they were banners that he flaunted with pride. He rose from the chair and walked over to within a few feet of the television set. The repairman looked up at him, smiling, and wiped his forehead.

'How are you today, Mr Finchley?'

Mr Finchley's left eyebrow shot up. 'I'll answer *that* burning question after you tell me what's wrong with that electronic boo-boo, and also acquaint me with how much this current larceny is going to cost me.'

The repairman rose and wiped his hands with a rag. He looked down at the set, then up to Mr Finchley. 'Two hours' labour,' he said, 'a broken set of tubes, new oscillator, new filter.'

Mr Finchley's face froze, his thin lips forming a taut line.

'How very technical,' he announced. 'How very nice! And I presume I'm to be dunned once again for three times the worth of the bloody thing?'

The repairman smiled gently and studied Mr Finchley. 'Last time I was here, Mr Finchley,' he said, 'you'd kicked your foot through the screen. Remember?'

Mr Finchley turned away and put a cigarette in a holder. 'I have a vivid recollection,' he announced. 'It was not working properly.' He shrugged. 'I tried to get it to do so in a normal fashion!'

'By kicking your foot through the screen?' the repairman shook his head. 'Why didn't you just horsewhip it, Mr Finchley? That'd show it who's boss.'

He started to collect his tools and put them into the box. Mr Finchley lit the cigarette in the holder, took a deep drag, and examined his nails.

'What do you say we cease this small talk and get down to some serious larceny? You can read me off the damages ... though I sometimes wonder exactly what is the purpose of the

Better Business Bureau when they allow you itinerant extortionists to come back week after week, move wires around, busily probe with ham-like hands, and accomplish nothing but the financial ruin of every customer on your route!'

The repairman looked up from the tool box, his smile fading. 'We're not a gyp outfit, Mr Finchley. We're legitimate repairmen. But I'll tell you something about *yourself* – '

'Spare me, please,' Mr Finchley interrupted him. 'I'm sure there must be some undernourished analyst with an ageing mother to care for whom I can contact for that purpose.'

The repairman closed the box and stood up. 'Why don't you hear me out. Mr Finchley? That set doesn't work because obviously you got back there and yanked out wires and God knows what else! You had me over here last month to fix your portable radio – because you'd thrown it down the steps.'

'It did not work properly,' Finchley said icily.

'That's the point, Mr Finchley. Why *don't* they work properly? Off-hand I'd say it's because you don't *treat* them properly.'

Mr Finchley let the cigarette holder dangle from his mouth as he surveyed the repairman much as a scientist would look at a bug through a microscope. 'I assume there's no charge for that analysis?' he inquired.

The repairman shook his head. 'What does go wrong with these things, Mr Finchley? Have you any idea?'

Mr Finchley let out a short, frozen chortle. 'Have *I* any idea? Now that's worth a scholarly ten lines in your *Repairman's Journal* ! Bilk the customer, but let him do the repairing!'

'The reason I asked that,' the repairman persisted, 'is because whatever it is that really bothers you about that television set *and* the radio ... you're not telling me.'

He waited for a response. Mr Finchley turned his back.

'Well?' the repairman asked.

Finchley drew a deep breath as if the last resisting pocket of his patience had been overrun and was being forced to capitulate. 'Aside from being rather an incompetent clod,' Finchley announced, turning back toward the repairman, 'you're a most insensitive man. I've explained to you already.

The television set simply did not work properly. And that rinky-dink original Marconi operating under the guise of a legitimate radio gave me nothing but static.'

The TV repairman flicked the set on, watched the picture, raised and lowered the volume, then shut it off. He turned toward Finchley.

'You're sure that's all that was wrong with it?'

Finchley made a gesture and started out of the room. The repairman, with a smile, followed him.

'I'll send you a bill, Mr Finchley,' he said as they walked toward the front hall.

'Of this I have no doubt,' Finchley responded.

At the front door, the repairman turned to look once again at Finchley who stood on the first step of the long sweeping stairway which led to the second floor.

'Mr Finchley ... what is it with you and machines?'

Finchley's eyes sought the ceiling as if this latest idiocy was more than he could bear. 'I will file *that* idiotic question in my memorabilia to be referred to at some future date when I write my memoirs. You will fill one entire chapter on The Most Forgettable Person I Have Ever Met!'

The repairman shook his head and left. Mr Finchley stood stock-still, his features working. For just one, single fleeting moment, his hauteur, his pre-emptive mastery of all situations, his snobbery seemed to desert the face, leaving behind a mask of absolute, undiluted terror.

'It just so happens, you boob,' Finchley called out into the empty hall, his voice shaking, 'it just so happens that every machine in my house is – '

He cut himself off abruptly, closed his eyes, shook his head, looked down at his hands that were shaking, grabbed them together, then turned and walked unsteadily into the living room. A clock on the mantelpiece chimed deep, resonant notes that filled the room.

'All right,' Finchley said, holding his voice down, 'that'll be about enough of that! Hear me?'

The clock continued to chime. Finchley walked over toward the mantel and shouted.

'*I said that'll be just about enough of that!* '

He reached up, grabbed the clock in both hands, ripped the

plug out of the wall, and slammed the clock down on the floor, stamping on it with his foot while the chimes continued to blare at him like the death rattle of some dying beast. It took several moments for the chimes to die out and Finchley stood over the wreckage of broken glass and dismembered fly wheels and springs, sweat pouring down his face, his whole body shaking as if with an ague. Then very slowly he recovered composure. The shaking stopped, and he went upstairs to his bedroom.

He closed the door and lay down on the bed, feeling limp, washed out and desperately vulnerable. Soon he fell into an uneasy twisting and turning, dream-filled sleep, full of all the nightmares that he lived with during the day and that were kept hidden underneath the icy facade of superiority which insulated him from the world.

Mr Bartlett Finchley at age forty-two was a practising sophisticate who wrote very special and very precious things for gourmet magazines and the like. He was a bachelor and a recluse. He had few friends – only devotees and adherents to the cause of tart sophistry. He had no interests – save whatever current annoyance he could put his mind to. He had no purpose to his life – except the formulation of day-to-day opportunities to vent his wrath on mechanical contrivances of an age he abhorred.

In short, Mr Bartlett Finchley was a malcontent, born either too late or too early in the century – he was unsure which. The only thing he was certain of as he awoke, drenched with perspiration, from his nap, was that the secret could not be held much longer. The sleepless nights and fear-filled days were telling on him, and this man with no friends and no confidants realized in a hidden portion of his mind that he urgently required both.

Late that afternoon he walked down the sweeping staircase from his sumptuous bedroom, attired in a smoking jacket, and directed himself to the small study off the living room where he could hear the sound of the electric typewriter. His secretary had come in a few hours before and was sitting at the desk typing from Finchley's notes.

Edith Rogers was an attractive thirty-year-old who had been with Finchley for over a year. In a history of some two dozen-odd secretaries, Miss Rogers held the record for tenure. It was rare that anyone stayed with Mr Finchley for over a month. She looked up as the master entered the room, cigarette in holder, holder dangling from mouth. He looked back insouciantly and walked behind her to stare over her shoulder at the page in the typewriter. He then picked up a stack of papers from the desk.

'This is all you've done?' he inquired coldly.

She met his stare, unyielding. 'That's all I've done,' she announced. 'That's forty pages in three and a half hours. That's the best *I* can do, Mr Finchley.'

He waggled a finger at the typewriter. 'It's that .., that idiotic gadget of yours. Thomas Jefferson wrote out the preamble to the Constitution with a feather quill and it took him half a day.'

The secretary turned in her chair and looked directly up into his face. 'Why don't you hire Mr Jefferson?' she said quietly.

Finchley's eyebrow, which was one of the most mobile features in a mobile face, shot up alarmingly. 'Did I ever tell you,' he asked, 'with what degree of distaste I view insubordination?'

Edith Rogers bent over the typewriter. 'Often and endlessly,' she said. Then she straightened up. 'I'll tell you what, Mr Finchley,' she said, rising and reaching for her bag, 'you get yourself another girl, somebody with three arms and with roughly the sensitivity of an alligator. Then you can work together till death do you part. As for me – ' she shut her pocketbook ' – I've had it!'

'And you are going where?' Finchley asked her as she started into the living room.

'Where?' the girl answered, turning toward him. 'I think I might take in Bermuda for a couple of weeks. Or Mexico City. Or perhaps a quiet sanitarium on the banks of the Hudson. Any place,' she continued, as she walked across the room toward the hall, 'where I can be away from the highly articulate, oh so sophisticated, *bon vivant* of America's winers and diners – Mr Bartlett Finchley.'

She paused for breath in the hall and found him staring at her from the living room.

'You've even got me talking like you,' she said angrily. 'But I'll tell you what you *won't* get me to do. You won't turn me into a female Finchley with a pinched little acorn for a heart and a mean, petty, jaundiced view of everybody else in the world!'

Finchley's instinct conjured up a tart, biting, cutting, and irreproachable reply, but something else deep inside shut it off. He stood for a moment with his mouth open, then he bit his lip and said very quietly in a tone she was quite unfamiliar with, 'Miss Rogers ... please don't leave.'

She noticed something in his face that she had never seen before. It was an unfrocked, naked fear so unlike him as to be unbelievable. 'I beg your pardon?' she asked very softly.

Finchley turned away, embarrassed. 'I do wish you'd ... you'd stay for a little bit.' He wavered an arm in the general direction of the study. 'I don't mean for work. All that can wait. I was just thinking ... well ... we could have dinner or something, or perhaps a cocktail.' He turned to her expectantly.

'I'm not very hungry,' she said after a pause. 'And it's too early for cocktails.' She saw the disappointment cross his face. 'What's your trouble, Mr Finchley?' she asked pointedly but not without sympathy.

Finchley's smile was a ghostly and wan attempt at recovery of aplomb, but his voice quickly took on the sharp, slicing overtones that were so much a part of him. 'Miss Rogers, my dear, you sound like a cave-dwelling orphan whose idea of a gigantic lark is a square dance at the local grange. I was merely suggesting to you that we observe the simple social amenities between an employer and a secretary. I thought we'd go out ... take in a show or something.'

She studied him for a long moment, not really liking the man either at this moment, but vaguely aware of something that was eating at him and forcing this momentary lapse into at least a semblance of courtesy.

'How very sweet, Mr Finchley,' she said. 'Thank you, but no thank you.'

Finchley half snorted as he turned his back to her and once again she felt the snobbery of the man, the insufferable ego, the unbearable superiority that he threw around to hurt and humiliate.

'Tonight,' she said, feeling no more pity or fascination, 'tonight I'm taking a hog-calling lesson. You know what a hog is, don't you, Mr Finchley? He's a terribly bright fathead who writes for gourmet magazines and condescends to let a few other slobs exist in the world for the purpose of taking his rudeness and running back and forth at his beck and call! Good night, Mr Finchley.'

She saw his shoulders slump and he was silent. Again she felt compelled to remain because this was so unlike him, so foreign to him not to top her, not to meet her barb head on, divert it, and send one of his own back at her, stronger, faster, and much more damaging. When he finally turned she saw again that his face had an odd look and there was something supplicating, something frightening and something, inconceivable though it was, lonely.

'Miss Rogers,' he said, his voice gentler than she'd ever heard it, 'before you do ... before you go – ' he made a kind of half-hearted gesture, ' – have a cup of coffee or something.' He turned away so that she would be unable to see his face. 'I'd like very much,' he continued, 'I'd like very much not to be alone for a while.'

Edith Rogers came back into the living room and stood close to him. 'Are you ill?' she asked.

He shook his head.

'Bad news or something?'

'No.'

There was a silence.

'What's your trouble?' she asked.

He whirled on her, his thin lips twisted. 'Does there have to be trouble just because I – '

He stopped, ran a hand over his face, and half fell into a chair. For the first time she observed the circles under his eyes, the pinched look of the mouth, the strangely haunted look.

'I'm desperately tired,' he said abruptly. 'I haven't slept for four nights and the very thought of being alone now – ' He grimaced, obviously hating this, feeling the reluctance of the strong man having to admit a weakness. 'Frankly,' he said, looking away, 'it's intolerable. Things have been happening, Miss Rogers, very odd things.'

'Go on.'

He pointed toward the TV set. 'That ... that thing over there. It goes on late at night and wakes me up. It goes on all by itself.' His eyes swept across the room toward the hall. 'And that portable radio I used to keep in my bedroom. It went on and off, just as I was going to sleep.'

His head went down and when he looked up his eyes darted around paranoically. 'There's a conspiracy in this house, Miss Rogers.' Seeing her expression, he raised his voice in rebuttal. 'That's exactly what it is – a conspiracy! The television set, the radio, lighters, electric clocks, that ... that miserable car I drive.'

He rose from the chair, his face white and intense. 'Last night I drove it into the driveway, mind you. Very slowly. Very carefully.' He took a step toward her, his fingers clinching and unclenching at his sides. 'The wheel turned in my hands. Hear me? *The wheel turned in my hand!* The car deliberately hit the side of the garage. Broke a headlight. – That clock up there on the mantelpiece!'

Edith looked at the mantelpiece. There was no clock there. She turned to him questioningly.

'I ... I threw it away,' Finchley announced lamely. Then, pointedly and forcefully he said, 'What I'm getting at, Miss Rogers, is that for as long as I've lived ... I've never been able to operate *machines*.' He spat out the last word as if it were some kind of epithet.

Edith Rogers stared at him, for the first time seeing a part of the man that had been kept hidden beneath a veneer and a smoking jacket.

'Mr Finchley,' she said very softly, 'I think you ought to see a doctor.'

Finchley's eyes went wide and the face and the voice were the Finchley of old. 'A *doctor*,' he shrieked at her. 'The universal panacea of the dreamless twentieth-century idiot! If you're depressed – see a doctor. If you're happy – see a doctor. If the mortgage is too high and the salary too low – see a doctor. You,' he screamed at her, 'Miss Rogers, *you* see a doctor.' Fury plugged up his voice for a moment and then he screamed at her again. 'I'm a logical, rational, intelligent man. I know what I see. I know what I hear. For the past three months I've been seeing and hearing a collection of wheezy Frankensteins whose whole purpose is to destroy me! Now what do you think about *that*, Miss Rogers?'

The girl studied him for a moment. 'I think you're terribly ill, Mr Finchley. I think you need medical attention.' She shook her head. 'I think you've got a very bad case of nerves from lack of sleep and I think that way down deep you yourself realize that these are nothing more than delusions.'

She looked down at the floor for a moment, then turned and started out of the room.

'Now where are you going?' he shouted at her.

'You don't need company, Mr Finchley,' she said from the hall. 'You need analysis.'

He half ran over to her, grabbed her arm, whirled her around.

'You're no different from a cog-wheeled, electrically generated metal machine yourself. You haven't an iota of compassion or sympathy.'

She struggled to free her arm. 'Mr Finchley, please let me go.'

'I'll let you go,' he yelled, 'when I get good and ready to let you go!'

Edith continued to struggle, hating the scene, desperately wanting to end it, and yet not knowing how.

'Mr Finchley,' she said to him, trying to push him off, 'this is ugly. Now please let me go.' She was growing frightened. '*Let go of me!*'

Suddenly, instinctively, she slapped him across the face. He dropped her arm abruptly and stared at her as if disbelieving that anything of this sort could happen to him. That he, Bartlett Finchley, could be struck by a woman. Again his lips trembled and his features worked. A burning fury took possession of him.

'Get out of here,' he said in a low, menacing voice, 'and don't come back!'

'With distinct pleasure,' Edith said, breathing heavily, 'and with manifest relief.' She whirled around and went to the door.

'Remember,' he shouted at her, 'don't come back. I'll send you a cheque. I will not be intimidated by machines, so it follows that no empty-headed little broad with a mechanical face can do anything to me either.'

She paused at the door, wanting air and freedom and most of all to get out of there. 'Mr Finchley,' she said softly, 'in this conspiracy you're suffering … this mortal combat between you and the appliances – *I hope you get licked!* '

She went out and slammed the door behind her. He stood there motionless, conjuring up some line of dialogue he could fling at her; some final cutting witticism that could leave him the winner. But no inspiration came and it was in the midst of this that he suddenly heard the electric typewriter keys.

He listened for a horrified moment until the sound stopped. Then he went to his study. There was a paper in the typewriter. Finchley turned the roller so that he could read the words on it. There were three lines of type and each one read, 'Get out of here, Finchley.'

That was what the typewriter had written all by itself. 'Get out of here, Finchley.' He ripped the paper from the machine, crumpled it, and flung it on the floor.

'Get out of here, Finchley,' he said aloud. 'Goddamn you. Who are you, to tell me to get out of here?' He shut his eyes tightly and ran a fluttery hand over a perspiring face. 'Why this is … this is absurd. It's a typewriter. It's a machine. It's a silly, Goddamn machine – '

He froze again as a voice came from the television set in the living room.

'Get out of here, Finchley,' the voice said.

He felt his heart pounding inside him as he turned and raced into the living room. There was a little Mexican girl on the screen doing a dance with a tambourine. He could have sworn that each time she clicked her heels past the camera she stared pointedly at him. But as the music continued and the girl kept on dancing, Finchley reached a point where he was almost certain that the whole thing was a product of his sleeplessness, his imagination, and perhaps just a remnant of the emotional scene he had just gone through with Edith Rogers.

But then the music stopped. The girl bowed to the applause

of an unseen audience and, when she had taken her bows, looked directly out of the screen into Finchley's face.

She smiled at him and said very clearly, 'You'd better get out of here, Finchley!'

Finchley screamed, picked up a vase, and threw it across the room. He did not think or aim, but the piece of ceramic smashed into the television set, splintering the glass in front to be followed by a loud noise and a puff of smoke. But clearly – ever so clearly from the smoking shambles of its interior – came the girl's voice again.

'You'd better get out of here, Finchley,' the voice said, and Finchley screamed again as he raced out of the room, into the hall and up the stairs.

On the top landing he turned and shouted down the stairs. 'All right! All right, you machines! You're not going to intimidate *me*! Do you hear me? You are not going to intimidate me! You ... you machines!'

And from down below in the study – dull, methodical, but distinctly audible – came the sound of typewriter keys and Finchley knew what they were writing. He started to cry, the deep, harsh sobs of a man who has gone without sleep, and who has closeted his fears deep inside.

He went blindly into his bedroom and shut the door, tears rolling down his face, making the room into a shimmering, indistinct pattern of satin drapes, pink walls, and fragile Louis XIV furniture, all blurred together in the giant mirror that covered one side of the room.

He flung himself on the bed and buried his face against the pillow. Through the closed door he continued to hear the sound of the typewriter keys as they typed out their message over and over again. Finally they stopped and there was silence in the house.

At seven o'clock that evening, Mr Finchley, dressed in a silk bathrobe and a white silk ascot, perched near the pillow of his bed and dialled a number on the ivory-coloured, bejewelled telephone.

'Yes,' he said into the phone. 'Yes. Miss Moore please. Agatha, Bartlett Finchley here. Yes, my dear, it has been a long time.' He smiled, remembering Miss Moore's former attachment to him. 'Which indeed prompts this call,' he explained. 'How about dinner this evening?' His face fell as the words came to him from the other end of the line. 'I see. Well, of course, it *is* short notice. But ... yes ... yes, I see. Yes, I'll call you again, my dear.'

He put the phone down, stared at it for a moment, then picked it up and dialled another number.

'Miss Donley, please,' he said, as if he were announcing a princess entering a state ball. 'Pauline, is this you?' (He was aware that his voice had taken on a false, bantering tone he was unaccustomed to and hated even as he used it.) 'And how's my favourite attractive young widow this evening?' He felt his hand shake. 'Bartlett,' he said. 'Bartlett Finchley. I was wondering if – Oh. I see. I see. Well I'm delighted. I'm simply delighted. I'll send you a wedding gift. Of course. Good night.'

He slammed the telephone down angrily. God, what could be more stupid than a conniving female hell-bent for marriage. He had a dim awareness of the total lack of logic for his anger. But disappointment and the prospect of a lonely evening made him quite unconcerned with logic. He stared at the phone, equating it with his disappointment, choosing to believe at this moment that in the cause and effect of things, this phone had somehow destroyed his plans. He suddenly yanked it out of the wall, flinging it across the room. His voice was tremulous.

'Telephones. Just like all the rest of them. Exactly like all the rest. A whole existence dedicated to embarrassing me or inconveniencing me or making my life miserable.'

He gave the phone a kick and turned his back to it. Bravado crept backwards into his voice.

'Well, who needs you?' he asked rhetorically. 'Who needs any of you? Bartlett Finchley is going out this evening. He's going out to have a wonderful dinner with some good wine and who knows what attractive young lady he may meet during his meanderings. Who knows indeed!'

He went into the bathroom. He studied the thin, aristocratic face that looked back at him from the mirror. Grey, perceptive eyes; thinning but still wavy brown hair; thin expressive lips. If not a strong face, at least an intelligent one. The face of a man who knew what he was about. The face of a thoughtful man of values and awareness.

He opened the medicine cabinet and took out an electric razor. Humming to himself, he plugged it into the wall, adjusted its head, then laid it aside while he put powder on his face. He was dusting off his chin when something made him look down at the electric razor. Its head was staring up at him for all the world like a kind of reptilian beast, gaping at him through a barbed, baleful opening in a grimacing face.

Finchley felt a fear clutch at his insides as he picked up the razor and held it half an arm's length away, studying it thoughtfully and with just a hint of a slowly building tension. This had to stop, he thought. This most definitely and assuredly had to stop.

That idiotic girl was brainless, stupid, and blind – but she had a point. It *was* his imagination. The TV set, the radio, and that damned phone in the other room. It was all part of his imagination. They *were* just machines. They had no entities or purpose or will. He grasped the razor more firmly and started to bring it toward his face. In a brief, fleeting, nightmarish instant the razor seemed to jump out of his hand and attack his face, biting, clawing, ripping at him.

Finchley screamed and flung it away from him, then stumbled backwards against the bathroom door. He scrambled for the ornate gold doorknob, pulled it open and ran stumbling into the bedroom. He tripped over the telephone cord, knocking the receiver off the cradle, and then gasped as a filtered voice came out of the phone.

'Get out of here, Finchley,' it trilled at him. 'Get out of here.'

Down below the typewriter started up again and from the destroyed television set the little Mexican dancer's voice joined the chorus. 'Get out of here, Finchley. Get out of here.'

His hands went to his head, pulling spasmodically at his hair, feeling his heart grow huge inside of him as if he were ready to explode and then, joining the rest of the chorus, was the sound of the front-door chimes. They rang several times and after a moment they were the only noises in the house. All the other voices and sounds had stopped.

Finchley tightened his bathrobe strap, went out of the room, and walked slowly down the stairs, letting bravado and aplomb surge back into him until by the time he reached the front door, his face wore the easy smirk of an animal trainer who has just completed placing thousand-pound lions on tiny stools. He adjusted his bathrobe, fluffed out the ascot, raised an eyebrow, then opened the door.

On the porch stood a policeman and, clustered behind him in a semicircle, a group of neighbours. Over their shoulder Finchley could see his car, hanging half over the curb, two deep furrows indicating its passage across the lawn.

'That your car?' the policeman asked him.

Finchley went outside. 'That's correct,' he said coldly. 'It's my car.'

'Rolled down the driveway,' the policeman said accusingly. 'Then across your lawn and almost hit a kid on a bike. You ought to check your emergency brake, mister.'

Finchley looked bored. 'The emergency brake *was* on.'

'I'm afraid it wasn't,' the policeman said, shaking his head. 'Or if it was – it's not working properly. Car rolled right into the street. You're lucky it didn't hit anyone.'

The neighbours made way for Finchley, knowing him to be a man of mercurial moods and an acid, destructive tongue. As he crossed the lawn toward his car, he gazed at a small boy with an all-day sucker in his mouth.

'And how are you this evening, Monstrous?' Mr Finchley said under his breath. He looked his car up and down, back and forth, and felt a cold spasm of fear as the thought came to him that, of all the machines, this was the biggest and the least controllable. Also, wasn't there an odd look about the front end of the thing? The headlights and grill, the bumper. Didn't it resemble a face? Again from deep inside Finchley there blossomed the beginning of hysteria that he had to choke down and hide from the people who were staring at him.

The policeman came up behind him. 'You got the keys?'

'They're in the house,' Finchley said.

'All right then, mister. You'd better pull her back into the garage and then you'd better have those brakes checked first chance you get. Understand?'

There was a pause as Finchley turned his back to him.

'Understand, mister?'

Finchley nodded perfunctorily, then turned and gazed at the circle of faces, his eyes slitted and suspicious. 'All right, dear friends,' he announced. 'You may remain on my property for another three and a half minutes goggling at this amazing sight. I shall then return with my automobile keys. At that time I should like all of you to be off my property or else I shall solicit the aid of this underpaid gendarme to forcibly evict you.' He looked along the line of people, raised an eyebrow and said, 'Understand, clods?'

He very carefully picked his way through the group and headed back toward the house, fastidiously avoiding any contact like a mediaeval baron fresh from a visit to an area of the black plague. Not really frightened of catching it, you understand, but playing it safe, just the same. When he reached his house and left the gaping neighbours behind, his shoulders slumped, the eyebrow went back to normal and his cold, rigidly controlled features suddenly became loose and pliable, the flesh white, the eyes nervous and haunted.

At nine o'clock in the evening, Bartlett Finchley had consumed three quarters of a bottle of excellent bourbon and had forgotten all about going out for the evening. He lay half-dozing on the couch, his well-tailored tuxedo crumpled and unkempt. There was a noise on the stairs and Finchley opened his eyes and turned his head so that he could stare across the room toward the hall. The telephone repairman was just coming down the steps. He paused at the entrance to the living room, looked in.

'She's operating all right now, Mr Finchley,' the repairman said.

'I'm deeply indebted,' Finchley answered acidly. 'Convey my best to Alexander Graham Bell.'

The telephone repairman lingered at the entrance. 'You tripped over the cord — is that what you said?'

'If that's what I said,' Finchley barked at him, 'that's precisely what happened.'

The repairman shrugged. 'Well, you're the boss, Mr Finchley. But those wires sure look as though they've been yanked out.'

Finchley rose to a sitting position on the couch and carefully smoothed back his hair. He took a cigarette from a hand-carved teakwood on the coffee table, careful that the repairman should not see how his fingers shook as he fitted the cigarette in the holder.

'Do they indeed?' Finchley said, concentrating on the cigarette. 'Proving what a vast storehouse of knowledge you've yet to acquire.' Then, looking up with disdain, he said, 'Good night!'

The repairman went out the front door and Finchley rose from the couch. He hesitated, then went to the television set. Its broken screen was a yawning abyss into the darkness beyond and Finchley hurriedly backed away from it.

At the bar in the corner of the room, he poured himself a large drink, downed half of it in a gulp, then stared almost challengingly at the television set. It stood in silent defeat, this time shattered beyond any repair and Finchley felt satisfaction. He was about to take another drink when the sound of the clock chimes suddenly clanged into the room. Finchley's glass dropped and broke on the bartop. Again the cold, clammy, impossible fear seized him as he looked toward the empty mantel where the clock had been and then down to the floor where he himself had smashed it into nothingness.

And yet there was the sound of the chimes, loud, deep, resonant and enveloping the room. He ran toward the hall and then stopped. From the study came the sound of the electric typewriter, the keys, then the carriage, then the keys again. And still the chimes of the clock joining as an obbligato and Finchley felt a scream building up in his throat.

He ran into the study in time to see the typewriter finishing a final line. He took a stumbling step and ripped the paper out of the carriage. 'Get out of here, Finchley.' It covered the page, line after line after line. And then suddenly came another horror from the living room. The little dancer's voice that he'd heard on the television set that afternoon.

'Get out of here, Finchley,' it called sweetly. 'Get out of here, Finchley.'

The chimes continued to ring and then, inexplicably, another chorus of voices joined the girls.

'Get out of here, Finchley,' it said, like some kind of vast *a capella* choir. 'Get out of here, Finchley.' Over and over again.

'Get out of here, Finchley. Get out of here, Finchley. *Get out of here, Finchley!* '

Finchley let out one gasping, agonizing sob and thrust his knuckles into his mouth as once again he ran into the living room and stared wildly around. He picked up a chair and threw it at the television set. It missed and shot past to smash against a fragile antique table holding an expensive lamp, both of which went to the floor with a loud clatter of broken wood and glass. And still the voices, the typewriter, the chimes.

And when Finchley, a steady, constant scream coming from his throat like a grotesque human siren, raced back into the hall and started upstairs, another nightmare was heading toward him from the top. There was the electric razor slithering down, step by step, like a snake with an oversized head.

Finchley's scream stopped and he was unable to conjure up another one, though his mouth was open and his eyes popped and he felt pain clawing the inside of his chest. He tripped and landed on his knees as he tried to reach the door. He yanked at it and finally got it open as the electric razor came unerringly after him.

He tore out into the night, the sounds of his house following him, a deafening chorus of, 'Get out of here, Finchley,' orchestrated for typewriter keys, clock chimes, and the hum of an electric razor.

He tripped again and landed in a heap on the sidewalk. He felt the needle of a rose bush through his trousers as he ran toward the garage and was able to scream once again, as the garage doors creaked open and the headlights of the car inside went on and bathed him in hot, white light.

The engine growled like a jungle beast as the car started to roll slowly out toward him. Finchley yelled for help, ran out to the street, tripped and fell, feeling the shock of protesting nerves as the curb tore a bleeding gash down the side of his face to his jaw.

But he had no time for concern because the car was pursuing him. He ran down the street and back and forth across it, and the car, all by itself, followed the contour of the street and refused to allow Finchley out of its sight. When he went on the sidewalk, the car jumped the curb and followed him. When he went back in the street the car did likewise. It was unhurried, calculating, and patient.

When Finchley reached the corner the car seemed to hesitate for a moment, but then it turned and followed him down the next block. Finchley knew his legs were beginning to give out and he could scarcely breathe. Calling on some hidden resource of logic and calculation to overcome his blinding, numbing fear, Finchley jumped over the white picket fence of one of the houses flanking the road and hid behind its front porch.

The car moved slowly past, stopped after a few yards, shifted itself into reverse and backed to a stop directly in front of the house where Finchley was hiding. It idled there at the curb, engine purring, a patient, unhurried stalker menacingly secure in the knowledge of its own superiority.

Finchley ran diagonally across the lawn back toward his own block. The car shifted its gears, made a U-turn in a wide arc, and again bore down on him. Bartlett Finchley made his legs move back and forth, but they grew heavier and heavier and became harder and harder to lift. His heart beat in spasmodic, agonizing thumps and his lungs were torn bellows wheezing hollowly with over-exertion and fast reaching that moment when they would collapse. Pain coursed through Finchley's body with every breath he took.

As he ran through the night it seemed to Finchley that he'd never done anything else all his life. He tried to prod his panicked mind into some kind of thought, rather than to succumb to the enveloping disaster that followed him with such precision and patience, as if never doubting for one moment that this was simply a cat-and-mouse game and that Finchley was the mouse.

He tripped over his feet and again ploughed head first into the street, causing the blood to run afresh down the side of his face. He lay there for a moment, sobbing and moaning.

But again there was the sound of the engine and again the bright lights played on him. He rose to his hands and knees and looked over his shoulder. The car was not a hundred feet away, moving slowly toward him, its headlights two unblinking eyes, the grill a metal mouth that leered at him.

Finchley got up again and ran, up one street and down another, across a lawn and then back onto the sidewalk, down another street, down another, then back to his own block.

How he kept going and moving and breathing, Finchley could not understand. Each breath seemed his last, each movement the final exertion, but he kept running.

Suddenly he realized he was once more in front of his own house. He turned sharply to run into the driveway, past the side of the house to the back yard. Its tyres shrieked as the car followed him up the driveway, picked up speed as it went into the garage, smashed through the opposite wall and into the back yard to meet Finchley just as he came around the corner.

All of the insides of Bartlett Finchley's body constricted at that moment. His throat, his lungs, his heart, the linings of his stomach. He fell once again to his hands and knees and began to crawl across a rock garden, tasting dirt and salty sweat, an hysterical animal, pleading over and over again to be left alone.

His voice was an insane, gurgling chant as he crawled across his patio, toppled sideways over a flight of concrete steps, and wound up on the edge of his swimming pool. The lights went on and the pool appeared a blue, shimmering square carved out of a piece of darkness.

Finchley's head slowly rose. The car slowly rolled down the small hill toward him, ploughing up the earth, the garden, pushing aside the patio furniture in its slow, steady, inexorable pursuit. And Finchley, on all fours, his face streaked with mud and torn flesh, his eyes glazed, his hair lying over his forehead in damp masses, his clothes flapping in torn fragments around him, had now reached the pinnacle of his fear. This was the climax of the nightmare. It was the ultimate fear barrier and he smashed through it with one final, piercing, inhuman scream.

He flung up his hands in front of his face, rose to his shaking feet as the car bore down on him. Then he felt himself falling through space. The wet surface of the pool touched him, gathered him in and sucked him down.

In that one brief, fragmentary moment that lay between life and death he saw the headlights of the car blinking down at him through the water and he heard the engine let out a deep roar like some triumphant shout.

Then he could see nothing more because he had reached the bottom of the pool and his eyes had become simply unfunctioning, useless orbs that stared out of a dead face.

A narrow, irregular line of water drops led from the pool to the ambulance where the body of Bartlett Finchley lay on a stretcher. A policeman with a notebook scratched his head and looked from the pool over to an intern who walked around the ambulance past the fascinated faces of neighbours and then closed the two rear doors.

'Heart attack, Doc?' the policeman asked him. 'Is that what you think?'

The intern looked up from his examination papers and nodded. 'That's what it appears.'

The policeman looked over toward the pool again, then up past the crushed garden and overturned patio chairs, to the big, gaping hole in the rear end of the garage where an automobile sat, mute and unrevealing.

'Neighbours said they heard him shouting about something during the night,' the policeman said. 'Sounded scared.' He scratched his head again. 'Whole Goddamn thing doesn't make much sense. The busted garage wall, those tyre tracks leading to the pool.' He shook his head. 'The whole Goddamned thing doesn't make any sense at all.'

The intern leaned against the closed ambulance doors, then looked down at the water drops that led to the pool's edge. 'Funny thing,' the intern said softly.

'What is?' asked the policeman.

'A body will float for a while after a drowning.'

'So?' the policeman inquired.

The intern jerked a thumb in the direction of the ambulance, 'This one wasn't floating. It was down at the bottom of the pool just as if it had been weighted or something. But that's the thing. It hadn't been weighted. It was just lying there down at the bottom. That'll happen, you know, after a couple of weeks when the body gets bloated and water-logged.' The intern pointed toward the pool. 'He hadn't been there but a few hours.'

'It was his face,' the policeman said with a shudder in his

voice. 'Did you look closely at his face, Doc? He looked so scared. He looked so God-awful scared. What do you suppose scared him?'

The intern shook his head. 'Whatever it was,' he said, 'it's a little item that he's taken with him!'

He folded the examination papers, went around to the passenger's seat of the ambulance and opened the door, motioning the driver to move out. The policeman folded up his notebook. He was suddenly conscious of all the neighbours.

'All right, everybody,' he said, putting firmness and authority into his voice, 'the show's over. Come on now ... everybody get out of here and go home!'

The crowd slowly dispersed in soft, whispering groups, voices muted by the fascination of death that all men carry with them in small pockets deep inside them. The policeman followed them toward the front yard, running over in his mind the nature of the report he'd have to write and wondering how in God's name he could submit such an odd-ball story to the powers that be and have it make any sense. A press photographer was the last man on the scene. He took pictures of the pool, the departing ambulance, a few of the neighbours. He asked a few questions of the latter, jotted them down hurriedly and, as an afterthought, took a picture of the car that was sitting in the garage. Then he got in his own car and drove away.

The following afternoon there was a funeral and only about nine people came because Bartlett Finchley had so few friends. It was a sombre but business-like affair with a very brief eulogy and a dry-eyed response. Bartlett Finchley was laid to rest, a lightly lamented minor character, who would be remembered more for his final torment than for his lifelong tartness. The conglomeration of odd and unrelated circumstances surrounding his death – the demolished garage, the destroyed garden, the wrecked patio – were grist for some gossip and conjecture. But they soon palled and were forgotten.

About a year later, the caretaker of the cemetery where Mr Finchley was interred, a taciturn, grim man, did tell an odd story to his wife one night at the dinner table. He had been using a power mower on the cemetery lawn, and two or three times it had shown a disconcerting tendency to veer off to the right and smash against Bartlett Finchley's tombstone.

It had elicited little concern on the part of the caretaker and he brought it up only as an additional support for a rather long standing contention, oft stated to his wife, that those Goddamned power mowers weren't worth their salt and a good old reliable hand mower was really a far better item, albeit slower. And after this briefest of colloquies with his wife, the caretaker had eaten a Brown Betty for dessert, watched television, and gone to bed.

Nothing more was said.

Nothing more needed to be said.

VIII

The Weird Tailor
Robert Bloch

It was in the late 1960s that I really began to put to use the knowledge I had gained from my years of absorbing horror from books, radio, television and the films. There was a reawakening of interest in the horror short story, and anthology followed anthology from my bulging library of material. Their popularity led to my being invited to act as a consultant on a number of radio and television programmes, and I also did some broadcasting – perhaps predictably finding myself much in demand every October 31, Halloween Night! In 1970, however, came my first invitation to enter the world of film-making. It came from Milton Subotsky, an American producer who had sensed a growing demand for horror films and formed Amicus Films specifically to cater to it. Although, of course, Hammer Films are undoubtedly the most famous British horror makers, with American International enjoying the accolade across the Atlantic, Amicus have in my opinion made some of the most stylish and varied films in the genre. What I believe they have done better than either of the other two companies are the 'anthology films' in which several stories are linked together. Milton Subotsky explains how they came to hit on this formula: 'Our series of multi-story films came about because I had always thought the British film Dead of Night *was the greatest horror film ever, and I wanted to do something like it. For the first one,* Dr Terror's House of Horrors, *I wrote five horror stories and connected them with a framework story. Since then I've preferred to do short stories instead of one long film.' During the years which followed, the work of one writer more than any other was to ensure Amicus's success – Robert Bloch, who had earlier written the original novel on which Alfred Hitchcock's movie* Psycho *was based. His stories had been favourites of mine for years, and the most unique of them were used in several of Amicus's multi-tale films including the best of all,*

Asylum, *made in 1972. This was based on a group of four of his gruesome yarns, including 'The Weird Tailor' which is reprinted here. It starred Peter Cushing as the mysterious Mr Smith who wants a suit made for a very strange purpose ...*

Only a connoisseur of horrors would have appreciated Erik Conrad's window dummy.

It had been a cheap model to begin with – and the passage of twenty years had not improved its crudely moulded features, its awkward stance, or the general air of clumsiness inherent in face and form. There was something grotesque about the dummy, as if it had been created by the alien art of another world; as though a life-form from Outside had deliberately set about to model a 'man' from a poor woodcut in an ancient book.

The brash smile, the jaunty little moustache, and the open candour of the staring blue eyes had all suffered the gnawings of Time, so that now the figure was minus an upper lip, the left corner of the moustache, and the entire right eye. A crack extended from the empty eye-socket up to the crown of the head and split the marcelled hair directly along the intended part. A chipped finger and a nick in the left wrist contributed to the gruesome aura of decay.

Certainly the suit Erik Conrad had draped over the dummy was just the garment which would be selected for the cheap client of a cheap mortician. It was eminently appropriate to the corpse-like pallor of the window dummy, but the effect of the ensemble was well calculated to disturb the eye of the sensitive observer.

Fortunately, Erik Conrad was not over-imaginative. He didn't mind the sight of the leering dummy slumped in the shadows at one corner of his dingy little tailoring establishment. He was not affected by the spectacle of its hideously progressive decay, any more than he was affected by his own.

For the years had not dealt kindly with Erik Conrad, merchant tailor. He had suffered a disintegration comparable to that of the dummy since setting up a shop of his own on this side street. His blue eyes were faded from endless peering, his fingers twisted and calloused from stitching, his shoulders bent from stooping over the pressing table. The sparse brown hairs plastered against his sloping skull were slowly turning grey, and hence were almost invisible against the grey pallor of his skin.

Erik Conrad was not conscious of these changes. He noted and bewailed only the steady decline of his business. Conrad's window dummy slumped a trifle with the years, and Conrad himself stooped more than a bit – but the business itself tottered on its last legs. Time had dealt most harshly with little independent merchant tailors. The popularity of the ready-made suit, the competition of stylish downtown tailoring establishments, the inroads made by modern cleaning and dyeing concerns – all had contributed to his loss of revenue.

Conrad saw it happen, and he found no solution. His only relief lay in cursing and grumbling as he went about his steadily decreasing daily tasks.

Then, a year ago, he had married.

Anna was a refugee; a young woman of great physical attraction and shy personal charm. A stranger in a new world, she readily consented to marriage, even though Erik Conrad was middle-aged and none too successful. She was grateful enough to stand in the steam-filled back room and assist in the pressing which now formed the bulk of Conrad's existing business.

Conrad, for his part, gave up cursing and grumbling after his marriage to Anna. Now, when he was discouraged or out of sorts, he merely smiled and shrugged, took his wife by the throat, and throttled her. Not too hard, of course, for she had her work to do. Anna did not complain too greatly, nor did she give way to tears. It is difficult to either scold or cry when one's throat has been thoroughly choked by gnarled and twisted fingers.

At first she had longed for a child to keep her company, but after coming to know her husband better, she was glad that there was no little one to suffer Conrad's mistreatment. Sometimes, when the tailor was out delivering pressed garments, she grew lonely in the deserted shop, and it was then that she talked to herself, in German. Sometimes, when she became self-conscious or apprehensive about this habit, she pretended that the window dummy was a person, and talked to it.

She even invented a name for it – 'Otto', after her cousin, the one who had been killed in the air-raid over Dresden, so many years ago. Otto had worn a moustache, too, and they would have been married. But a bomb had fallen from the sky, and when they found Otto in the ruins his head had been cracked like the dummy's – so – and on his face was the little wooden smile, beneath the waxen pallor.

Anna told Otto all about it, and Otto listened, looking at her through the steam-clouds with his one good eye. Anna knew there was harm in this pretending, but she needed something.

And so life went on, its currents diverted from the tiny side street where the little tailoring shop stood. The window dummy crouched corpse-like in the corner, Conrad choked his helpless, hopeless wife, and Anna's beauty faded and disappeared in wisps of hot steam. A fine cloud of grey dust descended to settle over bolts of cloth, racks of unclaimed garments, corners of the floor where no feet trod. The dust settled on the shoulders of the window dummy, sifted through Conrad's hair.

No connoisseur of horrors came to stare at the dummy or examine the sadistic secrets lurking behind the dingy exterior of the shop. Things might have gone on that way for years longer – the dummy could have continued to deteriorate, Conrad's fingers might have eventually left a permanent indentation in Anna's throat, and Anna would gradually have become a whining, half-mad harridan. The cloud of dust might have grown to an inch-deep layer upon the floor. The process could have continued indefinitely – but it didn't.

Mr Smith saw to that.

Mr Smith stepped into the tailoring shop one bright and sunny afternoon. Anna happened to be behind the counter in the outer room, and when she saw the stranger, one of her hands stole instinctively behind her head to tuck in the straggling hairs on her neck.

For Mr Smith inspired that sort of self-consciousness.

Mr Smith looked prosperous. His sleek, smooth, well-shaven features wore a smile of benevolent affluence. His manicured nails and carefully clipped little grey Van Dyke beard hinted of riches, and his heavy tweed suit fairly shouted wealth to the beholder. The heavy, confident tread of his custom-made shoes was somehow transformed into the merry tinkle of jangling gold-pieces.

He placed one plump hand carefully on the dusty counter, so that the errant sunbeams played over the massive diamond ring upon his third finger, and drummed authoritatively.

'Is the proprietor in?' he asked.

Anna smiled. She looked at his face, looked at the ring, then looked at his face once more.

'I'll call him, sir.'

Her step was strangely buoyant as she walked into the steam-filled back room. Conrad was dozing in a chair.

'Erik, there is a customer outside.'

He blinked and grunted in annoyance.

'Quickly. He is a very distinguished gentleman, I think.'

'Bill collector!' snarled Conrad. But he rose, brushed lint from his shabby coat, and shuffled out.

When he saw the stranger, he straightened up. He tried to look dapper and alert.

'Yes? What can I do for you, Mr – ?'

'Smith. Mr Smith,' said the man in tweeds. 'Do I understand correctly when I assume that you are prepared to custom-tailor a garment from material of my own selection?'

It took Erik Conrad several seconds to comprehend that this distinguished elderly gentleman was asking him if he could make a suit.

Then he understood, and immediately his mind conjured up visions of fabulous profits – ten dollars here, fifteen there, another twenty over-all on the basis of the fine fancy words this stranger had used.

'That is right, sir. You would like me to make you a suit? I imagine you'd want something special – '

'Correct. I want something very special.'

Mr Smith smiled with his eyes as well as his mouth when he answered the last question.

'Very well. If you'd give me an idea of what you have in mind, I could show you some very fine material. I've got a wonderful stock of woollens here.'

Conrad gabbled on, wondering to himself how he could

possibly dare to show any of his shabby bolts to such a rich and elegant customer. He tried to remember fragments of sales-talk long since fallen into disuse; he stalled for time, he perspired, he grew red and impassioned.

Mr Smith interrupted with an airy wave of the hand. The diamond sparkled as it flashed through the air, and Conrad's faded eyes followed it thirstily, as if seeking to draw fresh fire from its ageless brilliance.

'That won't be necessary,' said Mr Smith. 'I have the material already selected. Here, in my bag. Would you care to examine it?'

'Of course,' said Conrad. He was relieved and disappointed at the same time; relieved at being spared the ordeal of displaying his meagre stock, but disappointed because he could not profit on the sale of material.

Still he could make enough on tailoring the garment itself. This was a piece of luck. He eagerly awaited an inspection as Mr Smith opened the bag and spread a bolt of cloth on the counter. Conrad switched an overhead light into position.

'Take a look,' said Mr Smith. 'There's enough here for a suit, I believe.'

The cloth was grey. No, it couldn't be grey, because it had little flecks that reflected the light. It was gold. But gold does not shimmer in rainbow hues. It was a peculiar off-shade of tan. But tan is not green, and there was green in this cloth, also some red and blue. No, it was grey. It had to be grey.

Conrad stared at it, stared at the iridescent surface. Mr Smith seemed to notice nothing unusual, so Conrad forced himself to remain silent – but he had never looked upon this material before, in all his years of tailoring.

He spread the bolt out and fingered the material. It tingled to the touch, sliding through his hands with an electric crackling. It was not wool, or flannel, or cotton. The more Conrad saw of it, the less sure he became of what he saw. He could not discern a definite weave or texture. Neither eye nor finger could isolate a single thread for examination. Staring at it, Conrad began to experience a peculiar sensation – a tightness in his head.

But it was cloth, and Conrad was a tailor. He could make a suit from it, for this distinguished customer.

The distinguished customer eyed him closely as he examined the garment, and Conrad strove to remain impassive. 'It will be difficult to work with so unusual a fabric,' he commented. 'Still, I can promise you a suit. Now, if you'll slip off your coat, sir, I will take the measurements – '

Mr Smith held up his hand. The diamond's dazzling reflection gleamed from the single eye of the window dummy in the corner.

'The suit is not for me,' he told Conrad.

'No? Then what is it that you wish?'

'The suit is for my son,' the elderly man told him.

'Will he come in for a fitting, then?'

'No. It's to be a surprise. You see, I have all of his measurements written down here. Quite exact, they are. I shall require a most unusual fit for this garment.'

'And the style?'

'That, too, is noted.' Mr Smith pulled out a sheaf of papers, covered with fine, crabbed script. 'You understand all this must be done in strictest confidence, and exactly as I have indicated. I require a special suit. Of course, if you cannot handle it – '

Again the diamond described its glittering arc.

'I'm sure I can,' said Conrad, hastily. 'Anything you want, I'll give you.'

'Money is no object.' Mr Smith smiled confidentially. 'I expect you to bill me for your trouble. But these instructions, while they may seem peculiar to you, must be followed to the letter.'

Conrad nodded, and the two men bent over the sheaf of papers. Mr Smith read aloud, slowly, emphasizing certain matters and enlarging upon other details. The measurements must be thus and so. The cut must conform in this wise to the diagram. There must be no lining – none whatsoever – the technical problem involved here would have to be solved by Conrad's own ingenuity. Yes, and another thing; no vest would be required. Of course it might look a bit odd, but again Conrad must strive to turn out a suit of superficially conventional appearance and at the same time work within these limitations. Oh, and here was material for the buttons. Bone, to be turned and bored by hand.

Bye the bye, that was another very important stipulation. All work on this suit must be done by hand; no machine shortcuts were permissible. Of course Mr Smith realized what this entailed, and he expected to pay for the extra attention.

Conrad listened, comprehended finally the physical rudiments of what he must do, if not the reasons inherent in the instructions. But then, understanding was not required of him – merely strict obedience.

'And here are the dates,' Mr Smith concluded. 'The times during which you can work. As you see they are most carefully worked out; the hours and even the minutes calculated to a nicety. I beg of you to keep faith with me and sew on this suit only as directed. That is most important.'

Here Conrad could not withhold his curiosity. 'I can work only at these times?' he asked. 'But why?'

Mr Smith started to frown, then bit his lip until it curled back in a smile. 'It is natural that you should ask, I know. All I can tell you is that I happen to be a believer in astrology. As such, I am sure you will humour me in these requests. Set your own price for the service.'

Conrad shrugged. So be it. Perhaps this Mr Smith was mad. But no, with his fine clothes and big diamond – he was only eccentric. The rich are often so.

'Please, not a word to anyone,' the customer said, as he turned away from the counter. 'Take a month, six weeks, but conform to my schedule and keep silent. I am reposing my trust in you.'

'It shall be as you wish.' Conrad bent his head in the immemorial obeisance of servant to master, of artisan to aristocrat, of craftsman to burgher, of artist to patron.

So master-aristocrat-burgher-patron Mr Smith went away from the little shop and Conrad carefully wrapped and put away the strange bolt of cloth.

'Conrad, what is all this?' asked Anna, timidly slipping into the shop from the pressing room at the rear. 'Who was that man?'

'Never mind, woman, it doesn't concern you,' he told her.

'But I listened – I heard him talking to you about sewing at funny hours – '

'Be silent! It is nothing to you.'

'Conrad, I'm afraid. There is something not right in all this, something that will make trouble.'

'Trouble!' Conrad went over to her and gripped her thin shoulders. 'It is you who make trouble for me, you little fool!'

He beat her, then, until she whimpered and broke away to huddle in the corner of the shop. Conrad went out and sought the tavern where for a long time he sat mumbling to himself over his beer. In the beer-foam he saw the sparkling of diamonds.

Anna whispered to herself in the darkness, then whispered to Otto the dummy. In Otto's eye she saw not diamonds but the cold, empty glitter of glass.

The spider began to spin.

Squatting in the gloom, the web was woven with crabbed cunning, with squinting skill. Silently and ceaselessly the weaving went, the pattern emerged from fashioning fingers. Days, hours, minutes threaded past on single strands.

There were interruptions and distractions, of course. Conrad did not proceed with his work without making a futile effort to analyze the nature of the peculiar fabric. He placed it under a strong light, even used a pocket magnifying glass in order to observe the threads — but all he could conclude was that this was some cloth foreign to his knowledge. He tried wetting the material and found that moisture left no stain. There was no real reason for his inquiry, of course; but Conrad was curious and the mystery surrounding the making of the suit disturbed him.

He was more violently disturbed, during these weeks, by the sudden appearance of collection agents and small creditors, including the tavern-keeper down the street. He fobbed them off with promises or curses as suited their temperaments, and told himself that he must hasten and complete the garment. Often as he sewed he amused himself by idle computation. Should he charge two hundred dollars for the suit? Or three hundred? Why not — five hundred?

Once or twice he tried to hasten his task by working on the suit at times unspecified by Mr Smith's schedule. Strangely enough, he could not sew — not literally, but his stitches went awry, the cloth slipped through his fingers with that peculiar crackling feel of static electricity, and there were other mishaps. Insensitive as he was, Conrad felt a touch of fear as he considered the nature of the unusual garment he was fashioning. The hints about astrology were a clue, but Conrad guessed at other things. This was a most peculiar job, and a most peculiar suit. It began to take shape under his fingers, and as it did so, fears took shape in Conrad's mind.

Whatever Mr Smith intended, whatever his plans for the suit, Conrad meant to be out of the deal. All he wanted was to finish it and collect his – yes – five hundred dollars.

There were only two possible answers; either he was working for a crazy man or for a practitioner of Black Magic. Conrad relished neither speculation, and after long hours of toiling and brooding, it was small wonder that at times he lost his temper and raised his hand against Anna.

His wife received another, more thorough beating when at last the suit was completed. It hung from the hook, a strange, shimmering garment with high collar, unusual peaked lapels, a curious button arrangement, and no pockets whatsoever – sleeves of practically simian length, and curiously cuffless trousers. But it was the cloth more than the cut which contributed to the strangeness. In bolt form that fabric had disturbed Conrad's eyes. Now, in the shape of a suit, there was something quite odd and yet impelling to the eye. Conrad found himself glancing again and again at the new suit, trying to visualize it as it might appear when actually worn.

'Looks funny,' Anna commented.

'Of course,' Conrad nodded. 'That's because it isn't pressed. So get busy, woman.'

It was after this, when Anna returned and told him the suit just 'wouldn't take a press', that Conrad gave his wife a severe beating. When he took the garment and attempted, in vain, to do the job himself, he was tempted to strike Anna again.

Instead, he reminded himself that it would be wise to deliver the suit and collect his payment as soon as possible.

Placing the peculiar coat and trousers in a box, Conrad set out for the address Mr Smith had entrusted to him. It was in an unfamiliar section of the city, and he decided it would be best to go by taxi.

Jolting through the streets in the cab, Conrad conjured up a vision of the mansion in which Mr Smith must live. He would open a wrought iron gate, go up a long, tree-bordered walk to the big front door, grasp the bronze knocker and summon a butler. The butler would ask him to wait in the hall, then return to usher him into the big drawing room. And there was Mr Smith – so – seated before the huge open fireplace. Ah, it was a wonderful house, that one!

The cab jerked to a halt and Conrad was jarred out of his musings. He started as he peered out at the doorway of the ramshackle tenement dwelling huddled between two warehouses on the mean street. For a moment he considered cursing the cab driver, then hastily checked the address. No mistake, this was his destination.

Conrad paid the driver and darted through the entrance, lugging the garment box under his arm. At the tenant register in the hall he pressed the buzzer for 4A. He paused, buzzed again, waited. Sighing, he prepared to trudge up the stairs.

It was not a pleasant ascent; leg-muscles protested, hands clung to rickety railings, nose inhaled the stairwell reek of a dozen compounded unpleasantnesses. Conrad cursed the eccentricity of his customer. Why should a wealthy man choose to affect such poverty? Unless, of course, he was hiding out here.

There was some mystery connected with this whole affair, and it might very well be that Mr Smith had his reasons for choosing this squalid lodging.

Was that the answer?

Conrad considered the possibilities as he knocked on the door of 4A. He might be getting mixed up in some dirty business. Then again –

'Come in,' said Mr Smith. 'I've been expecting you.' The bright smile glittered, the diamond glittered, and Conrad's forebodings dissipated in the dazzle.

But there was nothing bright about the room. Toiling up the stairs, Conrad had wondered if perhaps his client might be concealing a luxurious hideaway beneath a grimy exterior. But this room was as filthy as the tenement in which it rotted.

Conrad noted a wooden table, a cot, a few chairs and a battered second-hand trunk in the corner beneath the single window overlooking the courtyard. A tattered curtain concealed a shallow alcove niche on the far side of the room. There was absolutely no sign of a fireplace, a butler, or any other figment of his daydreams.

Mr Smith, however, seemed real enough; and his eagerness at the sight of the box under Conrad's arm was quite genuine.

'You have brought it!' he boomed. 'Splendid! I can hardly believe that you managed, with all the difficult stipulations I found it necessary to impose.'

'It wasn't easy,' Conrad replied. 'Mighty strange, that material. And you wouldn't believe the trouble I had – '

'On the contrary, I would readily believe every word.' Mr Smith smiled and rubbed his hands, while the diamond zigzagged through the gloom. 'I hadn't really dared to hope for success, and yet you say the suit is complete?"

'Just like you ordered.'

'Fine. You have no idea how I've waited, what this means to me. And to my son.'

'Your son – where is he?' Conrad inquired.

'That does not matter, does it?'

'But don't you want a fitting, to make sure everything's all right?'

'I'll take your word for it,' said Mr Smith. 'If you followed instructions, the fit will be perfect. As a matter of fact, if you hadn't done exactly what I directed, you wouldn't have been able to complete the garment. So I know it's right.'

'Thanks.' Conrad bowed his head in acknowledgment. 'I did my best to turn out a good job.'

'I know you did, and it is I who should be thanking you.' Mr Smith also bobbed his head, at the same time extending both hands. 'Now, if you'll be good enough to leave the suit with me – '

The diamond came close to the box, but Conrad drew back. 'Wait a minute,' he said. 'What about money?'

'Ah, yes, the fee. How much did you say it was?'

Erik Conrad took a deep breath of musty air. 'Five hundred dollars,' he murmured.

'Very reasonable,' commented his customer. 'Send the bill along and I'll take care of it.'

'But – '

'Yes?'

'I have the bill made out, right here.' Conrad fumbled in his pocket. 'And if you don't mind, I need the money badly, and I was hoping that maybe today – '

Mr Smith shook his head, slowly but emphatically. 'I'm afraid that's out of the question. After all, it's not customary for one to pay tradesmen on delivery, is it? Why not mail your bill in the regular fashion – you'll get your money, never fear.'

Again he sought to take the package from Conrad, but the tailor retreated to the curtained alcove. 'I must have my money first,' he persisted. 'Look, if this was a regular job I wouldn't mind, but I've spent all these weeks working. And I have bills to pay. You wouldn't understand, because you're rich, but it's different with me. I got to eat.'

'My dear fellow.' Mr Smith advanced, cordially confidential. 'On the contrary, I can understand your situation only too well. For it so happens that at the moment, I am in the same fix.'

'You?'

'Precisely.' Mr Smith grinned as if he had just told the biggest joke in the world. 'Oh, don't misunderstand. In a very short while I should be in funds again. As soon as my son and I are re-united, in fact. But until then, I'm far from rich. In fact, I have no money, no money at all. So you'll have to wait – '

'But how can you say that?' Conrad wailed. 'A man like you, wearing a big diamond?'

Mr Smith drew the ring from his finger and tossed it on the table. It glinted its way over the wood, then rolled to the floor. Mr Smith did not bother to pick it up. 'A fake,' he said. 'A cheap, synthetic fake. Oh, at one time I had another, and the stone was real enough. But I was forced to place it in pawn, along with almost everything I possessed, in order to continue my studies. I have spent every penny on my son. Now, please, be reasonable and give me that suit.'

Again he reached for the package and again Conrad retreated – this time backing through the curtain veiling the alcove until his progress was halted by a waist-high obstruction.

Conrad turned and found himself confronting a gleaming

refrigerator – a big one, and obviously brand new.

'What's this?' the tailor accused. 'If you're so hard up for money, why do you need a big new refrigerator?'

'It's not for me,' Mr Smith placated, hastily. 'I had to buy it for my son. Like the suit. Now if you'll come over here and show me – ' and he attempted to grasp Conrad by the arm and draw him away.

But Conrad shrugged him off, still staring at the expensive refrigerator with a look of mingled puzzlement and disdain.

'Poor!' he muttered. 'Why, I'll bet it's full of fancy food and – '

Impulsively, the little tailor yanked at the handle. The door opened and he stared inside. An icy blast fanned his face.

There were no shelves in the refrigerator. The six-foot high interior consisted of bare walls framing a single object. The object was the rigid, frozen body of a man.

The corpse stood upright, a blue and naked horror with a youthful face congealed in the age-old grimace of death.

'Close that door!' screamed Mr Smith.

Conrad released the handle and jumped away. He pressed his back against the wall and bared his teeth. 'Murderer!' he gasped. 'So that's it!'

'No, you don't understand. I'm no murderer. He died a natural death. Can't you see? He is my son. He is the one I was working for, planning for. That's why I had you make the suit. It's for him. You can't stop me now, no one can stop me.'

Mr Smith advanced. His hands worked at his sides, then rose. 'Give me the suit,' he said. 'Give it to me.'

Conrad tried to move away, but Mr Smith blocked his path. 'Give it to me,' he repeated. And his hands moved out.

It had grown dark in the murky little room. Erik Conrad saw a diamond eye wink up through the shadows on the floor. It was watching him – watching him as he stood there with a dead man behind him and a madman before him. The dead man had grimaced, and now the madman was grimacing, too. Grimacing, and reaching for Erik Conrad in the dark, as the diamond eye stared.

There was nothing else. There was no five hundred dollars. There was no butler. There was no justice or mercy or hope. Only this maniac trapping him in the blackness and now he was hitting him across the side of the face, and from far away a panting voice said over and over again, 'Give it to me you fool give it to me you fool give it to me you fool – '

Until Erik Conrad struck back. The pudgy madman tried to choke him, tried to kick him, tried to squeeze him, and there was nothing else to do but strike back. Conrad said, 'Let me go,' but Mr Smith didn't even hear him because he began to scream and claw at Conrad's eyes. There was nothing else to do but strike back and it was only natural that Conrad pick up the wooden chair and swing it. He felt it land on Mr Smith's head and Mr Smith's scream died to a moan. Conrad raised the chair again and brought it down. Mr Smith's moan died to a gurgle. Conrad struck again, and again, and again, feeling the chair splinter and come apart in his hands. Mr Smith's gurgle died.

And so did Mr Smith.

Erik Conrad didn't know that until afterwards, of course. Not until he shook off his hysteria and turned on the light and bent down, panting, to examine Mr Smith's crushed and battered features as he lay sprawled on the grimy floor. Then the tailor understood.

He was a murderer.

The diamond eye had seen it all. The diamond eye knew it was a mistake, an accident. The diamond eye knew that Mr Smith was a madman who preserved his son's body in a refrigerator and had ordered a suit made up out of his own insane impulses. The diamond eye understood what had happened.

But the diamond eye was a fake. And the murderer was real. Soon the police would come –

Erik Conrad rose, grabbed at the suit package, and headed for the door. He had to get out of here. Everything was ruined now, everything was spoiled, there was no money, and he had risked his life forever in coming here. It was –

At the door, Conrad halted. He noted once again the presence of the battered trunk in the corner. A wild hope rose, and Conrad knelt.

The trunk was unlocked and opened easily. Conrad threw back the lid. This was the treasure-chest, the secret hiding-place, the source of riches; it had to be, it was only logical and right and just. Eagerly he surveyed the contents of the old trunk.

'Books!' Conrad groaned. 'Nothing but books!'

Nothing but books, and second-hand books at that – books with sprung spines, books with mildewed pages, books with torn bindings, books in foreign languages, books that appeared to be written by hand instead of printed. Junk. Rubbish. Good-for-nothing nonsense.

But wait – some of them were quite old. Some of them had iron hasps and locks. Some of them had worn vellum inserts. Didn't people collect old books? Conrad seemed to remember reading about auctions and sales at one time – there were people who foolishly paid a lot of money for things like that.

He stacked an armful hastily and stood up. After all, it wasn't really stealing. Mr Smith owed him five hundred dollars which he would never collect. Surely Conrad was entitled to a few wormy old books. These volumes were no longer of any use to Mr Smith. Dead men read no tales.

Conrad stepped into the hall, carrying the suit box and the books. The hall was dark and still as he tip-toed downstairs. No one had seen him come in, no one saw him leave. The taxi-driver wouldn't remember, would never connect Conrad with the killing in the ordinary course of events.

The ordinary course of events –

In that phrase Conrad recognized the key to salvation. He must only remember to behave naturally as if nothing had happened, to return to the shop and go about his business in the normal way, and there would be no trouble at all.

Conrad walked down the street, a little tailor carrying his bundles. He paused at corners, jostled and was jostled in return, obeyed traffic signals like the good citizen he was, and eventually arrived at his shop. Strangely enough, he was trembling.

The place was dark and nobody saw him enter. Nobody except Otto, the window dummy. And Otto's eye, like Mr Smith's diamond, was glass.

Conrad smiled as he shuffled down the hall into the bedroom. Glass, it was all glass, everything was a fake. And if everything was a fake, then nothing had happened. He hadn't killed anyone.

'It's a fake, just a fake,' Conrad murmured to himself as he fell face downward on the bed. 'Nothing to worry about – it was all a fake!' Then he began to cry.

Conrad wasn't conscious of the exact moment of transition from tears to terror. Sometime he must have roused himself and switched on the bedroom light. Somehow he must have begun to paw idly through the stack of battered books. Somewhere he must have noticed the volume printed in heavy black-letter German, and he had begun to read the text.

It was then that he remembered his early speculations concerning Mr Smith; the possibilities of the mysterious stranger's interest in Black Magic. Mr Smith had proven himself a madman, to be sure, but still, these volumes were books on sorcery. The treatise Conrad was reading dealt with spells and charms, with formulae and incantations designed to raise up demons. Erik Conrad found himself stumbling over the pronunciation of strange names – Azaziel, Samael, Yaddith. There was nothing particularly disconcerting about the way in which the book was written; everything was set down in a straightforward, matter-of-fact style. Only the subject-matter itself was grotesque and irrational.

Perhaps it was this very circumstance which caused Conrad's hands to tremble as he held the tome. This treatise on the summoning of evil entities was written in the style of a cookbook, filled with recipes. *Take the maiden's blood, take the heart torn from the infant's breast, take the eyes of the hanged man – mix and stir in the cauldron, add the corpse-fat, and evoke your fiend.* Simple. Easy. Anyone can do it.

It was absurd, it was insane, it was – convincing. Men had written this book, men had read this book, men had used this book for centuries. Men like Mr Smith, whatever his real name might be. They had used this book to produce – *what?*

It was then that Erik Conrad began to tremble. And it was then that Anna returned from her evening shopping; returned quietly and tiptoed into the room so as not to disturb Conrad as he read.

'Erik,' she murmured.

The tailor's face contorted with startled fear. He rose from the bed with a gasp which, as he faced and recognized the intruder, became transformed into a snarl of rage.

'What do you mean by sneaking in like that?' he choked. 'You stupid fool!'

'But what is wrong? I only wanted to ask about the suit. You sold it, eh?'

Conrad indicated the box on the bed. 'Does this look like I sold it?' he demanded.

'Was something wrong, then?'

'No, nothing was wrong. Don't bother me, woman!'

'But the money – I thought – '

'Be quiet!' Conrad glowered at her, but Anna persisted.

'After you left,' she continued, 'I told Mister Schwenk the butcher – he came after the money for the meat, you know – that he should come back tomorrow because you were getting paid by a customer. So – '

'You told him!' The tailor gripped Anna by the shoulder. 'But I warned you to say nothing to anyone. Nobody should know about the suit, understand? Do not mention it to a soul, do not mention it to me again, ever. And get it out of my sight, quick.'

Anna sank, gasping with incomprehension, in this torrent of violence. But Conrad's clawlike fingers bore her up. 'Not a word!' he screamed. 'Now take the suit and burn it, woman! Burn it in the furnace. And never speak of it again. Forget everything. Forget that I made it, forget Mr Smith, forget that I went out today!'

He raised the box from the bed and thrust it into Anna's arms. Then he slapped her across the face once, twice, three times. The third time he brought his hand away wet with tears. A fourth blow would bring blood, and for a moment he was tempted to deliver it.

Then suddenly all purpose left him. 'Get out!' he screamed. 'Get out and leave me alone.'

Anna stumbled out and closed the door. Conrad slumped to the bed once more and returned to his reading. He read for a long time. There were many subjects of outré interest.

Evocations – the runes of pestilence – the resurrection of vanished youth – the cloak of invisibility – the raising of the dead – the preservation of corpses and the use of mantic arts in restoring a semblance of life – the weaving of the cloth of Fate –

Conrad read the last sections again. It was all explained in prosaic detail. The bargain with the Powers. The sacrifice. The granting of the boon, the woven strands of Immortality with which to cloak the preserved corpse. The finished garment to impart life to any wearer bearing human guise. Conrad read it, and Mr Smith had read it, too. He had read it and acted on it.

Now at last, Erik Conrad knew the secret of the suit, the secret of the frozen corpse, the secret of the weaving and the shaping. Mr Smith had hoped to bring life back to his son.

Of course the old man had been mad, just as the author of this book had been mad. Best now to burn the book, and the other volumes, in case there should ever be any tracing, any questions.

Conrad loaded his arms with the ancient tomes and plodded down the dark hall to the basement stairs. He descended, knelt before the furnace, opened the door, recoiled momentarily before the blast of heat; then tossed the books into the fire.

There was no trace, no single shred of the strange suit. Apparently there had been no burning cloth odour, either. Anna had done her job well.

Anna – where was Anna? Conrad climbed the stairs, peered into the kitchen. Deserted. And the hall was dark. Was she out in the shop? She must be, but why?

Quietly, Erik Conrad walked down the hall. Yes, she was in the shop, he could hear her whispering. Talking to herself. He could distinguish words, phrases.

'... hates me, Otto. You're the ... friend I've got ... going crazy ... you had lived. Wish ... could talk ... tonight ... hit me. Sometimes ... dead.'

She was in there, talking to that window dummy again! Was the whole world going mad? Conrad pressed his hands against his skull. The temples were tight, bursting with rage.

He moved quickly into the shop, switching on the light. Anna turned. She was huddled in a heap at the feet of the wax dummy. Conrad stared at her, then at the mannikin. There was something strange about it, something different. It took a moment for him to comprehend and then he realized that Anna had put the crazy suit on the dummy.

'What are you doing?' Conrad was surprised when his voice came out so quietly. 'Didn't I tell you to burn the suit?' Why, he was talking calmly, sensibly.

'I was going to. I didn't mean any harm. I just wanted to look at it again – you acted so funny about it all that I wondered if there was a secret.'

Conrad nodded, still very quiet. He even helped Anna to her feet as she continued.

'So I thought I could see it better if I put it on Otto – I mean, on the dummy here. Did you notice it in the dark, Erik? It looks queer – so glowing – '

Conrad was gentle with her, quite gentle. 'Anna,' he said. 'This is not wise of you. To disobey my orders. To pry into things that do not concern you. To talk to clothing dummies. Are you sure you feel all right, Anna?'

She hid her face. 'I know,' she sighed. 'Sometimes I wonder if I'm out of my mind. But you are cruel, Erik. You beat me, and – '

'I will not beat you now,' said Conrad. 'If you will burn the suit at once. I only hit you because I was afraid. Perhaps if I tell you, you can understand.' It was odd how calm he felt, how quietly he could talk like this to her now.

'You see, the suit must be burned. And no one must ever hear about it, or about Mr Smith. Because this afternoon we quarrelled, and I killed him.'

'You killed – ?'

'An accident. Yes, an accident. He tried to take the suit away, it was self-defence, Anna. Mr Smith was crazy. He had his son's body in a refrigerator and he thought the suit would bring the boy back to life. You can't reason with such a man, Anna. And when he comes at you, you must strike back.'

Anna stared into his eyes. Conrad nodded gravely. 'So you see, it just happened that way. But the police wouldn't believe me if they knew. That's why I wanted the suit burned. That's why I wanted you to forget. Now. Do you understand me, woman?'

'Yes.' Anna came close. 'And I'm sorry, I didn't know what was upsetting you, Erik. Only – '

'Only?'

'Only I think you should tell the police. Tell them the truth, tell them everything. I'll make them believe you. Please, Erik! You cannot carry such a sin on your soul forever. For my sake, Erik, tell them what happened, that it was self-defence. I – I couldn't bear to go on living with a murderer.'

As she spoke, Conrad stared over her shoulder at the clothing dummy. It slumped ridiculously in the corner, its cracked waxen features stolid, its glass eye gleaming. The impossible suit hung in ill-fitting folds across its shoulders, giving an apelike aspect to the arms. All this Erik saw, and at the same time he was conscious of listening to Anna.

And when he heard what Anna was saying, he suddenly realized why he was so calm. It was necessary to be calm, necessary to move quietly so as not to frighten her. She had been talking to the window dummy, she had tried the suit on it, and now she wanted him to confess to the police. Obviously she was losing her sanity. Obviously she would never cease to urge him to confess and might even end up by going to the police herself with the story.

So, obviously he must remain calm. Remain calm now as he moved back to the wall and switched off the light. There. Now the shop was pitch dark. No one could see in from the street. No one could see as he did the obvious thing – take Anna by the throat and squeeze, so, and squeeze and squeeze –

'Help!' The gasp came out, and he had to squeeze harder, not so calmly. 'Erik – stop – oh – save me – Otto – save me!'

Crazy, to call on the dummy for help. Erik squeezed until she sagged and he could stare over her shoulders, stare into the pitch dark, which wasn't really pitch dark at all because something was glowing over there in the corner. Something with arms and legs. It was the suit, of course, Anna had said the suit glowed in the dark, and it did. Like phosphorus, like silver, like gold, glowing brighter and brighter, and every time Erik squeezed the glow increased.

It was only the crazy suit, the crazy suit ordered by the crazy man for a crazy purpose; there was nothing to fear. Erik Conrad could bring death to Anna, but the suit could not bring life. It couldn't!

But Conrad wasn't calm any more. Not when he saw the

silver arms stretch, saw the silver legs race forward, saw the leering eye of glass gleaming and flashing with a light that pierced brain and being.

He let Anna go, and turned to flee. Something caught him in the dark, then. There was nothing left to do but scream, and he tried that, but too late. There was a gleaming and a pressure and a spangle of silver fire that burst into final blackness.

Then there was nothing ...

Only a connoisseur of horrors would have appreciated Erik Conrad's window dummy as it loomed over him, clad in the silver suit of enchanted Life – with its waxen fingers clamped in a grip of death about Erik Conrad's throat.

IX

The Pit and the Pendulum
Edgar Allan Poe

*Once involved in the world of horror films, it was not long before I was becoming acquainted with its stars, and during the period from 1971 to 1977 I produced books with three of the best known actors, Vincent Prince (*The Ghouls, 1971), *Christopher Lee (*Christopher Lee's New Chamber of Horrors, 1974) *and Peter Cushing (*Tales of a Monster Hunter, 1977). *Despite their sinister and often frightening demeanours on the screen, all three men are charming and erudite people in real life. Vincent Price is a most cultured man with a quick, sardonic sense of humour, while Christopher Lee has a towering presence and the most courteous manners. Peter Cushing, by contrast, is quiet and reserved, with a sense of modesty and humility about his work which is most refreshing in a profession over-burdened with egos. Each of these three men has selected a favourite story for this collection. The first is picked by Vincent Price and perhaps not surprisingly is by his fellow countryman, Edgar Allan Poe. I say not surprisingly because of course Vincent has appeared in half a dozen films for American International based on Poe stories. 'The Pit and the Pendulum' is unique among these because prior to the film version (which he made in 1961) he had appeared in 1957 in a radio version for CBS's* Mystery Theatre *which all those who heard it remember was memorable for a sequence in which the prisoner has to ward off hordes of rats in the pit while the giant pendulum slowly but persistently swishes down on him. Of the story itself, Vincent says, 'I am a great admirer of Poe and for years have been going out as a lecturer trying to bring him to life for young people. I think he has incorporated more frights into "The Pit and the Pendulum" than any other writer in any other story. Read it with that in mind and you'll see why he is the master he is ...'*

I was sick – sick unto death with that long agony; and when they at length unbound me, and I was permitted to sit, I felt that my senses were leaving me. The sentence – the dread sentence of death – was the last of distinct accentuation which reached my ears. After that, the sound of the inquisitorial voices seemed merged in one dreamy indeterminate hum. It conveyed to my soul the idea of *revolution* – perhaps from its association in fancy with the burr of a mill-wheel. This only for a brief period; for presently I heard no more. Yet, for a while, I saw; but with how terrible an exaggeration! I saw the lips of the black-robed judges. They appeared to me white – whiter than the sheet upon which I trace these words – and thin even to grotesqueness; thin with the intensity of their expression of firmness – of immovable resolution – of stern contempt of human torture. I saw that the decrees, of what to me was Fate, were still issuing from those lips. I saw them writhe with a deadly locution. I saw them fashion the syllables of my name; and I shuddered because no sound succeeded. I saw, too, for a few moments of delirious horror, the soft and nearly imperceptible waving of the sable draperies which enwrapped the walls of the apartment. And then my vision fell upon the seven tall candles upon the table. At first they wore the aspect of charity, and seemed white slender angels who would save me; but then, all at once, there came a most deadly nausea over my spirit, and I felt every fibre in my frame thrill as if I had touched the wire of a galvanic battery, while the angel forms became meaningless spectres, with heads of flame, and I saw that from them there would be no help. And then there stole into my fancy, like a rich musical note, the thought of what sweet rest there must be in the grave. The thought came gently and stealthily, and it seemed long before it attained full appreciation; but just as my spirit came at length properly to feel and entertain it, the figures of the judges vanished, as if magically, from before me; the tall candles sank into nothingness; their flames went out utterly; the blackness of darkness supervened; all sensations appeared swallowed up in a mad rushing descent as of the soul into Hades. Then silence and stillness and night were the universe.

I had swooned; but still will not say that all of consciousness was lot. What of it there remained I will not attempt to define,

or even to describe; yet all was not lost. In the deepest slumber
– no! In delirium – no! In a swoon – no! In death – no! even in
the grave all *is not* lost. Else there is no immortality for man.
Arousing from the most profound of slumbers, we break the
gossamer web of *some* dream. Yet in a second afterward (so
frail may that web have been), we remember not that we have
dreamed. In the return to life from the swoon there are two
stages: first, that of the sense of mental or spiritual; secondly,
that of the sense of physical, existence. It seems probable that
if, upon reaching the second stage, we could recall the
impressions of the first, we should find these impressions
eloquent in memories of the gulf beyond. And that gulf is –
what? How at least shall we distinguish its shadows from
those of the tomb? But if the impressions of what I have
termed the first stage are not at will recalled, yet, after long
interval, do they not come unbidden, while we marvel whence
they come? He who has never swooned, is not he who finds
strange palaces and wildly familiar faces in coals that glow; is
not he who beholds floating in mid-air the sad visions that the
many may not view; is not he who ponders over the perfume of
some novel flower – is not he whose brain grows bewildered
with the meaning of some musical cadence which has never
before arrested his attention.

Amid frequent and thoughtful endeavours to remember;
amid earnest struggles to regather some token of the state of
seeming nothingness into which my soul had lapsed, there
have been moments when I have dreamed of success; there
have been brief, very brief periods when I have conjured up
remembrances which the lucid reason of a later epoch assures
me could have had reference only to that condition of seeming
unconsciousness. These shadows of memory tell, indistinctly,
of tall figures that lifted and bore me in silence down – down –
still down – till a hideous dizziness oppressed me at the mere
idea of the interminableness of the descent. They tell also of a
vague horror at my heart, on account of that heart's unnatural
stillness. Then comes a sense of sudden motionlessness
throughout all things; as if those who bore me (a ghastly
train!) had outrun, in their descent, the limits of the limitless,
and paused from the wearisomeness of their toil. After this I
call to mind flatness and dampness: and then all is *madness* –

the madness of a memory which busies itself among forbidden things.

Very suddenly, there came back to my soul motion and sound — the tumultuous motion of the heart, and, in my ears, the sound of its beating. Then a pause, in which all is blank. Then again, sound, and motion, and touch — a tingling sensation pervading my frame. Then the mere consciousness of existence, without thought — a condition which lasted long. Then, very suddenly, *thought* and shuddering terror, and earnest endeavour to comprehend my true state. Then a strong desire to lapse into insensibility. Then a rushing revival of soul and a successful effort to move. And now a full memory of the trial, of the judges, of the sable draperies, of the sentence, of the sickness, of the swoon. Then entire forgetfulness of all that followed; of all that a later day and much earnestness of endeavour have enabled me vaguely to recall.

So far, I had not opened my eyes. I felt that I lay upon my back, unbound. I reached out my hand, and it fell heavily upon something damp and hard. There I suffered it to remain for many minutes, while I strove to imagine where and *what* I could be. I longed, yet dared not, to employ my vision. I dreaded the first glance at objects around me. It was not that I feared to look upon things horrible, but I grew aghast lest there should be *nothing* to see. At length, with a wild desperation at heart, I quickly unclosed my eyes. My worst thoughts, then, were confirmed. The blackness of eternal night encompassed me. I struggled for breath. The intensity of the darkness seemed to oppress and stifle me. The atmosphere was intolerably close. I still lay quietly, and made effort to exercise my reason. I brought to mind the inquisitorial proceedings, and attempted from that point to deduce my real condition. The sentence had passed; and it appeared to me that a very long interval of time had since elapsed. Yet not for a moment did I suppose myself actually dead. Such a supposition, notwithstanding what we read in fiction, is altogether inconsistent with real existence; — but where and in what state was I? The condemned to death, I knew, perished usually at the *auto-da-fés*, and one of these had been held on the very night of the day of my trial. Had I been remanded to my dungeon, to await the next sacrifice, which would not take place for many months? This I at once saw could not be. Victims had been in immediate demand. Moreover, my dungeon, as well as all the condemned cells at Toledo, had stone floors, and light was not altogether excluded.

A fearful idea now suddenly drove the blood in torrents upon my heart, and for a brief period I once more relapsed into insensibility. Upon recovering, I at once started to my feet, trembling convulsively in every fibre. I thrust my arms wildly above and around me in all directions. I felt nothing; yet dreaded to move a step, lest I should be impeded by the walls of a *tomb*. Perspiration burst from every pore, and stood in cold big beads upon my forehead. The agony of suspense grew at length intolerable, and I cautiously moved forward, with my arms extended, and my eyes straining from their sockets, in the hope of catching some faint ray of light. I proceeded for many paces; but still all was blackness and vacancy. I breathed more freely. It seemed evident that mine was not, at least, the most hideous of fates.

And now, as I still continued to step cautiously onward, there came thronging upon my recollection a thousand vague rumours of the horrors of Toledo. Of the dungeons there had been strange things narrated – fables I had always deemed them – but yet strange, and too ghastly to repeat, save in a whisper. Was I left to perish of starvation in this subterranean world of darkness; or what fate, perhaps even more fearful, awaited me? That the result would be death, and a death of more than customary bitterness, I knew too well the character of my judges to doubt. The mode and the hour were all that occupied or distracted me.

My outstretched hands at length encountered some solid obstruction. It was a wall, seemingly of stone masonry – very smooth, slimy, and cold. I followed it up; stepping with all the careful distrust with which certain antique narratives had inspired me. This process, however, afforded me no means of ascertaining the dimensions of my dungeon; as I might make its circuit, and return to the point whence I set out, without being aware of the fact; so perfectly uniform seemed the wall. I therefore sought the knife which had been in my pocket when led into the inquisitorial chamber, but it was gone; my clothes had been exchanged for a wrapper of coarse serge. I had thought of forcing the blade in some minute crevice of the masonry, so as to identify my point of departure. The difficulty, nevertheless, was but trivial; although in the disorder of my fancy, it seemed at first insuperable. I tore a part of the hem from the robe and placed the fragment at full length, and at right angles to the wall. In groping my way around the prison, I could not fail to encounter this rag upon completing the circuit. So, at least, I thought: but I had not counted upon the extent of the dungeon, or upon my own weakness. The ground was moist and slippery. I staggered onward for some time, when I stumbled and fell. My excessive fatigue induced me to remain prostrate; and sleep soon overtook me as I lay.

Upon awaking, and stretching forth an arm, I found beside me a loaf and a pitcher with water. I was too much exhausted to reflect upon this circumstance, but ate and drank with avidity. Shortly afterward, I resumed my tour around the prison, and with much toil, came at last upon the fragment of the serge. Up to the period when I fell, I had counted fifty-two paces, and, upon resuming my walk, I had counted forty-eight more – when I arrived at the rag. There were in all, then, a hundred paces; and, admitting two paces to the yard, I presumed the dungeon to be fifty yards in circuit. I had met, however, with many angles in the wall, and thus I could form no guess at the shape of the vault; for vault I could not help supposing it to be.

I had little object – certainly no hope – in these researches; but a vague curiosity prompted me to continue them. Quitting the wall, I resolved to cross the area of the enclosure. At first, I proceeded with extreme caution, for the floor, although seemingly of solid material, was treacherous with slime. At length, however, I took courage, and did not hesitate to step firmly – endeavouring to cross in as direct a line as possible. I had advanced some ten or twelve paces in this manner, when the remnant of the torn hem of my robe became entangled between my legs. I stepped on it, and fell violently on my face.

In the confusion attending my fall, I did not immediately apprehend a somewhat startling circumstance, which yet, in a few seconds afterwards, and while I still lay prostrate, arrested my attention. It was this: my chin rested upon the floor of the prison, but my lips, and the upper portion of my head, although seemingly at a less elevation than the chin, touched nothing. At the same time, my forehead seemed bathed in a clammy vapour, and the peculiar smell of decayed fungus arose to my nostrils. I put forward my arm, and shuddered to find that I had fallen at the very brink of a circular pit, whose extent, of course, I had no means of ascertaining at the moment. Groping about the masonry just below the margin, I succeeded in dislodging a small fragment, and let it fall into the abyss. For many seconds I hearkened to its reverberations as it dashed against the sides of the chasm in its descent: at length, there was a sullen plunge into water, succeeded by loud echoes. At the same moment there came a sound resembling the quick opening and as rapid closing of a door overhead, while a faint gleam of light flashed suddenly through the gloom, and as suddenly faded away.

I saw clearly the doom which had been prepared for me, and congratulated myself upon the timely accident by which I had escaped. Another step before my fall, and the world had seen me no more. And the death just avoided, was of that very character which I had regarded as fabulous and frivolous in the tales respecting the Inquisition. To the victims of its tyranny, there was the choice of death with its direst physical agonies, or death with its most hideous moral horrors. I had been reserved for the latter. By long suffering my nerves had been unstrung, until I trembled at the sound of my own voice, and had become in every respect a fitting subject for the species of torture which awaited me.

Shaking in every limb, I groped my way back to the wall – resolving there to perish rather than risk the terrors of the wells, of which my imagination now pictured many in various positions about the dungeon. In other conditions of mind, I might have had courage to end my misery at once by a plunge into one of these abysses; but now I was the veriest of cowards. Neither could I forget what I had read of these pits – that the *sudden* extinction of life formed no part of their most horrible plan.

Agitation of spirit kept me awake for many long hours; but at length I again slumbered. Upon arousing, I found by my side, as before, a loaf and a pitcher of water. A burning thirst consumed me, and I emptied the vessel at a draught. It must have been drugged – for scarcely had I drunk, before I became irresistibly drowsy. A deep sleep fell upon me – a sleep like that of death. How long it lasted, of course I know not; but when, once again, I unclosed my eyes, the objects around me were visible. By a wild, sulphurous lustre, the origin of which I could not at first determine, I was enabled to see the extent and aspect of the prison.

In its size I had been greatly mistaken. The whole circuit of its walls did not exceed twenty-five yards. For some minutes this fact occasioned me a world of vain trouble; vain indeed – for what could be of less importance, under the terrible circumstances which environed me, than the mere dimensions of my dungeon? But my soul took a wild interest in trifles, and I busied myself in endeavours to account for the error I had committed in my measurement. The truth at length flashed upon me. In my first attempt at exploration, I had counted fifty-two paces, up to the period when I fell: I must then have been within a pace or two of the fragment of serge; in fact, I had nearly performed the circuit of the vault. I then slept – and, upon awaking, I must have returned upon my steps – thus supposing the circuit nearly double what it actually was. My confusion of mind prevented me from observing that I began my tour with the wall to the left, and ended it with the wall to the right.

I had been deceived, too, in respect to the shape of the enclosure. In feeling my way, I had found many angles, and thus deduced an idea of great irregularity; so potent is the effect of total darkness upon one arousing from lethargy or sleep! The angles were simply those of a few slight depressions, or niches, at odd intervals. The general shape of the prison was square. What I had taken for masonry, seemed now to be iron, or some other metal, in huge plates, whose sutures or joints occasioned the depression. The entire surface of this metallic enclosure was rudely daubed in all the hideous and repulsive devices to which the charnel superstition of the monks has given rise. The figures of fiends in aspects of menace, with skeleton forms, and other more really fearful images, overspread and disfigured the walls. I observed that the outlines of these monstrosities were sufficiently distinct, but that the colours seemed faded and blurred, as if from the effects of a damp atmosphere. I now noticed the floor, too, which was of stone. In the centre yawned the circular pit from whose jaws I had escaped; but it was the only one in the dungeon.

All this I saw indistinctly and by much effort, for my personal condition had been greatly changed during slumber. I now lay upon my back, and at full length, on a species of low framework of wood. To this I was securely bound by a long strap resembling a surcingle. It passed in many convolutions about my limbs and body, leaving at liberty only my head and my left arm to such extent that I could, by dint of much exertion, supply myself with food from an earthen dish which lay by my side on the floor. I saw, to my horror, that the pitcher had been removed. I say to my horror, for I was consumed with intolerable thirst. This thirst it appeared to be the design of my persecutors to stimulate, for the food in the dish was meat pungently seasoned.

Looking upward, I surveyed the ceiling of my prison. It was some thirty or forty feet overhead, and constructed much as the side walls. In one of its panels a very singular figure riveted my whole attention. It was the painted figure of Time as he is commonly represented, save that, in lieu of a scythe, he held what, at a casual glance, I supposed to be the pictured image of a huge pendulum, such as we see on antique clocks. There was something, however, in the appearance of this machine which caused me to regard it more attentively. While I gazed directly upward at it (for its position was immediately over my own), I fancied that I saw it in motion. In an instant afterward the fancy was confirmed. Its sweep was brief, and of course slow. I watched it for some minutes, somewhat in fear, but more in wonder. Wearied at length with observing its dull movement, I turned my eyes upon the other objects in the cell.

A slight noise attracted my notice, and, looking at the floor, I saw several enormous rats traversing it. They had issued from the well, which lay just within view to my right. Even then, while I gazed, they came up in troops, hurriedly, with ravenous eyes, allured by the scent of the meat. From this it required much effort and attention to scare them away.

It might have been half an hour, perhaps even an hour (for I could take but imperfect note of time), before I again cast my eyes upward. What I then saw, confounded and amazed me. The sweep of the pendulum had increased in extent by nearly a yard. As a natural consequence, its velocity was also much greater. But what mainly disturbed me was the idea that it had perceptibly *descended*. I now observed – with what horror it is needless to say – that its nether extremity was formed of a crescent of glittering steel, about a foot in length from horn to horn; the horns upward, and the under edge evidently as keen as that of a razor. Like a razor also it seemed massy and heavy, tapering from the edge into a solid and broad structure above. It was appended to a weighty rod of brass, and the whole *hissed* as it swung through the air.

I could no longer doubt the doom prepared for me by monkish ingenuity in torture. My cognizance of the pit had become known to the inquisitorial agents – *the pit*, whose horrors had been destined for so bold a recusant as myself – *the pit*, typical of hell, and regarded by rumour as the Ultima Thule of all their punishments. The plunge into this pit I had avoided by the merest of accidents, and I knew that surprise, or entrapment into torment, formed an important portion of all the grotesquerie of these dungeon deaths. Having failed to fall, it was no part of the demon plan to hurl me into the abyss; and thus (there being no alternative) a different and a milder destruction awaited me. Milder! I half smiled in my agony, as I thought of such application of such a term.

What boots it to tell of the long, long hours of horror more than mortal, during which I counted the rushing oscillations of the steel! Inch by inch – line by line – with a descent only appreciable at intervals that seemed ages – down and still down it came! Days passed – it might have been that many days passed – ere it swept so closely over me as to fan me with its acrid breath. The odour of the sharp steel forced itself into my nostrils. I prayed – I wearied heaven with my prayer for its more speedy descent. I grew frantically mad, and struggled to force myself upward against the sweep of the fearful scimitar. And then I fell suddenly calm, and lay smiling at the glittering death, as a child at some rare bauble.

There was another interval of utter insensibility; it was

brief; for, upon again lapsing into life, there had been no perceptible descent in the pendulum. But it might have been long – for I knew there were demons who took note of my swoon, and who could have arrested the vibration at pleasure. Upon my recovery, too, I felt very – oh, inexpressibly – sick and weak, as if through long inanition. Even amid the agonies of that period, the human nature craved food. With painful effort I outstretched my left arm as far as my bonds permitted, and took possession of the small remnant which had been spared me by the rats. As I put a portion of it to my lips, there rushed to my mind a half-formed thought of joy – of hope. Yet what business had *I* with hope? It was, as I say, a half-formed thought – man has many such, which are never completed. I felt that it was of joy – of hope; but I felt also that it had perished in its formation. In vain I struggled to perfect – to regain it. Long suffering had nearly annihilated all my ordinary powers of mind. I was an imbecile – an idiot.

The vibration of the pendulum was at right angles to my length. I saw that the crescent was designed to cross the region of the heart. It would fray the serge of my robe – it would return and repeat its operations – again – and again. Notwithstanding its terrifically wide sweep (some thirty feet or more), and the hissing vigour of its descent, sufficient to sunder these very walls of iron, still the fraying of my robe would be all that, for several minutes, it would accomplish. And at this thought I paused. I dared not go farther than this reflection. I dwelt upon it with a pertinacity of attention – as if, in so dwelling, I could arrest *here* the descent of the steel. I forced myself to ponder upon the sound of the crescent as it should pass across the garment – upon the peculiar thrilling sensation which the friction of cloth produces on the nerves. I pondered upon all this frivolity until my teeth were on edge.

Down – steadily down it crept. I took a frenzied pleasure in contrasting its downward with its lateral velocity. To the right – to the left – far and wide – with the shriek of a damned spirit! to my heart, with the stealthy pace of the tiger! I alternately laughed and howled, as the one or the other idea grew predominant.

Down – certainly, relentlessly down! It vibrated within three inches of my bosom! I struggled violently – furiously – to free my left arm. This was free only from the elbow to the hand. I could reach the latter, from the platter beside me, to my mouth, with great effort, but no farther. Could I have broken the fastenings above the elbow, I would have seized and attempted to arrest the pendulum. I might as well have attempted to arrest an avalanche!

Down – still unceasingly – still inevitably down! I gasped and struggled at each vibration. I shrunk convulsively at its every sweep. My eyes followed its outward or upward whirls with the eagerness of the most unmeaning despair; they closed themselves spasmodically at the descent, although death would have been a relief, oh, how unspeakable! Still I quivered in every nerve to think how slight a sinking of the machinery would precipitate that keen, glistening axe upon my bosom. It was *hope* that prompted the nerve to quiver – the frame to shrink. It was *hope* – the hope that triumphs on the rack – that whispers to the death-condemned even in the dungeons of the Inquisition.

I saw that some ten or twelve vibrations would bring the steel in actual contact with my robe – and with this observation there suddenly came over my spirit all the keen, collected calmness of despair. For the first time during many hours – or perhaps days – I *thought*. It now occurred to me that the bandage, or surcingle, which enveloped me, was *unique*. I was tied by no separate cord. The first stroke of the razor-like crescent athwart any portion of the band, would so detach it that it might be unwound from my person by means of my left hand. But how fearful, in that case, the proximity of the steel! The result of the slightest struggle, how deadly! Was it likely, moreover, that the minions of the torturer had not foreseen and provided for this possibility? Was it probable that the bandage crossed my bosom in the track of the pendulum? Dreading to find my faint, and, as it seemed, my last hope frustrated, I so far elevated my head as to obtain a distinct view of my breast. The surcingle enveloped my limbs and body close in all directions – *save in the path of the destroying crescent*.

Scarcely had I dropped my head back into its original position when there flashed upon my mind what I cannot better describe than as the unformed half of that idea of deliverance to which I have previously alluded, and of which a moiety only floated indeterminately through my brain when I raised food to my burning lips. The whole thought was now present – feeble, scarcely sane, scarcely definite – but still entire. I proceeded at once, with the nervous energy of despair, to attempt its execution.

For many hours, the immediate vicinity of the low framework upon which I lay, had been literally swarming with rats. They were wild, bold, ravenous – their red eyes glaring upon me as if they waited but for motionlessness on my part to make me their prey. 'To what food,' I thought, 'have they been accustomed in the well?'

They had devoured, in spite of all my efforts to prevent them, all but a small remnant of the contents of the dish. I had fallen into an habitual see-saw, or wave of the hand, about the platter; and, at length, the unconscious uniformity of the movement deprived it of effect. In their voracity, the vermin frequently fastened their sharp fangs in my fingers. With the particles of the oily and spicy viand which now remained, I thoroughly rubbed the bandage wherever I could reach it; then, raising my hand from the floor, I lay breathlessly still.

At first, the ravenous animals were startled and terrified at the change – at the cessation of movement. They shrank alarmedly back; many sought the well. But this was only for a moment. I had not counted in vain upon their voracity. Observing that I remained without motion, one or two of the boldest leaped upon the framework, and smelt at the surcingle. This seemed the signal for a general rush. Forth from the well they hurried in fresh troops. They clung to the wood – they overran it, and leaped in hundreds upon my person. The measured movement of the pendulum disturbed them not at all. Avoiding its strokes, they busied themselves with the anointed bandage. They pressed – they swarmed upon me in ever-accumulating heaps. They writhed upon my throat; their cold lips sought my own; I was half stifled by their thronging pressure; disgust for which the world has no name swelled my bosom, and chilled, with a heavy clamminess, my heart. Yet one minute, and I felt that the struggle would be over. Plainly I perceived the loosening of the bandage. I knew that in more than one place it must be already severed. With a more than human resolution I lay *still*.

Nor had I erred in my calculations – nor had I endured in vain. I at length felt that I was *free*. The surcingle hung in ribands from my body. But the stroke of the pendulum already pressed upon my bosom. It had divided the serge of the robe. It had cut through the linen beneath. Twice again it swung, and a sharp sense of pain shot through every nerve. But the moment of escape had arrived. With a wave of my hand my deliverers hurried tumultuously away. With a steady movement – cautious, sidelong, shrinking, and slow – I slid from the embrace of the bandage and beyond the reach of the scimitar. For the moment, at least, *I was free*.

Free! – and in the grasp of the Inquisition! I had scarcely stepped from my wooden bed of horror upon the stone floor of the prison, when the motion of the hellish machine ceased, and I beheld it drawn up, by some invisible force, through the ceiling. This was a lesson which I took desperately to heart. My every motion was undoubtedly watched. Free! – I had but escaped death in one form of agony, to be delivered unto worse than death in some other. With that thought I rolled my eyes nervously around on the barriers of iron that hemmed me in. Something unusual – some change which, at first, I could not appreciate distinctly – it was obvious, had taken place in the apartment. For many minutes of a dreamy and trembling abstraction, I busied myself in vain, unconnected conjecture. During this period I became aware, for the first time, of the origin of the sulphurous light which illumined the cell. It proceeded from a fissure, about half an inch in width, extending entirely around the prison at the base of the walls, which thus appeared, and were completely separated from the floor. I endeavoured, but of course in vain, to look through the aperture.

As I arose from the attempt, the mystery of the alteration in the chamber broke at once upon my understanding. I have observed that, although the outlines of the figures upon the walls were sufficiently distinct, yet the colours seemed blurred and indefinite. These colours had now assumed, and were momentarily assuming, a startling and most intense brilliancy, that gave to the spectral and fiendish portraitures an aspect that might have thrilled even firmer nerves than my own. Demon eyes, of a wild and ghastly vivacity, glared upon me in a thousand directions, where none had been visible before, and gleamed with the lurid lustre of a fire that I could not force my imagination to regard as unreal.

Unreal! – Even while I breathed there came to my nostrils the breath of the vapour of heated iron! A suffocating odour pervaded the prison! A deeper glow settled each moment in the eyes that glared at my agonies! A richer tint of crimson diffused itself over the pictured horrors of blood. I panted! I gasped for breath! There could be no doubt of the design of my tormentors – oh! most unrelenting! oh! most demoniac of men! I shrank from the glowing metal to the centre of the cell. Amid the thought of the fiery destruction that impended, the idea of the coolness of the well came over my soul like balm. I rushed to its deadly brink. I threw my straining vision below. The glare from the enkindled roof illumined its inmost recesses. Yet, for a wild moment, did my spirit refuse to comprehend the meaning of what I saw. At length it forced – it wrested its way into my soul – it burned itself in upon my shuddering reason. Oh! for a voice to speak! – oh! horror! – oh! any horror but this! With a shriek, I rushed from the margin, and buried my face in my hands – weeping bitterly.

The heat rapidly increased, and once again I looked up, shuddering as with a fit of the ague. There had been a second change in the cell – and now the change was obviously in the *form*. As before, it was in vain that I at first endeavoured to appreciate or understand what was taking place. But not long was I left in doubt. The Inquisitorial vengeance had been hurried by my twofold escape, and there was to be no more dallying with the King of Terrors. The room had been square. I saw that two of its iron angles were now acute – two, consequently, obtuse. The fearful difference quickly increased with a low rumbling or moaning sound. In an instant the apartment had shifted its form into that of a lozenge. But the alteration stopped not here – I neither hoped nor desired it to stop. I could have clasped the red walls to my bosom as a garment of eternal peace. 'Death,' I said, 'any death but that of the pit!' Fool! might I not have known that *into the pit* it was the object of the burning iron to urge me? Could I resist its glow? or if even that, could I withstand its pressure? And now flatter and flatter grew the lozenge, with a rapidity that left me no time for contemplation. Its centre, and, of course, its greatest width, came just over the yawning gulf. I shrank back – but the closing walls pressed me resistlessly onward. At length for my seared and writhing body there was no longer an inch of foothold on the firm floor of the prison. I struggled no more, but the agony of my soul found vent in one loud, long, and final scream of despair. I felt that I tottered upon the brink – I averted my eyes –

There was a discordant hum of human voices! There was a loud blast as of many trumpets! There was a harsh grating as of a thousand thunders! The fiery walls rushed back! An outstretched arm caught my own as I fell, fainting, into the abyss. It was that of General Lasalle. The French army had entered Toledo. The Inquisition was in the hands of its enemies.

X

Perez
W.L. George

*Christopher Lee is, of course, particularly identified in the public's mind with Dracula, the vampire Count, but in actual fact horror films represent only a small proportion of his film output, and indeed in recent years he has turned his back almost completely on such pictures. His reason for this has been simple enough: he wants to avoid becoming type-cast, and in pursuit of this aim he recently moved from London to Hollywood where he now lives and works. With him, though, has gone his impressive library of over 12,000 books, many of which are stories of the macabre, and as a result of building this collection he has a profound knowledge of 'terror tales' as he prefers to call such literature. He admires a number of writers, several of whose work he has appeared in on the screen, including Bram Stoker (*Dracula*), Mary Shelley (*Frankenstein*), Sax Rohmer (*Fu Manchu*), Sir Arthur Conan Doyle (creator of Sherlock Holmes: Christopher has played both Holmes and his brother, Mycroft, in films), Dennis Wheatley (*The Devil Rides Out*) and the Americans, Robert Bloch and Ray Bradbury, who are now personal friends. A few years ago Christopher set up his own film company, Charlemagne Productions (named after an ancestor on his mother's side, the Emperor Charlemagne), and for a while before he left for America I worked as a consultant searching for screen properties. Among the short-list of stories which Christopher now has of tales he would like to film, this story 'Perez' is right at the top. I believe when you have read it you will see why it appeals so strongly to him ...*

'And that,' said Mr Warlingham, holding up a few sheets of quarto paper, 'is the end. The end,' he repeated meditatively, his fingers playing with the manuscript as if he could not bear to hand it to his secretary.

'May I congratulate you, Mr Warlingham?' said Miss Medhurst. 'I'm sure it will be a great success. A greater success than any of your novels.' Mr Warlingham raised a modest hand, and Miss Medhurst hastened to repair possible error. 'I don't mean that your novels haven't been successful, no one could say that; you remember how America went mad over *The Four Frontiersmen* ... and there was *Juliana* too: eleven editions in nine weeks!'

'You forget the private limited edition on Japan paper,' said Mr Warlingham with some severity. 'Yes, I haven't done badly.' The novelist leant back in his arm-chair, finger-tips joined, staring at the ceiling with a certain complacency. He was a shortish, stoutish man, aged about forty, with a rosy complexion, well-kept hands, a neatly clipped moustache, and a noticeable baldness. Upon his rather thick, not unpleasant, mouth lingered a little private smile, as if he were remembering obstacles easily overcome, were listing in his mind past triumphs; as if confident in merits that had not been overlooked by praise. Mr Warlingham was successful. Mr Warlingham looked successful.

Then again he played with those manuscript sheets. He had dictated the whole of the book to Miss Medhurst except the last page, for he knew that the highest skill is obtained only when the hand labours with the brain. Still, at that moment Mr Warlingham was conscious of some uneasiness. It was an indefinable feeling which had come upon him during the last few days, a sense of ... how could he put it? Secret criticism? No, not exactly that. True, he had found that last page incredibly difficult to write; he had been held back by some doubt which his mind could not analyse. And now the strange sensation grew stronger.

He felt as if he were not alone, as if something faintly hostile stood by his side. He wrinkled his brows crossly. 'Ridiculous,' he murmured. Indeed, his surroundings were strictly normal. Here he sat in his familiar study, his typical study: the deep red-and-blue carpet, the crowded bookshelves, the excellent appliances, the files, the scales, the typewriter in the corner, everything in his comfortable room cried out to him that he sat in the midst of ordinary life. But then? What? Tired, he supposed. Anyhow, he mustn't brood.

'Well,' said Mr Warlingham briskly, 'here are the last sheets, Miss Medhurst. Please type them out, and I will revise them with the rest.'

Miss Medhurst held out a wiry little hand and took the manuscript with an air of devotion. Her author's words thrilled her always, but conveyed in his own handwriting they took on an air of sanctity. Then Mr Warlingham reached across the desk and took back the sheets. 'I will read you the last page,' he said, and Miss Medhurst wondered at a tone of defiance which had come into his voice. She could not know that Mr Warlingham was reacting against a sudden growth of that secret feeling. As he gave her the sheets he had again experienced it, and determined to read the page aloud. After all there *might* be something wrong with the stuff.

'Oh,' she gasped, 'please do. Like that,' she added hurriedly, 'I shan't make any mistakes in typing.' But a faint flush rose in her pale cheeks as she grew conscious of her own excitement. Miss Medhurst was of indeterminable age, between thirty and forty; she was small, thin, with little features that had once been pretty; dressed always in dark colours she looked even more insignificant than she was; her hair was of a neutral brown shade; only her eyes, that all mankind could, if it cared, describe as yellow-grey, grew large and soft as she gazed upon the man whose secretary she had been for ten years, yet was still to her marvellous and inspired. Mr Warlingham did not observe any change in those neutral eyes. He cleared his throat and read. The first few sentences Miss Medhurst did not hear, for her heart beat fast, but after a moment the old spell worked, and as in a purple cloud the phrases of Mr Warlingham took shape for her:

... The six men stood undecided about the long shape that lay upon the ground. It was as if they feared to touch that sumptuously wild buccaneer, heavy-breeched, scarlet-sashed, so dark, and fierce, and beautiful, lest the slightest movement should release the mortal spark that lingered still in the faintly heaving breast. At last Moreno spoke: 'We cannot leave him here,' he said. 'The sun is too hot.'

Indeed, from the purple vault above, the Mexican sun felt like a heavy hand, and the air was filled with the buzzing of insects; the air was crowded with life; Moreno, pitiless and crime-stained, felt his heart grow big and painful as he thought that Nature was filled with life, yet could not afford another hour to Perez, Perez the man without fear, his comrade who lay there dying. 'Come,' he said gently, 'let us carry him into the house.'

A few minutes later they stood a little away from the bedside. Perez breathed more hurriedly. He grew yet paler, and Moreno stepped forward, an anguish upon him. Then for one moment his comrade opened his eyes, those soft, lustrous eyes; his lips twisted into a crooked smile as for the last time he met the gaze of Moreno; but, very slowly, his head sank down and was still. Thus he lay, his dark face sharp outlined against the pillow, as an ancient bronze, black beard erect, in death defiant as in life.

Moreno fell upon his knees: 'Good-bye, eagle-heart, good-bye,' he cried. One by one the others stole away; Perez lay still and aloof. And his soul, winging its way through space, carried as a last memory the sound of his comrade's weeping.

Miss Medhurst did not move; her yellow-grey eyes were dim, for she too loved the eagle-hearted buccaneer. So she did not notice that as Mr Warlingham pronounced the last word he started so violently that his knees rapped against the desk. Nor did she see him furtively glance to the right and left, eyes dilated, or fumble for his handkerchief with an unsteady hand. For Mr Warlingham had distinctly heard a voice – a loud, indignant voice. And what it said was: 'Nonsense!'

Nonsense? Somebody had said 'Nonsense'. With sudden suspicion Mr Warlingham stared at Miss Medhurst, then was ashamed, for his secretary sat in the same rapt attitude, and her eyes were swimming in tears. But then, what? Oh, if only his hand wouldn't shake so. Wherever had he put his handkerchief? He swore silently, still casting into the corners of the room a frightened gaze.

'It's wonderful,' murmured Miss Medhurst, 'wonderful. Oh, it'll be a great success. It's better than anything Henry

James ever did. It's better than Hall Caine. But why must Perez die? Yes, I suppose it's artistic truth and that he had to die that – '

'Miss Medhurst,' said Mr Warlingham in a voice suddenly metallic and laboured, 'if you don't mind ... I won't do any more today ... I'm not very well.'

She bent forward with quick sympathy. 'Yes, of course, work like yours takes all your strength. I'll go. And, please, please, Mr Warlingham, rest. Go into the park. And I'm sure a tonic ...'

Mr Warlingham was not listening. He sat with clenched hands. When Miss Medhurst said, 'Why must Perez die?' a voice had grumbled: 'He didn't.'

For a long time Mr Warlingham sat with his face in his hands. The silence was complete, no ghostly voice assailed his ears, but at any moment he knew that it might speak. Haunted! He was haunted. An hour passed while his excited brain revolved horrid stories; he thought of phantoms that rattle chains, of the death dog, of riding witches. At length, only as the study grew dark and he hurriedly switched on the electric light, he forced himself into a balanced state of mind.

'This won't do,' he said aloud. 'If I go on like this I'll get worse, and then ...' he shuddered, 'I'll find myself in a private nursing-home, to call it by a polite name. How can you be so absurd?' he asked himself. 'You let yourself become the prey of your nerves just because you're a little overworked. Old Medhurst is right; she's been at me for months to take a rest. Anyhow ...' Mr Warlingham suddenly grew defiant and addressed the wall: 'Speak up! Now's your chance. I'm listening.' There was no reply, and, nearly comforted, Mr Warlingham got into his evening clothes and went to his club. He ate an excellent dinner; conscious of the rights of an invalid he drank a pint of champagne.

This helped him to find the company attractive; his satisfaction was increased after dinner, for he made up a four at bridge with Draycott, Lord Langwith, and the club bore, and as fortune gave him almost uniformly good hands he grew to like the club bore. At twelve o'clock Mr Warlingham unlocked his front door, meeting the darkness with a slight tremor that passed away at once; faintly conscious of uneasiness as he undressed, he for a moment feared that he would have the horrors. But he slept almost at once, and awoke only to find that his valet had gone out, leaving by his side his letters, the newspapers, and the morning tea, while brilliant spring sunshine lit up every part of the room. Almost at once he remembered.

'Ah,' he thought, as he stretched, 'I feel better,' and began to drink his tea. Then, quite suddenly, as the cup fell crashing and unnoticed to the ground, Mr Warlingham found his brow wet. Somebody was standing at the foot of his bed. He clenched his fists, staring.'Yes, this was no illusion. The door had not opened, and yet a man stood looking at him with a disagreeable expression. Mr Warlingham made a violent effort to speak, but found his tongue palsied. Then a voice, the familiar voice that had haunted him, grew audible:

'Well,' said the shape. 'Surprised to see me, I suppose.' Mr Warlingham did not reply. 'You've given me a lot of trouble,' the Thing went on; 'materializing isn't as easy as you novelists make out. When I think of the weeks of bother I've had over this business, I've a good mind ...' It visibly snarled. 'Still, that's not what I've really come for. Warlingham, that ending of yours is nonsense. Bunkum. Pure bunkum.'

'What do you want?' asked Mr Warlingham feebly, for this insult to his literary powers galvanized him.

'I want you to alter the ending. And you'll do it, sure as my name's Perez.'

Mr Warlingham still stared at the Thing. Perez! He had known at once that tall, black-bearded shape with the lustrous dark eyes, had recognized the full trousers and the scarlet sash. His buccaneer! But this was awful. Was he going mad? Perez was talking again.

'Look here,' he said. 'I've got no time to waste. It's all I can do to hold my molecules together, so let's get down to business. That ending of yours is bunkum because I didn't die. Understand? *I didn't die.* It's quite true that Moreno, whom you have the audacity to call my friend, the scab who cheated me out of thirty-three dollars at euchre last night, so that I had to let the moonlight through him ... Well, Moreno, as I was saying, carried me in. But that's where what you call your imagination failed. Mercedes was in the house; for a fortnight she fed me on milk and I got perfectly well. As soon as I felt strong enough I murdered her and took charge of her savings, which I am glad to say were considerable.'

'You ... murdered the woman who saved your life!' cried Mr Warlingham, his fear expelled by surprise.

'Of course. You may think it ungrateful of me. But I'm not a respectable character; you made me like that, and if I killed Mercedes it's your fault.'

'Well, I like your cheek!' said Mr Warlingham. 'You say that Mercedes – '

'I'm tired of Mercedes,' grumbled Perez. 'And don't interrupt. With her savings I went to Mexico City and bought myself a small saloon at No 11 Calle Berganza. I'm doing quite well; I've a man to help me, and by and by I expect to develop a bit. Before I'm done I'll be running a big café; I'll call it the Café Warlingham. I'll always be pleased to see you. My place is near the street car depot. So you see your ending won't do.'

For a moment Mr Warlingham was silent. He was still frightened, but interested. 'All this,' he said loftily, 'has nothing to do with me.'

'Nothing to do with you? Don't be silly. You've no right to create a character and end him up wrong. Especially you've no right to kill him off to save yourself the trouble of writing a few hundred pages more.'

'I'd like to see you do it,' protested Mr Warlingham. 'You talk as if one could write a few hundred pages in a week.'

'Nothing to do with me. Anyhow, I didn't die. I'm alive today, so your ending isn't true; it isn't artistic truth.'

'What!' shouted Mr Warlingham, springing up in bed, 'you dare to stand there and lecture me on artistic truth. Please remember to whom you're talking.'

'Don't brag; keep that for Miss Medhurst. Obviously the ending's inartistic; if you'll just look up Chapter VIII and observe the psychology of ...'

Here the discussion grew confused, and Mr Warlingham found himself at a disadvantage, for Perez knew a great many things about the psychology of the other characters (and of Perez) which had never occurred to the novelist. They ended by shouting:

'Thoroughly inartistic ...'

'I know more about novels than you'll ...'

'I want another seven chapters at least.'

'Leave the room at once, sir.'

There was a tap at the door. As Mr Warlingham sank down upon the pillow the valet came in and said: 'Your bath is ready, sir,' then withdrew, Perez being obviously invisible to him.

'All right,' said Perez. 'Go and have your bath. I know you think best in your bath. Besides, every molecule of me is aching, so I'll dissolve for an hour or so. But,' he added threateningly, 'I'll come back and resume the discussion. I'll teach you ...' He began to grow dim. 'You'll thank me for this some day.' The voice grew faint. 'I'll teach you artistic truth.'

'Mr Warlingham,' said Miss Medhurst as she buttoned her gloves prior to going out to lunch, 'please don't think me impertinent, but I'm sure you're working too hard. You *must* have a holiday.'

'You mean,' said the novelist in an acid tone, 'that my work isn't up to standard?'

'I don't mean anything of the kind,' protested the little spinster. 'I think you're wonderful. Only I thought yesterday, and again this morning ... well, you know, you had to stop dictating, and – '

'Yes, I know, I know.' Mr Warlingham had indeed been paralysed for several minutes while Perez stood behind Miss Medhurst's chair and made ferocious faces. When at last Mr Warlingham decided to affront him and tremblingly resumed an incoherent dictation, Perez had punctuated every other sentence with loud cries of 'Rot!', while Miss Medhurst shrank from her author's livid face. 'Inspiration,' she thought, 'is a beautiful, terrible thing.'

'Just for a few days.' Miss Medhurst's tone grew wheedling, and as she bent forward her yellow-grey eyes grew tender. 'In the country. Think of it; here is the spring. Daffodils, primroses, and ... daffodils in the fields.'

'Perhaps I will,' said Mr Warlingham harshly. 'I'll see whether he ... I mean, I'll see how I feel.'

But the days that followed brought no improvement in Mr Warlingham's condition. Perez had begun by appearing twice in one day; within a week he took to materializing every four hours or so. This seemed to please the phantom. 'I say, Warlie, old boy,' he remarked as he leant against the tobacconist's counter while his victim tried to buy cigarettes, 'this materializing isn't as difficult as it looks. It's a matter of practice; now that I know how to control my molecules I can bring it off every two hours. In time I may be able to keep it up day and night; and then I'll never leave you at all.'

Mr Warlingham groaned and rushed out of the shop, leaving his change in front of the amazed salesman, Perez running by his side with long, easy strides.

'Steady,' said the phantom, 'there's no hurry. You won't get away from me.'

Soon Mr Warlingham realized that Perez was right. He appeared in the park and followed his author all the way to the publisher, arguing incessantly. He was beginning to develop theories. 'You've made a mess of the whole thing,' said Perez. 'On thinking it over carefully I don't think I should have killed Pepita before eloping with Inez. As for Isabel, I rather think I shot her father, so you should say in Chapter V – '

'I wish you'd go away,' moaned Mr Warlingham. 'If you go on bothering me I'll burn the book and you'll be snuffed out.'

'I shan't. You'll write it over again in the right way. Now, Warlie, pull yourself together. I'll make a celebrity of you when you've learned artistic truth.'

Thereupon followed acrid argument, for Mr Warlingham no longer feared Perez; he merely looked upon him as an intolerable nuisance whose literary criticisms outraged his pride. But on this occasion the victim soon was silenced, for a policeman turned round and stared as Mr Warlingham told the empty air not to be a fool. As time passed the oppressor almost realized his threats; his molecular control became so great that in one day he managed to lunch with Mr Warlingham, to make a fifth at bridge (which cost Mr Warlingham a good deal of money and the friendship of his partner), and to enter a crowded omnibus, where he sat upon an unmoved old lady and loudly lectured the apparently blind and deaf passengers on the defects of Mr Warlingham's style. The author felt a dull brutalization creep over him; Miss Medhurst openly wept. 'He doesn't seem to care about anything,' she whimpered to herself; 'I don't think he hears.'

She was wrong. Mr Warlingham heard too much. His ruddy colour was leaving him, and his waistcoat began to sag. 'I'm wasting away,' he thought, and did not care. But his nervous system was working independently of his will, and only his pride forbade that he should surrender to the ever more insistent Perez; an incident brought about the breakdown. Mr Warlingham went to a fashionable luncheon party and found himself seated between a very pretty American Duchess and a well-known actress. Anxious to make himself agreeable he garnished his conversations with epigrams, and for a time all went well; he was alone. Who could say? Perhaps it was all over. Then he saw Perez, seated on the rose bowl, his heavy boots in the middle of a basket of crystallized violets. He seemed to enjoy the scene, but as Mr Warlingham remarked: 'Don't do unto others as you would be done by, for they may not have the same taste,' the phantom informed the party that the epigram was not by Mr Warlingham, but by Mr Bernard Shaw.

For a few minutes the novelist ground his teeth and plodded on his witty way, but the shameless Perez gravely followed every epigram by: 'As Whistler put it,' or 'That's the best thing Anatole France ever said'; at last Mr Warlingham grew blackly silent. Later the American Duchess confided to her husband that after the first ten minutes well-known novelists turned out to be dull dogs. Meanwhile Mr Warlingham sat in his study, his face in his hands, while Miss Medhurst fluttered about him. 'Tell me what's the matter,' she implored. Mr Warlingham looked at her wildly; perhaps something of her immense tenderness touched him, for suddenly he spoke:

'Don't think me mad … I don't know what to do. It keeps following me about, and arguing. Oh, what shall I do?' The horror of the past days was released as he told Miss Medhurst everything, little details of time and place, literary arguments the phantom had used, and gripping the wiry little hand that

trembled and yielded he cried out as a child: 'Oh, I'm right,
I'm right, tell me I'm right.'

'Yes,' whispered Miss Medhurst. 'Of course you're right.
Who could teach you anything? Don't alter your novel; it
doesn't belong to you, it belongs to humanity. But you are
overwrought, worn out. I'm going to pack for you, and you
must go to the seaside for a week. Promise?'

Mr Warlingham nodded. He did not notice that for a
moment his secretary laid upon his arm fingers light as a
butterfly's wing.

A week later Miss Medhurst entered the study, her heart
beating. Oh, how ill he looked! 'Well?' she asked tensely.

'It's no good,' said Mr Warlingham in a gloomy tone.
'Perez and I went ... bathing.'

For a moment Miss Medhurst was tempted to laugh, then
was ashamed. This was terrible. The man chosen of the muses
was dying before her eyes; worse, his reason was dying,
because of a wretched illusion. Oh, if she could only take it
upon herself! She wrung her little hard hands, and as she
peered into corners, seized by a sense of the uncanny, the
hatred of a true partisan held her: if only Perez could appear
to her ... she would outrage him, blot him out. Yes, blot him
out. The words raised in the little spinster an incredible
excitement; medical memories taken from the newspapers
invaded her mind, wonderful cures brought about by
suggestion, by self-suggestion. *By self-suggestion!* Aghast at her
own audacity she put her hand on the stricken man's
shoulder.

'Mr Warlingham,' she whispered, 'do you hear me? It is an
illusion. Do you understand it is an illusion?'

'Yes,' said the novelist, without raising his eyes.

'Then if it is an illusion let us face it. Prove to yourself that it
is only an illusion.'

'Prove?' uttered Mr Warlingham. 'How?'

'He said he lived in Mexico, that he kept a saloon. Well ...
go and see. Go to Mexico.'

'Go to Mexico,' shouted Mr Warlingham, leaping to his
feet.

'Yes. Go. Go and see. It's an illusion. When you get there,
very likely you'll find a bank at the address he gave you. And

then you'll know it was only an illusion. You'll be free.'

Mr Warlingham thought for a long time, then gently took her hand and said: 'Perhaps you're right. But don't let me go alone. Come with me.'

A sickly man wrapped in a travelling rug staggered on to the platform, hanging with a curious air of helplessness to the arm of a slim, capable little woman. Behind them, in procession, came several swarthy porters laden with baggage; the commissionaire of the *Hotel de las Cuatro Naciónes*, disguised as a full general, led the way. The little woman erupted into the Spanish she had acquired on board ship, directed the porters to wait with the *equipaje*, gave the commissionaire five pesos to help the heavy luggage through the customs, and gently led the grey-faced man to the waiting omnibus.

'Now, Mr Warlingham,' she said briskly, half an hour later, 'you must stay in bed and rest. Nothing can be done today; first you must sleep. I must go to my hotel, but I'll come back for dinner. You'll stay in bed? Promise?'

'All right,' said Mr Warlingham wearily. He shut his eyes as if half asleep or exhausted. With a sudden fond gesture Miss Medhurst smoothed the creases from the pillow and left the room.

But she stayed only a few minutes at her hotel, just long enough to wash her thin, intelligent face, and to smile as she powdered her nose, for this was a new habit. For a moment, on the steps, she shrank from the broad expanse of the *plaza*, crowded with black-garbed men crowned by sombreros, bare-headed women whose hair shone like oiled silk, lounging *peones*, wild, half Indian, always about to be run over by the prancing buggy horses or the clanging electric cars. Then she clenched her little fists and called a cab. Her course was fixed in advance: the driver must carry her to a church selected from the plan of Mexico City and must inevitably pass through the Calle Berganza; yet she would not arouse suspicion by naming the street of doom. Her excitement was so powerful that the broad white streets became to her mere symbols. She saw only name-plates: *C. de Tampico* ... *C. de Santa Fe* ... then at last, in the mist, *C. Berganza* ... 27 ... 25 ...

a little street of old, mean houses ... 19 ... a dog rooting in a
dustbin ... 13 ...

She passed Number 11, was conscious horribly of the bush
over the door. Indeed, it was not a bank but a little bar. Miss
Medhurst ground her teeth as she dropped her sunshade in
the road, stopped the driver by a violent tug at the coat-tail
(for not a word of Spanish could she remember), leaped out,
ran back. As she bent she stared into the little bar. For a
moment she could see nothing through the dirty panes, then a
shape. Miss Medhurst tottered as she walked away with the
sunshade: she had recognized the tall, dark man with the soft
eyes and the black beard.

All through the night Miss Medhurst tossed in the high
Spanish bed. Perez! It was Perez. It was madness, death for
Mr Warlingham. Miss Medhurst wept into the pillow, bit it so
as not to scream. And later she lit all the candles, seized by the
dread of the supernatural. When morning came and she crept
to the *Cuatro Naciónes* she was paler than Mr Warlingham. As
she came in he was speaking to the shade, and for a moment
she thought that she, too, could now glimpse Perez against the
flowered curtain. Mad! Both mad! But a savage purpose told
her to gain time, to make Mr Warlingham dress, to drive him
wildly through the town, into the suburbs, only to gain time to
think. The novelist did not resist, seemed to have lost even the
desire to hasten to the place of trial, or to flee from it.
Obediently, when lunch was done, he lay down for a siesta.
All he said was:

'If you're going out, remember this is Mexico and take your
revolver.' He had given her the weapon and loaded it himself.
For Mr Warlingham's novels were slightly sensational, and he
expected life to equal them. Miss Medhurst went out into the
heat that struck up from the stones (she remembered Mr
Warlingham's metaphor) like a heavy hand. She hardly felt it,
nor the molten shafts of light from the purple sky. She sped
through the desert streets, a grim, earnest little figure, careless
of sights, on the route of yesterday. At the corner of Calle
Berganza she paused, then ran. Number 11 stood open, and
without an apparent tremor she went in. As her eyes, sun-
blind, recovered sight, she took in the few details, the wooden

tables, the few iron chairs, the counter, the armchair on which slumbered a man of destiny. Her limbs shook, but Miss Medhurst rapped a table with her knuckles until Perez half opened his eyes.

'*Te!* ' she said harshly, '*con leche.*'

Perez stared at her. Tea, with milk? At half past two? He expressed this view. Also the *mozo* had gone home for a siesta. He was alone in the café.

'*Te con leche,*' snapped Miss Medhurst.

Perez reflected that she was English, therefore a lunatic, therefore also rich, and after some time brought in an amazingly vile liquid. The little spinster watched his face, his hands. 'Am I mad?' she thought. Then: 'No, it is he.' She drank the tea. She had nothing to say. This was the end. And yet she could not go. Time, gain time; she must. Desperately she asked if this were an old inn.

'*No se,*' replied Perez sleepily.

She found herself explaining that her employer was an antiquarian who studied old inns. Might she visit the inn? Perez was about to refuse, but observed in Miss Medhurst's hand a twenty pesos note. Lunatic, he thought; shrugged his shoulders and led the way up steep wooden stairs.

They stood in a dark, shuttered bedroom. A carved oak chest ran up to the black beams. On the mantelpiece stood a cheap statuette of a saint. In an alcove she saw the high white bed.

'The carpet,' said Perez, proudly pointing at the horror from Brussels, 'is new.' He turned to her, smiling. She did not know what had happened. She did not know what she did. She heard a shot, a cry, found herself, laughing and crying, on her knees by the side of the man she had slain, found her tiny strength tenfold multiplied as she hauled him to the bed, set upon the pillow the limp head. But before she fled through the lonely, brilliant streets, she thrust the revolver into the relaxed hand.

She found Mr Warlingham up and excited.

'Where have you been all this time? I've been waiting,' he cried crossly. 'I feel so funny. I was talking to him a quarter of an hour ago, and he vanished in the middle of a word. Oh, I feel so ill.'

'Come with me,' said Miss Medhurst firmly. 'Come now. I have found the way. Now! Quick; hurry!'

Her new cunning told her to make him walk to arouse no notice. That cunning led her and her trembling charge into the bar where a dirty *mozo* now sat and smoked. It told her to make her scanty Spanish incomprehensible, until at last the *mozo* said he must fetch his master. He called up the wooden stairs, and Miss Medhurst's fingers entered like claws into Mr Warlingham's arm. There was no reply. '*Señor!*' called the *mozo* again. Again no reply. The man's feet sounded loud as he went up the stairs. A moment later they heard him cry out, and as if drawn by a predominant will they ran up the stairs.

'Ah!' screamed the waiter.

But there was no horror in Mr Warlingham's face. With enraptured eyes he gazed at the long, red-sashed body, at the black beard that stood erect, outlined against the pillow. Colour rushed into his cheeks. He looked erect, confident in his fame.

'I was right!' he cried. 'It was artistic truth!' His voice rose; he shouted into a realm now devoid of phantoms. 'I was right! Right! Artistically right!'

XI

The Pond
Nigel Kneale

Peter Cushing is perhaps even more totally identified with horror films than either Vincent Price or Christopher Lee, yet while both of them are anxious to work in other genres, Peter is perfectly happy to continue with the kind of roles that have made him so popular around the world. As I mentioned earlier, Peter is the most gentle and reserved of men off screen, and to take tea with him in the old world London hotel where he stays when filming, or to visit his secluded cottage home near the coast in Kent, is like stepping back into a more tranquil and peaceful time such as the Victorian era. This said, it is no surprise to find that Peter's favourite authors are Sir Arthur Conan Doyle and E.R. Delderfield. He finds the latter's family sagas engrossing and has been a collector of Conan Doyle's work for many years – and now possesses an enviable library of bound volumes of the Strand Magazine *in which Sherlock Holmes first appeared. He has, of course, appeared as Holmes in films and on television, and in many people's opinion has given the most authentic portrayals of the Great Detective. Peter is also an admirer of the work of Nigel Kneale, the scriptwriter who became famous as a result of his television serial.* The Quatermass Experiment *and its sequels. He also starred in a film written by Kneale,* The Abominable Snowman *(1957) which he considers had one of the best scripts he ever worked with. Consequently Peter selected a story by Kneale, and one which also reflects a hobby of his, model making. In his spare time, little as it is, he delights in creating tiny, exquisite figurines. This said, I am sure that he would never indulge in quite the same variation of this hobby as the old man who features in the story of 'The Pond'.*

It was deeply scooped from a corner of the field, a green stagnant hollow with thorn bushes on its banks.

From time to time something moved cautiously beneath the prickly branches that were laden with red autumn berries. It whistled and murmured coaxingly.

'Come, come, come, come,' it whispered. An old man, squatting frog-like on the bank. His words were no louder than the rustling of the dry leaves above his head. 'Come now. Sssst – ssst! Little dear – here's a bit of meat for thee.' He tossed a tiny scrap of something into the pool. The weed rippled sluggishly.

The old man sighed and shifted his position. He was crouching on his haunches because the bank was damp.

He froze.

The green slime had parted on the far side of the pool. The disturbance travelled to the bank opposite, and a large frog drew itself half out of the water. It stayed quite still, watching; then with a swift crawl it was clear of the water. Its yellow throat throbbed.

'Oh! – little dear,' breathed the old man. He did not move.

He waited, letting the frog grow accustomed to the air and slippery earth. When he judged the moment to be right, he made a low grating noise in his throat.

He saw the frog listen.

The sound was subtly like the call of its own kind. The old man paused, then made it again.

This time the frog answered. It sprang into the pool, sending the green weed slopping, and swam strongly. Only its eyes showed above the water. It crawled out a few feet distant from the old man and looked up the bank, as if eager to find the frog it had heard.

The old man waited patiently. The frog hopped twice, up the bank.

His hand was moving, so slowly that it did not seem to move, towards the handle of the light net at his side. He gripped it, watching the still frog.

Suddenly he struck.

A sweep of the net, and its wire frame whacked the ground about the frog. It leaped frantically, but was helpless in the green mesh.

'Dear! Oh, my dear!' said the old man delightedly.

He stood with much difficulty and pain, his foot on the thin rod. His joints had stiffened and it was some minutes before he could go to the net. The frog was still struggling desperately. He closed the net around its body and picked both up together.

'Ah, big beauty!' he said. 'Pretty. Handsome fellow, you!'

He took a darning needle from his coat lapel and carefully killed the creature through the mouth, so that its skin would not be damaged; then put it in his pocket.

It was the last frog in the pond.

He lashed the water with the handle, and the weed swirled and bobbed: there was no sign of life now but the little flies that flitted on the surface.

He went across the empty field with the net across his shoulder, shivering a little, feeling that the warmth had gone out of his body during the long wait. He climbed a stile, throwing the net over in front of him, to leave his hands free. In the next field, by the road, was his cottage.

Hobbling through the grass with the sun striking a long shadow from him, he felt the weight of the dead frog in his pocket, and was glad.

'Big beauty!' he murmured again.

The cottage was small and dry, and ugly and very old. Its windows gave little light, and they had coloured panels, dark-blue and green, that gave the rooms the appearance of being under the sea.

The old man lit a lamp, for the sun had set; and the light became more cheerful. He put the frog on a plate, and poked the fire, and when he was warm again, took off his coat.

He settled down close beside the lamp and took a sharp knife from the drawer of the table. With great care and patience, he began to skin the frog.

From time to time he took off his spectacles and rubbed his eyes. The work was tiring; also the heat from the lamp made them sore. He would speak aloud to the dead creature, coaxing and cajoling it when he found his task difficult. But in time he had the skin neatly removed, a little heap of tumbled, slippery film. He dropped the stiff, stripped body into a pan of boiling water on the fire, and sat again, humming and fingering the limp skin.

'Pretty,' he said. 'You'll be so handsome.'

There was a stump of black soap in the drawer and he took it out to rub the skin, with the slow, over-careful motion that showed the age in his hand. The little mottled thing began to stiffen under the curing action. He left it at last, and brewed himself a pot of tea, lifting the lid of the simmering pan occasionally to make sure that the tiny skull and bones were being boiled clean without damage.

Sipping his tea, he crossed the narrow living-room. Well away from the fire stood a high table, its top covered by a square of dark cloth supported on a frame. There was a faint smell of decay.

'How are you, little dears?' said the old man.

He lifted the covering with shaky scrupulousness. Beneath the wire support were dozens of stuffed frogs.

All had been posed in human attitudes; dressed in tiny coats and breeches to the fashion of an earlier time. There were ladies and gentlemen and bowing flunkeys. One, with lace at his yellow, waxen throat, held a wooden wine-cup. To the dried forepaw of its neighbour was stitched a tiny glassless monocle, raised to a black button eye. A third had a midget pipe pressed into its jaws, with a wisp of wool for smoke. The same coarse wool, cleaned and shaped, served the ladies for their miniature wigs; they wore long skirts and carried fans.

The old man looked proudly over the stiff little figures.

'You, my lord – what are you doing, with your mouth so glum?' His fingers prised open the jaws of a round-bellied frog dressed in satins; shrinkage must have closed them. 'Now you can sing again, and drink up!'

His eyes searched the banqueting, motionless party.

'Where now – ? Ah!'

In the middle of the table three of the creatures were fixed in the attitudes of a dance.

The old man spoke to them. 'Soon we'll have a partner for the lady there. He'll be the handsomest of the whole company, my dear, so don't forget to smile at him and look your prettiest!'

He hurried back to the fireplace and lifted the pan; poured off the steaming water into a bucket.

'Fine, shapely brain-box you have.' He picked with his knife, cleaning the tiny skull. 'Easy does it.' He put it down on the table, admiringly; it was like a transparent flake of ivory. One by one he found the delicate bones in the pan, knowing each for what it was.

'Now, little duke, we have all of them that we need,' he said at last. 'We can make you into a picture indeed. The beau of the ball. And such an object of jealousy for the lovely ladies!'

With wire and thread he fashioned a stiff little skeleton, binding in the bones to preserve the proportions. At the top went the skull.

The frog's skin had lost its earlier flaccidness. He threaded a needle, eyeing it close to the lamp. From the table drawer he now brought a loose wad of wool. Like a doctor reassuring his patient by describing his methods, he began to talk.

'This wool is coarse, I know, little friend. A poor substitute to fill that skin of yours, you may say: wool from the hedges, snatched by the thorns from a sheep's back.' He was pulling the wad into tufts of the size he required. 'But you'll find it gives you such a springiness that you'll thank me for it. Now, carefully does it – '

With perfect concentration he worked his needle through the skin, drawing it together round the wool with almost untraceable stitches.

'A piece of lace in your left hand, or shall it be a quizzing-glass?' With tiny scissors he trimmed away a fragment of skin. 'But wait – it's a dance and it is your right hand that we must see, guiding the lady.'

He worked the skin precisely into place round the skull. He would attend to the empty eye-holes later.

Suddenly he lowered his needle.

He listened.

Puzzled, he put down the half-stuffed skin and went to the door and opened it.

The sky was dark now. He heard the sound more clearly. He knew it was coming from the pond. A far-off, harsh croaking, as of a great many frogs.

He frowned.

In the wall cupboard he found a lantern ready trimmed, and lit it with a flickering splinter. He put on an overcoat and hat, remembering his earlier chill. Lastly he took his net.

He went very cautiously. His eyes saw nothing at first, after working so close to the lamp. Then, as the croaking came to him more clearly and he grew accustomed to the darkness, he hurried.

He climbed the stile as before, throwing the net ahead. This time, however, he had to search for it in the darkness, tantalised by the sounds from the pond. When it was in his hand again, he began to move stealthily.

About twenty yards from the pool he stopped and listened.

There was no wind and the noise astonished him. Hundreds of frogs must have travelled through the fields to this spot; from other water where danger had arisen, perhaps, or drought. He had heard of such instances.

Almost on tiptoe he crept towards the pond. He could see nothing yet. There was no moon, and the thorn-bushes hid the surface of the water.

He was a few paces from the pond when, without warning, every sound ceased.

He froze again. There was absolute silence. Not even a watery plop or splashing told that one frog out of all those hundreds had dived for shelter into the weed. It was strange.

He stepped forward, and heard his boots brushing the grass.

He brought the net up across his chest, ready to strike if he saw anything move. He came to the thorn bushes, and still heard no sound. Yet, to judge by the noise they had made, they should be hopping in dozens from beneath his feet.

Peering, he made the throaty noise which had called the frog that afternoon. The hush continued.

He looked down at where the water must be. The surface of the pond, shadowed by the bushes, was too dark to be seen. He shivered, and waited.

Gradually, as he stood, he became aware of a smell.

It was wholly unpleasant. Seemingly it came from the weed, yet mixed with the vegetable odour was one of another kind of decay. A soft, oozy bubbling accompanied it. Gases must be rising from the mud at the bottom. It would not do to stay in this place and risk his health.

He stooped, still puzzled by the disappearance of the frogs, and stared once more at the dark surface. Pulling his net to a ready position, he tried the throaty call for the last time.

Instantly he threw himself backwards with a cry.

A vast, belching bubble of foul air shot from the pool. Another gushed up past his head; then another. Great patches of slimy weed were flung high among the thorn branches.

The whole pond seemed to boil.

He turned blindly to escape, and stepped into the thorns. He was in agony. A dreadful slobbering deafened his ears: the stench overcame his senses. He felt the net whipped from his hand. The icy weeds were wet on his face. Reeds lashed him.

Then he was in the midst of an immense, pulsating softness that yielded and received and held him. He knew he was shrieking. He knew there was no one to hear him.

An hour after the sun had risen, the rain slackened to a light drizzle.

A policeman cycled slowly on the road that ran by the cottage, shaking out his cape with one hand, and half-expecting the old man to appear and call out a comment on the weather. Then he caught sight of the lamp, still burning feebly in the kitchen, and dismounted. He found the door ajar, and wondered if something was wrong.

He called to the old man. He saw the uncommon handiwork lying on the table as if it had been suddenly dropped; and the unused bed.

For half an hour the policeman searched in the neighbourhood of the cottage, calling out the old man's name at intervals, before remembering the pond. He turned towards the stile.

Climbing over it, he frowned and began to hurry. He was disturbed by what he saw.

On the bank of the pond crouched a naked figure.

The policeman went closer. He saw it was the old man, on his haunches; his arms were straight; the hands resting between his feet. He did not move as the policeman approached.

'Hallo, there!' said the policeman. He ducked to avoid the thorn bushes catching his helmet. 'This won't do, you know. You can get into trouble – '

He saw green slime in the old man's beard, and the staring eyes. His spine chilled. With an unprofessional distaste, he quickly put out a hand and took the old man by the upper arm. It was cold. He shivered, and moved the arm gently.

Then he groaned and ran from the pond.

For the arm had come away at the shoulder: reeds and green water-plants and slime tumbled from the broken joint.

As the old man fell backwards, tiny green stitches glistened across his belly.

XII

The Ferryman
Kingsley Amis

My most recent advisory work has kept me busy in television, and consequently my final two selections reflect this involvement − in particular with two of the best received series to feature macabre stories, Haunted *and* Tales of the Unexpected, *both the handiwork of independent television companies.* Haunted *was the brainchild of Granada TV producer, Derek Granger, and it was certainly responsible for sending shivers up the spines of a great many viewers in 1974 and 1975. The highlight of the series was, I thought, 'The Ferryman' by Kingsley Amis which went out just before Christmas in 1974. The production was all the more intriguing because it was based on a story by Amis in which he described a strange series of unnerving events that occurred to him in an old rural inn not long after he had written his supernatural novel* The Green Man. *Whether they were true or not was a matter of conjecture. In the television dramatisation of the story, Jeremy Brett starred as a novelist who finds himself in an old inn acting out the very same mysterious events he had written about in his latest macabre novel. Natasha Parry played his increasingly nervous and bewildered young wife. But I won't give away any more details of what happened: I'll let Kingsley Amis do that right now ...*

I want to tell you about a very odd experience I had a few months ago − not so as to entertain you, but because I think it raises some very basic questions about, you know, what life is all about and to what extent we run our own lives. Rather worrying questions. Anyway, what happened was this ...

My wife and I had been staying the weekend with her uncle and aunt in Westmorland, near a place called Milnethorpe. Both of us − Jane and I, that is − had things to do in London on the Monday morning, and it's a long drive from there down to Barnet, where we live, even though a good half of it is on the M6. So I said: 'Look, don't let's break our necks trying to get home in the light' (this was in August). 'Let's take it easy and stop somewhere for dinner and reckon to get home about half-past ten or 11.' Jane said okay.

So we left Milnethorpe in the middle of the afternoon, took things fairly easily, and landed up about half-past seven or a quarter to eight at the place we'd picked out of one of the food guides before we started. I won't tell you the name of the place, because the people who run it wouldn't thank me if I did. Please don't go looking for it. I'd advise you not to.

Anyway, we parked the car in the yard and went inside. It was a nice-looking sort of place: pretty old, built a good time ago, I mean, done up in a sensible sort of way, no muzak and no bloody silly blacked-out lighting, but no olde-worlde nonsense either. I got us both a drink in the bar and went off to see about a table for dinner. I soon found the right chap, and he said: 'Table for two in half an hour – certainly, sir. Are you in the bar? I'll get someone to bring you the menu in a few minutes.' Pleasant sort of chap, a bit young for the job.

I was just going off when a sort of paunchy business-type came in and said something like 'Mr Allington not in tonight?' and the young fellow said: 'No, sir, he's taken the evening off.' 'All right, never mind.'

Well, I'll tell you why in a minute, but I turned back to the young fellow and said, 'Excuse me, but is your name Palmer?' and he said: 'Yes, sir.' I said, 'Not David Palmer by any chance?' and he said: 'No, sir. Actually, the name's George.' I said, or rather burbled: 'A friend of mine was telling me about this place, said he'd stayed here, liked it very much, mentioned you – anyway, I got half the name right, and Mr Allington is the proprietor, isn't he?' 'That's correct, sir.'

I went straight back to the bar, went up to the barman and said: 'Fred?' He said: 'Yes, sir.' I said, 'Fred Soames?' and he said: 'Fred Browning, sir.' I just said, 'Wrong Fred' – not very polite, but it was all I could think of. I went over to where my wife was sitting and I'd hardly sat down before she asked: 'What's the matter?'

What was the matter calls for a bit of explanation. In 1969 I published a novel called *The Green Man*, which was not only the title of the book but also the name of a sort of classy pub, or inn, where most of the action took place – very much the kind of establishment we were in that evening. Now the landlord of The Green Man was called Allington, and his deputy was called David Palmer, and the barman was called Fred Soames. Allington is a very uncommon name – I wanted that for reasons nothing to do with this story. The other two aren't, but to have got Palmer and Fred right, so to speak, as well as Allington was a thumping great coincidence – staggering, in fact. But I wasn't just staggered, I was very alarmed. Because The Green Man wasn't only the name of the pub in my book: it was also the name of a frightening creature, a sort of solid ghost, conjured up out of tree branches and leaves and so on, that very nearly kills Allington and his young daughter. I didn't want to find I was right about that too.

Jane was very sensible, as always. She said stranger coincidences had happened and still been just coincidences, and mightn't I have come across an innkeeper called Allington somewhere, half-forgotten about it and brought it up out of my unconscious mind when I was looking for a name for an innkeeper to put in the book, and now the real Allington had moved from wherever I'd seen him before to this place. And Palmer and Fred really are very common names. And I'd got the name of the pub wrong. (I'm still not telling you what it's called, but one of the things it isn't called is The Green Man.) And my pub was in Hertfordshire and this place was ... off the M6. All very reasonable and reassuring.

Only I wasn't very reassured. I mean, I obviously couldn't just leave it there. The thing to do was get hold of this chap Palmer and see if there was, well, any more to come. Which was going to be tricky if I wasn't going to look nosey or mad or something else that would shut him up. Neither of us ate much at dinner, though there was nothing wrong with the food. We didn't say much, either. I drank a fair amount.

Then, half-way through, Palmer turned up to do his everything-all-right routine, as I'd hoped he would, and as he would have done in my book. I said yes, it was fine, thanks, and then I said we'd be very pleased if he'd join us for a brandy afterwards if he'd got time, and he said he'd be delighted. Jolly good, but I was still stuck with this problem of how to dress the thing up.

Jane had said earlier on, why didn't I just tell the truth, and I'd said that since Palmer hadn't reacted at all when I gave him my name when I was booking the table, he'd only have my word for the whole story and might think I was off my rocker. She'd said that of course she'd back me up, and I'd said he'd just think he'd got two loonies on his hands instead of one. Anyway, now she said: '*Some* people who've read *The Green Man* must have mentioned it – fancy that, Mr Palmer, you and Mr Allington and Fred are all in a book by somebody called Kingsley Amis.' Obvious enough when you think of it, but like a lot of obvious things, you have got to think of it.

Well, that was the line I took when Palmer rolled up for his brandy: I'm me and I wrote this book and so on. Oh really? he said, more or less. I thought we were buggered, but then he said, 'Oh yes, now you mention it, I do remember some chap saying something like that, but it must have been two or three years ago' – as if that stopped it counting for much. 'I'm not much of a reader, you see,' he said.

'What about Mr Allington,' I said, 'doesn't he read?' 'Not what you'd call a reader,' he said. Well, that was one down to me, or one up, depending on how you look at it, because *my* Allington was a tremendous reader – French poetry and all that. Still, the approach had worked after a fashion, and Palmer very decently put up with being cross-questioned on how far this place corresponded with my place in the book. Was Mrs Allington blonde? There wasn't a Mrs Allington any more: she'd died of leukemia quite a long time ago. Had he got his widowed father living here? (Allington's father, that is.) No, Mr Allington senior, and his wife, lived in Eastbourne. Was the house, the pub, haunted at all? Not as far as Palmer knew, and he'd been there three years. In fact, the place was only about two hundred years old, which completely clobbered a good half of my novel, where the ghosts had been hard at it more than a hundred years earlier still.

Nearly all of it was like that. Of course, there were some questions I couldn't ask, for one reason or another. For instance, was Allington a boozer, like my Allington, and, even more so, had this Allington had a visit from God? In the book, God turns up in the form of a young man to give Allington some tips on how to deal with the ghosts, who he, God, thinks are a menace to him. No point in going any further into that part.

I said nearly all the answers Palmer gave me were straight negatives. One wasn't, or rather there were two points where I scored, so to speak. One was that Allington had a 15-year-old daughter called Marilyn living in the house. My Allington's daughter was 13, and called Amy, but I'd come somewhere near the mark – too near for comfort. The other thing was a bit harder to tie down. When I'm writing a novel, I very rarely have any sort of mental picture of any of the characters, what they actually look like. I think a lot of novelists would say the same. But, I don't know why, I'd had a very clear image of what my chap David Palmer looked like, and now I'd had a really good look at George Palmer, this one here, he was nearly the same as I'd imagined: not so tall, different nose, but still nearly the same. I didn't care for that.

Palmer, George Palmer, said he had things to see to and took off. I told Jane about the resemblance. She said I could easily have imagined that, and I said I supposed I might. 'Anyway,' she said, 'what do you think of it all?' I said it could still all be coincidence. What could it be if it isn't coincidence?' she asked. I'd been wondering about that while we were talking to Palmer. Not an easy one. Feeling a complete bloody fool, I said I thought we could have strayed into some kind of parallel world that slightly resembles the world I have made up – like in a Science Fiction story. She didn't laugh or back away. She looked round and spotted a newspaper someone had left on one of the chairs. It was that day's *Sunday Telegraph*. She said: 'If where we are is a world that's parallel to the real world, it's bound to be different from the real world in all sorts of ways. Now you read most of the *Telegraph* this morning, the real *Telegraph*. Look at this one and see if it's any different.' Well, I did, and it wasn't: same front page, same article on the trade unions by Perry, that's Peregrine Worsthorne, same readers' letters, same crossword down to the last clue. Well, that was a relief.

But I didn't stay relieved, because there was another

coincidence shaping up. It was a hot night in August when all this happened, and Allington was out for the evening. It was on a hot night in August, after Allington had come back from an evening out, that the monster, the Green Man, finally takes shape and comes pounding up the road to tear young Amy Allington to pieces. That bit begins on page 225 in my book, if you're interested.

The other nasty little consideration was this. Unlike some novelists I could name, I invent all my characters, except for a few minor ones here and there. What I mean is, I don't go in for just renaming people I know and bunging them into a book. But, of course, you can't help putting *something* of yourself into all your characters, even if it's a surly bus-conductor who only comes in for half a page. Obviously, this comes up most of all with your heroes. None of my heroes, not even old Lucky Jim, are me, but they can't help having pretty fair chunks of me in them, some more than others. And Allington in that book was one of the some. I'm more like him than I'm like most of the others: in particular, I'm more like my Maurice Allington in my book than the real Allington, who, by the way, turned out to be called John, seemed (from what I'd heard) to be like my Maurice Allington. Sorry to be long-winded, but I want to get that quite clear.

So, if, by some fantastic chance, the Green Man, the monster, was going to turn up here, he, or it, seemed more likely to turn up tonight than most nights. Furthermore, I seemed better cast for the part of the young girl's father, who manages in the book to save her from the monster, than this young girl's father did.

I tried to explain all this to Jane. Evidently I got it across all right, because she said straight away: 'We'd better stay here tonight, then.' 'If we can,' I said, meaning if there was a room. Well, there was, and at the front of the house too – which was important, because in the book that's the side the monster appears on.

While one of the blokes was taking our stuff out of the car and upstairs, I said to Jane: 'I'm not going to be like a bloody fool in a ghost story who insists on seeing things through alone, not if I can help it – I'm going to give Bob Conquest a ring. Bob's an old chum of mine, and about the only one I felt

I could ask to come belting up all this way (he lives in Battersea) for such a ridiculous reason. It was just after ten by this time, and the Green Man wasn't scheduled to put in an appearance till after 1 a.m., so Bob could make it all right, if he started straight away. Fine, except his phone didn't answer: I tried twice.

Jane said: 'Get hold of Monkey. I'll speak to him.' Monkey, otherwise known as Colin, is her brother: he lives with us in Barnet. Our number answered all right, but I got my son Philip, who was staying the weekend there. He said Monkey was out at a party, he didn't know where. So all I could do was the necessary but not at all helpful job of saying we wouldn't be home till the next morning. So that was that. I mean, I just couldn't start getting hold of George Palmer and asking him to sit up with us into the small hours in case a ghost came along. Could any of you? I should have said that Philip hasn't got a car.

We stayed in the bar until it closed. I said to Jane at one point: 'You don't think I'm mad, do you? Or silly or anything?' She said: 'On the contrary, I think you're being extremely practical and sensible.' Well, thank God for that. Jane believes in ghosts, you see. My own position on that is exactly that of the man who said: 'I don't believe in ghosts, but I'm afraid of them.'

Which brings me to one of the oddest things about this whole business. I'm a nervous type by nature: I never go in an aeroplane; I won't drive a car (Jane does the driving); I don't even much care for being alone in the house. But, ever since we'd decided to stay the night at this place, all the uneasiness and, let's face it, the considerable fear I'd started to feel as soon as these coincidences started coming up, it all just fell away. I felt quite confident, I felt I knew I'd be able to do whatever might be required of me.

There was one other thing to get settled. I said to Jane – we were in the bedroom by this time: 'If he turns up, what am I going to use against him?' You see, in the book, Maurice Allington has dug up a sort of magic object that sort of controls the Green Man. I hadn't. Jane saw what I was driving at. She said she'd thought of that, and took off and gave me the plain gold cross she wears round her neck, not for religious reasons: it was her grandmother's. That'll fix him, I thought, and, as before, I felt quite confident about it.

After that, we more or less sat and waited. At one point a car drove up and stopped in the car park. A man got out and went in the front door. It must have been Allington. I couldn't see much about him except that he had the wrong colour hair, and when I looked at my watch it was eight minutes to midnight, the exact time when the Allington in the book got back after his evening out the night he coped with the creature. One more bit of ... call it confirmation.

I opened our bedroom door and listened. Soon I heard footsteps coming upstairs and going off towards the back of the house, then a door shutting, and then straight away the house seemed totally still. It can't have been much later that I said to Jane: 'Look, there's no point in me hanging round up here. He might be early, you never know. It's a warm night, I might as well go down there now.' She said: 'Are you sure you don't want me to come with you?'

'Absolutely sure,' I said, 'I'll be fine. But I do want you to watch from the window here.'

'Okay,' she said. She wished me luck and we clung to each other for a bit, and then off I went.

I was glad I'd left plenty of time, because getting out of the place turned out to be far from straightforward. Everything seemed to be locked and the key taken away. Eventually I found a scullery door with the key still in the lock. Outside it was quite bright, with a full moon, or not far off, and a couple of fairly powerful lights at the corners of the house. It was a pretty lonely spot, with only two or three other houses in sight. I remember a car went by soon after I got out there, but it was the only one. There wasn't a breath of wind. I saw Jane at our window and waved, and she waved back.

The question was, where to wait. If what was going to happen – assuming something was – went like the book, then the young girl, the daughter, was going to come out of the house because she'd thought she'd heard her father calling her (another bit of magic), and then this Green Man creature was going to come running at her from one direction or the other. I couldn't decide which was the more likely direction.

A bit of luck: near the front door there was one of those

heavy wooden benches. I sat down on that and started keeping watch, first one way, then the other, half a minute at a time. Normally, ten minutes of this would have driven me off my head with boredom, but that night somehow it was all right. After some quite long time, I turned my head from right to left on schedule and there was a girl, standing a few yards away: she must have come round that side of the house. She was wearing light-green pyjamas – wrong colour again. I was going to speak to her, but there was something about the way she was standing ...

She wasn't looking at me: in fact, I soon saw she wasn't looking at anything much. I waved my hand in front of her eyes, the way they do in films when they think someone's been hypnotised or something. I felt a perfect idiot, but her eyes didn't move. Sleepwalking, presumably: not in the book. Do people walk in their sleep? Apparently not: they only pretend to, according to what a psychiatrist chum told me afterwards, but I hadn't heard that then. All I knew, or thought I knew, was this thing everybody's heard somewhere about it being dangerous to wake a sleepwalker. So I just stayed close to the girl and went on keeping watch. A bit more time went by, and then, sure enough, I heard, faintly but clearly, the sound I'd written about: the rustling, creaking sound of the movement of something made of tree branches, twigs and clusters of leaves. And there it was, about a hundred yards away, not really much like a man, coming up at a clumsy, jolting sort of jog-trot on the grass verge, and accelerating.

I knew what I had to do. I started walking to meet it, with the cross ready in my hand. (The girl hadn't moved at all.) When the thing was about twenty yards away I saw its face, which had fungus on it, and I heard another sound I'd written about coming from what I suppose you'd have to call its mouth, like the howling of wind through trees. I stopped and steadied myself and threw the cross at it, and it vanished – immediately. That wasn't like the book, but I didn't stop to think about it. I didn't stop to look for the cross, either. When I turned back, the girl had gone. So much the better. I rushed back into the inn and up to the bedroom and knocked on the door – I'd told Jane to lock it after me.

There was a delay before she came and opened it. I could

see she looked confused or something, but I didn't bother with that, because I could feel all the calm and confidence I'd had earlier, it was all just draining away from me. I sat her down on the bed and sat down myself on a chair and just rattled off what had happened as fast as I could. I must have forgotten she'd been meant to be watching.

By the time I'd finished I was shaking. So was Jane. She said: 'What made you change your mind?'

'Change my mind – what about?'

'Going out there,' she said: 'getting up again and going out.'

'But,' I said, 'I've been out there all the time.'

'Oh no you haven't,' she said. 'You came back up here after about twenty minutes, and you told me the whole thing was silly and you were going to bed, which we both did.' She seemed quite positive.

I was absolutely shattered. 'But it all really happened,' I said. 'Just the way I told you.'

'It couldn't have,' she said. 'You must have dreamed it. You certainly didn't throw the cross at anything because it's here, you gave it back to me when you came back the first time.'

And there it was, on the chain round her neck.

I broke down then. I'm not quite clear what I said or did. Jane got some sleeping-pills down me and I went off in the end. I remember thinking rather wildly that somebody or other with a funny sense of humour had got me into exactly the same predicament, the same mess, as the hero of my book had been in: seeing something that must have been supernatural and just not being believed. Because I knew I'd seen the whole thing: I knew it then and I still know it.

I woke up late, feeling terrible. Jane was sitting reading by the bed. She said: 'I've seen young Miss Allington. Your description of her fits and, she said, she used to walk in her sleep.' I asked her how she'd found out, and she said she just had: she's good at that kind of thing. Anyway, I felt better straight away. I said it looked as if we'd neither of us been dreaming, even if what I'd seen couldn't be reconciled with what she'd seen, and she agreed. After that we rather dropped the subject in a funny sort of way. We decided not to look for the cross I'd thrown at the Green Man. I said we wouldn't be able to find it. I didn't ask Jane whether she was thinking what I was thinking: that looking would be a waste of time because she was wearing it at that very moment.

We packed up, made a couple of phone-calls rearranging our appointments, paid the bill and drove off. We still didn't talk about the main issue. But then, as we were coming off the Mill Hill roundabout – that's only about ten minutes from home – Jane said: 'What do you think happened to sort of make it all happen?' I said: 'I think someone was needed there to destroy that monster. Which means I was guided there at that time, or perhaps the time could be adjusted. I must have been, well, sent all that stuff about the Green Man and about Allington and the others.'

'To make sure you recognised the place when you got there and knew what to do,' she said. 'Who did all the guiding and the sending and so on?'

'The same chap who appeared in my book to tell Allington what he wanted done.'

'Why couldn't he have fixed the monster himself?'

'There are limitations to his power.'

'There can't be many,' she said, 'if he can make the same object be in two places at the same time.'

Yes, you see, she'd thought of that too. It's supposed to be a physical impossibility, isn't it? Anyway, I said, probably the way he'd chosen had been more fun. 'More fun,' Jane repeated. She looked very thoughtful.

As you'll have seen, there was one loose end, of a sort. Who or what was it that had taken on my shape to enter that bedroom, talk to Jane with my voice, and share her bed for at any rate a few minutes? She and I didn't discuss it for several days. Then one morning she asked me the question more or less as I've just put it.

'Interesting point,' I said. 'I don't know.'

'It's more interesting than you think,' she said. 'Because when ... whoever it was got into bed with me, he didn't just go to sleep.'

I suppose I just looked at her.

'That's right,' she said. 'I thought I'd better go and see John before I told you.' (That's John Allison, our GP.)

'It was negative, then,' I said.

'Yes,' Jane said.

Well, that's it. A relief, of course. But in one way, rather disappointing.

XIII

De Mortuis
John Collier

As I complete work on this collection in the Autumn of 1980, Tales of
the Unexpected *is undoubtedly the most successful horror series ever
presented on television: already there have been two lengthy seasons of
plays and a third one is on the way. Nor has this success just been
confined to Britain – the series is already being shown abroad and is
tremendously popular in America. The series was initially based solely
on the superb short stories of Roald Dahl, all of which invariably have
some quite unexpected twist in the ending which gives the programme its
name. Once the series was well underway, however, the producer, Sir
John Woolf of Anglia Television, found he had a real winner on his
hands – but unfortunately a rapidly dwindling supply of Roald Dahl's
stories which he could use. So, a number of experts, myself included, were
called in to track down other tales with similarly unexpected endings. To
close this anthology, then, I'd like to leave you with the story I like best
of those I selected for the series, 'De Mortuis' by John Collier, a writer
with an equally seductive and ultimately startling style like Roald Dahl.
The tales of both men seem ideally suited to share the same series.*

Dr Rankin was a large and rawboned man on whom the
newest suit at once appeared outdated, like a suit in a
photograph of twenty years ago. This was due to the
squareness and flatness of his torso, which might have been
put together by a manufacturer of packing cases. His face also
had a wooden and a roughly constructed look; his hair was
wiglike and resentful of the comb. He had those huge and
clumsy hands which can be an asset to a doctor in a small
upstate town where people still retain a rural relish for
paradox, thinking that the more apelike the paw, the more

precise it can be in the delicate business of a tonsillectomy.

This conclusion was perfectly justified in the case of Dr Rankin. For example, on this particular fine morning, though his task was nothing more ticklish than the cementing over of a large patch on his cellar floor, he managed those large and clumsy hands with all the unflurried certainty of one who would never leave a sponge within or create an unsightly scar without.

The Doctor surveyed his handiwork from all angles. He added a touch here and a touch there till he had achieved a smoothness altogether professional. He swept up a few last crumbs of soil and dropped them into the furnace. He paused before putting away the pick and shovel he had been using, and found occasion for yet another artistic sweep of his trowel, which made the new surface precisely flush with the surrounding floor. At this moment of supreme concentration the porch door upstairs slammed with the report of a minor piece of artillery, which, appropriately enough, caused Dr Rankin to jump as if he had been shot.

The Doctor lifted a frowning face and an attentive ear. He heard two pairs of heavy feet clump across the resonant floor of the porch. He heard the house door opened and the visitors enter the hall, with which his cellar communicated by a short flight of steps. He heard whistling and then the voices of Buck and Bud crying, 'Doc! Hi, Doc! They're biting!'

Whether the Doctor was not inclined for fishing that day, or whether, like others of his large and heavy type, he experienced an especially sharp, unsociable reaction on being suddenly startled, or whether he was merely anxious to finish undisturbed the job in hand and proceed to more important duties, he did not respond immediately to the inviting outcry of his friends. Instead, he listened while it ran its natural course, dying down at last into a puzzled and fretful dialogue.

'I guess he's out.'

'I'll write a note – say we're at the creek, to come on down.'

'We could tell Irene.'

'But she's not here, either. You'd think *she'd* be around.'

'Ought to be, by the look of the place.'

'You said it, Bud. Just look at this table. You could write your name – '

'Sh-h-h! Look!'

Evidently the last speaker had noticed that the cellar door was ajar and that a light was shining below. Next moment the door was pushed wide open and Bud and Buck looked down.

'Why, Doc! There you are!'

'Didn't you hear us yelling?'

The Doctor, not too pleased at what he had overheard, nevertheless smiled his rather wooden smile as his two friends made their way down the steps. 'I thought I heard someone,' he said.

'We were bawling our heads off,' Buck said. 'Thought nobody was home. Where's Irene?'

'Visiting,' said the Doctor. 'She's gone visiting.'

'Hey, what goes on?' said Bud. 'What are you doing? Burying one of your patients, or what?'

'Oh, there's been water seeping up through the floor,' said the Doctor. 'I figured it might be some spring opened up or something.'

'You don't say!' said Bud, assuming instantly the high ethical standpoint of the realtor. 'Gee, Doc, I sold you this property. Don't say I fixed you up with a dump where there's an underground spring.'

'There was water,' said the Doctor.

'Yes, but, Doc, you can look on that geological map the Kiwanis Club got up. There's not a better section of subsoil in the town.'

'Looks like he sold you a pup,' said Buck, grinning.

'No,' said Bud. 'Look. When the Doc came here he was green. You'll admit he was green. The things he didn't know!'

'He bought Ted Webber's jalopy,' said Buck.

'He'd have bought the Jessop place if I'd let him,' said Bud. 'But I wouldn't give him a bum steer.'

'Not the poor, simple city slicker from Poughkeepsie,' said Buck.

'Some people would have taken him,' said Bud. 'Maybe some people did. Not me. I recommended this property. He and Irene moved straight in as soon as they were married. I wouldn't have put the Doc on to a dump where there'd be a spring under the foundations.'

'Oh, forget it,' said the Doctor, embarrassed by this

conscientiousness. 'I guess it was just the heavy rains.'

'By gosh!' Buck said, glancing at the besmeared point of the pickaxe. 'You certainly went deep enough. Right down into the clay, huh?'

'That's four feet down, the clay,' Bud said.

'Eighteen inches,' said the Doctor.

'Four feet,' said Bud. 'I can show you on the map.'

'Come on. No arguments,' said Buck. 'How's about it, Doc? An hour or two at the creek, eh? They're biting.'

'Can't do it, boys,' said the Doctor. 'I've got to see a patient or two.'

'Aw, live and let live, Doc,' Bud said. 'Give 'em a chance to get better. Are you going to depopulate the whole darn town?'

The Doctor looked down, smiled, and muttered, as he always did when this particular jest was trotted out. 'Sorry, boys,' he said. 'I can't make it.'

'Well,' said Bud, disappointed, 'I suppose we'd better get along. How's Irene?'

'Irene?' said the Doctor. 'Never better. She's gone visiting. Albany. Got the eleven o'clock train.'

'Eleven o'clock?' said Buck. 'For Albany?'

'Did I say Albany?' said the Doctor. 'Watertown, I meant.'

'Friends in Watertown?' Buck asked.

'Mrs Slater,' said the Doctor. 'Mr and Mrs Slater. Lived next door to 'em when she was a kid, Irene said, over on Sycamore Street.'

'Slater?' said Bud. 'Next door to Irene. Not in *this* town.'

'Oh, yes,' said the Doctor. 'She was telling me all about them last night. She got a letter. Seems this Mrs Slater looked after her when her mother was in the hospital one time.'

'No,' said Bud.

'That's what she told me,' said the Doctor. 'Of course, it was a good many years ago.'

'Look, Doc,' said Buck. 'Bud and I were raised in this town. We've known Irene's folks all our lives. We were in and out of their house all the time. There was never anybody next door called Slater.'

'Perhaps,' said the Doctor, 'she married again, this woman. Perhaps it was a different name.'

Bud shook his head.

'What time did Irene go to the station?' Buck asked.

'Oh, about a quarter of an hour ago,' said the Doctor.

'You didn't drive her?' said Buck.

'She walked,' said the Doctor.

'We came down Main Street,' Buck said. 'We didn't meet her.'

'Maybe she walked across the pasture,' said the Doctor.

'That's a tough walk with a suitcase,' said Buck.

'She just had a couple of things in a little bag,' said the Doctor.

Bud was still shaking his head.

Buck looked at Bud, and then at the pick, at the new, damp cement on the floor. 'Jesus Christ!' he said.

'Oh, God, Doc!' Bud said. 'A guy like you!'

'What in the name of heaven are you two bloody fools thinking?' asked the Doctor. 'What are you trying to say?'

'A spring!' said Bud. 'I ought to have known right away it wasn't any spring.'

The Doctor looked at his cement-work, at the pick, at the large worried faces of his two friends. His own face turned livid. 'Am I crazy?' he said. 'Or are you? You suggest that I've – that Irene – my wife – oh, go on! Get out! Yes, go and get the sheriff. Tell him to come here and start digging. You – get out!'

Bud and Buck looked at each other, shifted their feet, and stood still again.

'Go on,' said the Doctor.

'I don't know,' said Bud.

'It's not as if he didn't have the provocation,' Buck said.

'God knows,' Bud said.

'God knows,' Buck said. 'You know. I know. The whole town knows. But try telling it to a jury.'

The Doctor put his hand to his head. 'What's that?' he said. 'What is it? Now what are you saying? What do you mean?'

'If this ain't being on the spot!' said Buck. 'Doc, you can see how it is. It takes some thinking. We've been friends right from the start. Damn good friends.'

'But we've got to think,' said Bud. 'It's serious. Provocation or not, there's a law in the land. There's such a thing as being an accomplice.'

'You were talking about provocation,' said the Doctor.

'You're right,' said Buck. 'And you're our friend. And if ever it could be called justified – '

'We've got to fix this somehow,' said Bud.

'Justified?' said the Doctor.

'You were bound to get wised up sooner or later,' said Buck.

'We could have told you,' said Bud. 'Only – what the hell?'

'We could,' said Buck. 'And we nearly did. Five years ago. Before ever you married her. You hadn't been here six months, but we sort of cottoned to you. Thought of giving you a hint. Spoke about it. Remember, Bud?'

Bud nodded. 'Funny,' he said. 'I came right out in the open about that Jessop property. I wouldn't let you buy that, Doc. But getting married, that's something else again. We could have told you.'

'We're that much responsible,' Buck said.

'I'm fifty,' said the Doctor. 'I suppose it's pretty old for Irene.'

'If you was Johnny Weissmuller at the age of twenty-one, it wouldn't make any difference,' said Buck.

'I know a lot of people think she's not exactly a perfect wife,' said the Doctor. 'Maybe she's not. She's young. She's full of life.'

'Oh, skip it!' said Buck sharply, looking at the raw cement. 'Skip it, Doc, for God's sake.'

The Doctor brushed his hand across his face. 'Not everybody wants the same thing,' he said. 'I'm a sort of dry fellow. I don't open up very easily. Irene – you'd call her gay.'

'You said it,' said Buck.

'She's no housekeeper,' said the Doctor. 'I know it. But that's not the only thing a man wants. She's enjoyed herself.'

'Yeah,' said Buck. 'She did.'

'That's what I love,' said the Doctor. 'Because I'm not that way myself. She's not very deep, mentally. All right. Say she's stupid. I don't care. Lazy. No system. Well, I've got plenty of system. She's enjoyed herself. It's beautiful. It's innocent. Like a child.'

'Yes. If that was all,' Buck said.

'But,' said the Doctor, turning his eyes full on him, 'you seem to know there was more.'

'Everybody knows it,' said Buck.

'A decent, straightforward guy comes to a place like this and marries the town floozy,' Bud said bitterly. 'And nobody'll tell him. Everybody just watches.'

'And laughs,' said Buck. 'You and me, Bud, as well as the rest.'

'We told her to watch her step,' said Bud. 'We warned her.'

'Everybody warned her,' said Buck. 'But people get fed up. When it got to truck-drivers – '

'It was never us, Doc,' said Bud, earnestly. 'Not after you came along, anyway.'

'The town'll be on your side,' said Buck.

'That won't mean much when the case comes to trial in the county seat,' said Bud.

'Oh!' cried the Doctor, suddenly. 'What shall I do? What shall I do?'

'It's up to you, Bud,' said Buck. 'I can't turn him in.'

'Take it easy, Doc,' said Bud. 'Calm down. Look, Buck. When we came in here the street was empty, wasn't it?'

'I guess so,' said Buck. 'Anyway, nobody saw us come down cellar.'

'And we haven't been down,' Bud said, addressing himself forcefully to the Doctor. 'Get that, Doc? We shouted upstairs, hung around a minute or two, and cleared out. But we never came down into this cellar.'

'I wish you hadn't,' the Doctor said heavily.

'All you have to do is say Irene went out for a walk and never came back,' said Buck. 'Bud and I can swear we saw her headed out of town with a fellow in a – well, say in a Buick sedan. Everybody'll believe that, all right. We'll fix it. But later. Now we'd better scram.'

'And remember, now. Stick to it. We never came down here and we haven't seen you today,' said Bud. 'So long!'

Buck and Bud ascended the steps, moving with a rather absurd degree of caution. 'You'd better get that ... that thing covered up,' Buck said over his shoulder.

Left alone, the Doctor sat down on an empty box, holding his head with both hands. He was still sitting like this when the porch door slammed again. This time he did not start. He listened. The house door opened and closed. A voice cried, 'Yoo-hoo! Yoo-hoo! I'm back.'

The Doctor rose slowly to his feet. 'I'm down here, Irene!' he called.

The cellar door opened. A young woman stood at the head of the steps. 'Can you beat it?' she said. 'I missed the damn train.'

'Oh!' said the Doctor. 'Did you come back across the field?'

'Yes, like a fool,' she said. 'I could have hitched a ride and caught the train up the line. Only I didn't think. If you'd run me over to the junction, I could still make it.'

'Maybe,' said the Doctor. 'Did you meet anyone coming back?'

'Not a soul,' she said. 'Aren't you finished with that old job yet?'

'I'm afraid I'll have to take it all up again,' said the Doctor. 'Come down here, my dear, and I'll show you.'